SAVED

Fear makes a terrible compass.

♡ Hazel

HAZEL JAMES

ISBN-13: 978-1719551564
ISBN-10: 1719551561

Editing by JaVa Editing

Cover Design by Pink Ink Designs
www.pinkinkdesigns.com

Formatting by Champagne Book Design
www.champagnebookdesign.com

Cover photo by Charles Grubbs. Used with permission.

Dear Reader,

I almost didn't finish Clay and Leilani's story because depression is a bitch who stole my words and my creativity and my love for books.

But here's the thing—I was already on an antidepressant. *I'd already gotten help.* Turns out, I needed to ask again. I went up a dose on my medication and held on to the knot at the end of my rope until it wasn't so high above the ground anymore.

There is NO SHAME in asking for help. None. Nada. Zero. Zilch.

I've included a self-assessment for depression at the end of this book. If you think you may be suffering from depression, or if you know someone who could be, please consider looking over the questions and discussing your responses with a medical professional.

All my love,
Hazel

To Alyson Santos, Jennifer Mock, and Imagine Dragons.
Thank you for being the beauty in my darkness.

Leilani

OklaHOMEa

KIKI NUDGES THE LAPTOP IN MY DIRECTION. "THESE?"

"Too pointy," I say, my eyes barely leaving my swear word coloring book. Mom wasn't happy I bought it, but that's more her fault than mine. If she would've let me go to the store by myself like a normal adult, she wouldn't have seen it in the first place.

"Okay, how 'bout these?"

I shake my head. "Too round."

"Picky, picky," Kiki grumbles, typing in a new search.

Exchanging the yellow pencil for orange, I shade the outer edges of each letter. Coloring was part of my physical therapy years ago. I felt like a preschooler when I started, but it's something I grew to love. It's also why my handwriting looks halfway

1

decent. Some of the other survivors in my group never got past the "blind doctor" phase of their penmanship journey.

"I got it!" Kiki shifts herself on my bed and angles the screen toward me with a victorious smile. I almost feel bad for hating these too, though in all fairness, I told her I didn't feel like doing this tonight.

I muster as much gentleness as possible and say, "Too *Xena: Warrior Princess*."

"Oh, come on, Goldilocks," she huffs. "You can't hate them *all*. Sooner or later, you're going to have to pick something that's not too hot or too cold."

"It's been a while, but wasn't it *Goldilocks and the Three Bears*, not the *Three Boobs*? That would make me an even bigger freak than I already am," I add under my breath, returning to my coloring page. Just a little more pink and it'll be done.

Kiki sighs and flops onto her back. "If I have to tell you you're not a freak one more time, I'm going to slap you." We both know she won't. The only time she hit me was in middle school when I borrowed her favorite shirt, then spilled ketchup on it. After that we resorted to more passive-aggressive tactics, like hiding the other's toothbrush.

"Says the whole one."

"You mean the smart one," she retorts.

Of course, she had to bring that up. It's her failsafe in any argument. Still, I smile. We might be identical in looks, but no matter how hard I studied, Kiki always beat me on tests. "You're never going to let me live that down, are you?"

"Not a chance. Now quit coloring the word 'fuck' and pick out your new boobs."

"Jeez," I mutter, "the girl gets a two-minute head start in life and thinks she's the boss of me." With a playful side-eye, I close my coloring book and scooch toward her.

Nearly an hour later, I find the perfect pair—teardrop shaped and slightly bigger than my old ones, but still natural looking. And thanks to a private browser window and the digital crop tool, no one will ever know it came from a porn site.

"Knock, knock!" My bedroom door swings open, and Mom breezes through without actually knocking. I think she only says that to make herself feel better for invading my privacy, which she does at least once an hour while I'm awake. Who knows how many times she checks on me at night. "What are my girls up to?" Her footsteps start toward my bed, and I swap my X-rated website for Facebook faster than she can say "Sunday sermon."

"Just checking on a few friends back home." Kiki holds her phone up, covering for me. She texted her roommate and some of the newspaper staff a couple of hours ago, so she's not technically lying, but we both know Mom is better left clueless when it comes to the details of my reconstruction research. "They're all fine. Just some minor damage at Sergeant Brower's house."

"Tornadoes on Mother's Day morning. Can you imagine?" Mom tsks, lowering herself beside me. "Even if it is Oklahoma, that doesn't seem very nice of Mother Nature." She shakes her head as if funnel clouds are a crime against moms.

"Maybe Mother Nature was tired of her own mother breathing down her back," I mutter.

"Nonsense," Mom says, completely missing the point. "Mother Nature doesn't have a mother. And if she did, I'm sure she'd appreciate her, just like my girls appreciate me." *Ugh.* She runs her hand over my forehead and face, assessing me. She used to do the same thing when we were sick as kids. Except I'm not a kid, and I'm not sick. Well, not anymore.

But don't tell her that. Her instincts never got the message that the chemo worked and I don't need her hovering over me like a fucking Chinook helicopter. I wouldn't be surprised if she had asked my surgeon to reattach my umbilical cord when he did my mastectomy.

"I have an idea," Kiki interjects, lifting Mom's hand off me. God bless the twin psychic-connection thing. That, or my resting bitch face has gotten out of control in the last two minutes. "I'm taking you for an impromptu Mother's Day manicure." Kiki stands and pulls Mom to her feet.

"That's sweet," Mom says, patting Kiki's back, "but not necessary. Having you home for the weekend is enough of a gift for me." Saccharine alert.

Undeterred, Kiki links arms with her and heads toward the door. "I insist. We haven't had any one-on-one time since I got here, and I'm driving back to Fort Sill tomorrow." Mom is three words into her protest when Kiki plays the trump card. "Besides, I'm sure Leilani is worn out. It'll be good for her to rest while we're gone so she's fresh for dinner."

She's got a point. Dad made reservations at Mom's favorite restaurant tonight. The food is great, and now that my appetite is coming back, I plan on taking full advantage of the menu. Hopefully my taste buds cooperate. Tasting food is still hit-or-miss, thanks to chemo.

"Well, that is true," Mom says. "Honey, are you feeling tired?"

I glance up in time to see Kiki fake-wink behind Mom. "Yeah, a nap would do me some good," I fib, adding a yawn. "You two go ahead and I'll rest up." Mom studies me for a full ten seconds, no doubt calculating my current health status and wondering whether any rogue cancer cells will pop up while she's away. "I'm fine, Mom. I promise." I even offer a reassuring smile.

Satisfied, she turns toward Kiki and giggles. "Looks like we have a date! I'll grab my purse and tell your dad bye." As soon as she leaves the room, I sigh with relief.

"Thanks, Kiki. I owe you big."

"Well, you know what they say… you can't spell 'smother' without 'mother.' I figured you could use a break."

"I told you she was getting worse. If she's not checking me for a fever, she's treating me like I'm an invalid. Twice last week she pre-cut my food!" I hold up two fingers to drive my point home. "I know she means well, but damn, I wish I could go with you tomorrow." I don't bother hiding the wistfulness in my voice. Moving back in with my parents was not my idea, and even though it's only been a few months, I'm ready to pull my hair out.

Well, the smidgen that's grown back anyway.

Kiki offers a sympathetic smile. "I wish you could, too, but at least you have a couple hours of solitude now." I settle back against my pillows after she shuts the door but don't fully relax until her 4Runner backs out of the driveway with Mom in the passenger seat.

Feeling victorious and not at all tired, I continue scrolling through my Facebook feed, stopping at a post one of Kiki's friends tagged her in.

Here's what you missed today! Too bad this guy is married. He's cute ;)

The link takes me to a video on a news website.

Local Man Delivers Daughter as Tornado Sweeps Through Moore

"The line of thunderstorms that pushed through central

Oklahoma this morning produced three confirmed tornadoes between Lawton and Oklahoma City. Amateur storm chaser DH Rhoads is no stranger to extreme weather, but even he wasn't prepared for what this Mother's Day storm would bring. News 9's Jill Baker has the story."

The clip continues with aerial footage of the damage across the state, then switches to a reporter interviewing a man whose wife went into labor overnight. By the time she was ready to go to the hospital, the tornado sirens started, so they went to their storm shelter instead. The story itself is nuts, but it's what the reporter says when she's done with her interview that has me sitting up.

"Longtime viewers of News 9 might recognize DH from his involvement in VETSports and other community events. I asked him for an update on Operation: OklaHOMEa, the housing program he launched last fall to give veterans the fresh start they deserve. He said over the past nine months, they've helped four veterans, and they'll have another vacancy next month. We'll post a link on our website—"

Too excited to watch the rest of the video, I scroll down and find the information I'm searching for.

The transition from military service to civilian life can be tough. We want to help. Operation: OklaHOMEa gives veterans:

- *Up to six months of free housing in Moore, Oklahoma*
- *Employment*
- *Access to mental health services*
- *Free gym membership*

It's like the universe just handed me a ticket to freedom.

I skim the rest of the application and complete it as fast as a one-handed person can type.

> **Name:** *Leilani Moretti*
> **Age:** *27*
> **Address:** *303 Badger St. Colorado Springs, Colorado 80919*
> **Phone number:** *719-555-1125*
> **Years of military service:** *2012-2015*
> **Branch:** *Army*
> **Military Occupational Specialty:** *36B, financial management technician*
> **Reason for applying to Operation: OklaHOMEa:** *Because I might strangle my overprotective mother if I don't move out of her house and the state. Yes, I said state. She'll still come over every day if I'm within a 100-mile radius.*

My finger hovers over the submit button as I re-read the last part. It's one hundred percent true, but I don't want these people to get the wrong idea about her. Or me. I quickly add another line, just in case.

> *She means well, and I love her, but seriously. Please pick me. I'll even bake cookies.*

With a silent prayer on my lips, I hit send.

"Are you sure?" Mom asks for the millionth time. She's gone back and forth, packing me snacks and drinks one minute, then offering to help me unload my Wrangler the next. I know this is hard on her. Hell, the last four months have been brutal on everyone in our family. Cancer's a bitch like that.

"I'm sure."

"What if you hate your roommate?"

"I lived with roommates in college and in the Army. I'll be fine." I toss my purse next to the box on the passenger seat, then turn to face my parents. Mom looks two seconds away from bursting into tears—again—and Dad is his usual serene self. I hug him first.

"I'm proud of you, Limp," he says. I smile into his chest at the sound of my childhood nickname. I was six, and he'd gotten home from a deployment a couple of days before my first gymnastics class. I begged him to drive me there and spent the whole ride talking about how I was going to be in the Olympics like the girls in the Magnificent Seven.

I'd perfected cartwheels in our front yard that summer, so I was showing off in class by only using one arm. Turns out, those were much harder. I landed wrong, hurt my leg, and demanded that he take me home. He refused and said something he's repeated more times over the years than I can count: '*Fear makes a terrible compass.*' Then he said Olympians got their name because they had to learn how to get up and try again, even if they were limping.

I ended up falling in love with gymnastics, and while I never went to the Olympics, I did score a college scholarship and graduated as a national champion. "Thanks, Dad," I whisper. With a final squeeze, he releases me and I shift to my mom. She cups my face in her hands and gives me a tearful smile.

"Call me when you stop for gas, or if you get tired, or if you just want to talk."

"I will, I promise." Mom had been in my room—big surprise—when I got the call from Operation: OklaHOMEa saying I'd been accepted. She'd looked offended that I'd even considered applying for the program, much less having done it without consulting her first. Dad had reminded her that I was a grown woman and, up until my diagnosis, had been living on my own just fine.

When that didn't work, he went into the story about the young Hawaiian girl who fell in love with the Italian soldier wearing U.S. Army boots. Dad had met Mom at the end of his assignment in Oahu in the early eighties. They'd dated for a short time and eloped right before he left for his next duty station. "So at least our daughter isn't marrying a stranger and running away to live with him," he'd said. That shut Mom up for a while.

The truth is, my love life is another reason I want to move away. Dating is hard enough, but doing it as an amputee is especially challenging; most guys don't know how to act around a girl who's missing half her arm. But Travis McKay had been different. He'd interviewed me during a live broadcast from my bank's fiftieth anniversary celebration. Thank God it was radio and not television, because I hadn't been able to stop staring at him. The best part? He'd been the first man who made me feel as confident as I was before my accident. Our relationship had been amazing… right up until Valentine's Day. What had started as a promising night of dinner, drinks, and love making turned into him feeling a lump on my left breast.

It went downhill from there. Once my diagnosis was confirmed, Travis broke things off. His mom died of cancer several years ago, and he said he couldn't watch someone he cared about go through that again. I felt equal parts understanding and betrayed.

Okay, maybe a *little* more betrayed.

Mom nudges my shoulder. "Leilani, have you heard anything I said?"

I blink once and shake my head, dismissing the memory of my failed relationship. "Sorry, no."

"See, Leonard! She's about to fall asleep on her feet. There's no way she can drive in this condition." Mom's hands are all over my face and head again, checking me for the slightest excuse to take my keys.

"She's fine, Mother Hen." Dad wraps his arms around Mom and eases her backward, allowing me to adjust the beanie concealing my kiwi fuzz and escape to my Jeep. I don't know what I'm looking forward to most on my nine-hour drive—not having to talk to anyone, or not hearing Mom complain about my choice in music. For Christ's sake, a little Eminem and Jay-Z never hurt anybody.

With a final wave, I pull out of the driveway and start my journey toward freedom.

Kiki gasps. "You didn't."

"I did. I'll probably go to hell for it, but what's the fun of having cancer if you can't use it to your benefit?" In my defense, I didn't plan for it to happen. All I did was slide my beanie off to scratch my head. When I caught the officer glancing between my stump and lack of hair, I might have thrown in a couple of coughs and a weak smile.

He disappeared back to his cruiser and returned with a written warning for speeding and best wishes on my recovery. "Hey, at least I didn't try to flash him to get out of a ticket. I wouldn't have gotten very far."

"You're rotten," she says, laughing. "How's the new place?"

I tuck my suitcase in the closet and glance around my room. "Surprisingly... cute. Definitely had a woman's touch on the décor." The creams and browns in the bedding pick up the colors of the magnolia print above the bed. It's rustic but feminine, making me feel like I'm living at a southern plantation instead of above an auto shop.

"My roommate will be back tomorrow, and I met the guy who owns the building when I got here. I think his name is Kirk. He said someone else would be stopping by later this evening to make sure I get settled. In fact—" I glance at the clock on the dresser "—I should probably go so I have time to grab some groceries before they get here." My stomach growls with approval.

We disconnect and I head down to retrieve the last few items from my Jeep. A fully furnished apartment means I only needed to bring my clothes and essentials—great news for someone who doesn't have a lot of cargo space. The way things have fallen into place is... strange. Not only did I get a free ticket out of Colorado Springs, but I got one that put me an hour and a half away from my sister. Maybe it's a sign that the universe is finally done fucking with me.

Halfway up the stairs, I hear crunching gravel and a car door slamming. That's not alarming, considering my location, but the chipper voice of the driver? That's something I could do without.

"Hey there! You need a hand?" I shift my box to my left arm and hold up my stump as I turn around.

"Just one!" I pause long enough to watch his face transform from a cheerful smile to sheer panic, then continue my path up the steps, laughing the whole way.

Clay

Porcupines

S *HIT!*

On a list of the worst things to say to an amputee, that's got to land somewhere in the top five. Not that I knew she was missing a limb, but still.

"I'm so sorry," I say, trailing after her two steps at a time. "I didn't mean that the way it came out." She sandwiches the box between her stump and her chest and opens the screen door with her left arm, letting it slam behind her as I reach the landing. "I hope I didn't offend you," I call through the mesh.

"You're forgiven," she shouts from somewhere inside.

"Do you have anything else that needs to come up?"

Several seconds later, she appears in the living room, zipping a hoodie. Why she's wearing a hoodie and a beanie in

12

June is beyond me. "Just my guitar." My eyes flick from the flat expression on her face to the sleeve concealing her right arm. She's kidding, right? Getting back at me for making an unintentional joke?

I tip my head and smile. "Nice try."

"Suit yourself." She shrugs and pushes the door open, forcing me to jump into the corner of the small landing, and treks down the stairs. And fuck me if she doesn't pull a guitar case from the back seat. It's almost as big as she is, but she carries it with ease. I open my mouth to say something—*anything*—but the only noise that escapes my lips is a faint wheezing. Sheer stupidity has me rooted in place as she goes inside again. For a man who prides himself on his people skills, I've never struck out so hard in my life. Frustrated and mostly embarrassed, I plod two steps back to the screen.

"So, this has obviously gone well." I pause, waiting for her to return to the entryway, but she doesn't. "If I promise not to offer any more help, do you think you could come out of hiding?"

"Don't give yourself too much credit," she finally says, emerging from her bedroom. "I was going pee and getting my purse."

Sensing her next move, I open the door. "Hi, I'm Clay." I don't bother holding out my hand. I don't know if that's considered rude, and I'd rather not find out right now.

"Hi, Clay." Skipping her half of the introduction, she locks the deadbolt and starts toward her Jeep. Jesus, why is she making this so difficult? I follow her down and grab the top corner of her door before she can close it.

"I'm here to welcome you to Oklahoma."

Her eyebrows inch toward her beanie. "Right. Okay then. I'm welcomed. Now, if you'll excuse me." She tugs on the door handle, but I don't loosen my grip. Does she think I'm just a random auto shop customer who parked in the back by mistake?

"I don't think you understand. I'm Clay, from Operation: OklaHOMEa."

Her eyes narrow as she studies me. "You're not the guy from the news."

I chuckle. "You're thinking of DH. He's in colicky newborn hell right now, so I told him I'd come over instead and make sure you had everything you needed."

Nodding, she reaches through the steering wheel with her left hand and starts the engine. "I will in about thirty minutes. Thanks for stopping by." She offers up a stilted smile.

"Wait," I say, gripping the door even tighter. "We don't want to throw you to the wolves on your first day. If you'll give me a second, I have a welcome packet for you with information on—"

She throws her hand up. "There aren't any wolves, and I'm not being thrown. I'm just hangry and need to get some food. Again, if you'll excuse me." This time I let her close her door, because the sliver of silver over her shoulder tells me the other door is unlocked.

She greets me with a quizzical look when I walk around to the passenger side and climb in. "Excuse me? What are you doing?"

"Usually these introductions go something like this—DH comes over, meets with his new tenant, goes over some basic information, answers a few questions, and leaves. But since you're hell-bent on not cooperating, I'm improvising." I pause to buckle my seatbelt. "By the way, Leilani, you still haven't introduced yourself."

The furrow in her brow deepens. "Why do I need to

introduce myself if you already know who I am?"

"Because that's the polite thing to do."

"Don't take this the wrong way, but you're annoying."

I don't know how else I'm supposed to take that, but I've been called much worse. "Don't take this the wrong way, but you remind me of a porcupine," I counter. She holds my gaze, her milk chocolate daggers boring holes into my eyes, but it doesn't faze me. I've done this dance many times as a trainer and counselor. I'm nothing if not persistent.

"I don't think I like you," she finally says, rolling up her right sleeve.

"I don't think that matters. I came here to do a job, and I'll stay here until that's done." I make a show of getting comfortable in her seat.

Her eyes roll in resignation. "Fine," she huffs, retrieving her phone to snap a picture of me. "What's your last name?"

"Prescott."

Her thumb flies over the screen. For a one-handed woman, she's remarkably efficient with texting. "Age?"

"Thirty-four."

More typing. "If you try to rape me or kill me, my sister's gonna call the cops. She'll also call if she hasn't heard from me in two hours."

"You expect me to believe that you'd let a potential rapist or murderer inside your Jeep? Please," I scoff.

Shrugging, Leilani puts her stump into a cup attached to the top of her gear shifter and steps on the clutch. "You never know. A lot of people thought Ted Bundy was a nice guy."

I chuckle as we round the front of Rhoads Auto Shop. "So, where are we headed?"

"The grocery store."

"Okay, there's one about five minutes that way," I point out my window, "and another one—"

"A few miles down this road, across the street from Sonic and Wells Fargo. I know. I drove by it on the way in. I just didn't have any room for extra stuff." Her tone dances on the line between brusque and bitchy, emphasizing my earlier assessment.

Total porcupine.

Needing to find neutral ground, I opt for small talk. "Your license plate says you're from Colorado. What made you want to move down here?"

She cuts a glance at me. "I thought you knew all about me already."

"Nope, just your name. DH handles everything. Like I said, I'm just helping out." I prop my arm on the windowsill and tap my fingers to the beat of Outkast quietly pumping through her speakers. I didn't peg Leilani for a hip hop fan.

"I'd been there for a few years and was ready for a change of pace. The military itch or whatever," she says, waving her hand. "This seemed like a good place to start."

"Air Force?"

"Army," she corrects.

I nod. "What'd you do?"

"I was a thirty-six bravo."

My ears perk up. "Finance, huh?" They held the power over when and how I got paid, so I always tried to make friends with them.

Leilani's eyes find me again, but this time she's surprised. "How'd you know that?"

"I was a ninety-two romeo." Her mouth moves like she wants to ask me a question, but closes just as quickly. The gentleman in me wants to take it easy on her and give her the answers she's looking for. The counselor part of me overrules. If she wants to know more about my service or my job as a parachute rigger, she'll have to put her quills away and ask. "Where were you stationed?" I continue as we pull into the parking lot.

"Fort Lewis. I deployed from there and got out in 2015."

I point to her arm. "Medical retirement?"

"Yup." She doesn't elaborate and I don't pry. We'll have time for that later.

We exit her Jeep in silence, and she leads the way into Homeland, yanking a buggy from the row closest to the door. Her unseasonable attire earns a few double takes from the customers shucking corn in the produce section, but Leilani doesn't seem to notice. She's oblivious to everything but the signs hanging at the end of each aisle. I match her footsteps all the way to the cereal section, where she loads up on four boxes of Fruity Pebbles and a box of Kix.

"Well that explains why you're so short. All that sugar stunted your growth."

She juts her chin out. "Kix doesn't have sugar."

"Oh, but it does." I turn the orange box on its side and point to the nutrition panel.

"Barely," is all she says before steering to the snack aisle. She drops a family sized bag of caramel popcorn into the basket and cocks an eyebrow, daring me to say something. I don't. The health and beauty display on the endcap gives me an even better idea.

It's time for some passive-aggressive supermarket fun.

Leilani's desire to ignore me works to my benefit; she presses forward, leaving me with the golden opportunity to snag a bottle of anti-diarrheal medicine from the shelf. I wait until her back is turned to slip it behind the popcorn. "So, the paperwork

DH gave me said you were undecided about a job. Have you given that any more thought?"

"Not really. I figured I'd drive around to a few banks and see if anyone is hiring." She pulls up to the peanut butter and scans the labels, then tosses a jar into the buggy.

Chunky. Interesting. "Want any help?"

"Nope." Standing on her tip toes, Leilani reaches into the void on the shelf where the Nutella should be. "Dammit," she whispers.

"Problem?"

Her eyes track upward to the surplus of chocolate hazelnut spread perched on the top shelf. "No." She uses her foot to nudge a few jars of marshmallow fluff out of her way and steps on the bottom ledge. Her stump finds purchase under the lip of the peanut butter shelf and then she's scaling aisle three like a sugar-crazed Spiderwoman. Her determination is only half as impressive as her smile when she lands on the linoleum with a jar of Nutella in her hand. And just like that, I know all I need to know about Leilani Moretti.

For now, anyway.

"What do you think about working at a gym?" I ask as we continue our treasure hunt through the store.

"Doing what? Training?" She grabs a package of Oreos.

"Numbers. I'm opening up a second location in a few months, and I need someone to help me get my shit together."

She stops. "You own a gym?"

"Should I be offended by your tone?" I tease. "Yes, I own a gym. A very successful one, hence the new location. I thought you might like doing the same type of job in a more relaxed atmosphere, but if you want to pull a nine-to-five in business suits…" I lift a shoulder.

Leilani takes the bait in the frozen foods section. "How many hours each week?"

"Depends on whether you want part-time or full-time."

She raises an eyebrow as she haphazardly tosses a supreme pizza into the basket. "And the pay?"

"Negotiable, based on experience."

She leads us to the dairy case for a gallon of milk, then moves to the front of the store. "What's the catch?"

"No catch. Just a job offer. You also have one from Kurt, the owner of the auto shop below your apartment. You can read more about that in your welcome packet." I unload the contents of Leilani's buggy onto the conveyor belt before she can tell me not to, then pluck a grocery store gift card from the display above the candy and step into the line next to her. When it's my turn, I take a five from my wallet and hand it to the cashier.

And that's when I hear it.

"What the hell? I didn't—" I move back to Leilani's lane just in time to see her cashier scan the jumbo-sized bottle of anti-diarrheal medicine.

"Good thinking," I say. "With all that junk food, your stomach's bound to get messed up."

Leilani's eyes snap to me. I can tell she wants to say something not meant for polite company, but she holds her tongue and finishes her transaction while I load her bags in the buggy. I save the one with the medicine for last, making a show of placing it on top. Her scowl remains in place as she steers the buggy past me, but the reflection in the dome-shaped mirrors above the exit gives her away.

She's smiling.

Leilani

First Impressions

A LOW RUMBLE OF THUNDER VIBRATES THE SMALL kitchen window above the sink, a bass line to the melody of raindrops pinging against the glass. The storm has held steady all morning, as have Mom's calls and texts making sure I'm not in danger of tornadoes or lightning or flash flooding in my second-story apartment. I find it relaxing, though.

The rain, not her calls.

Before my accident, I loved playing my guitar in the barracks—the unsightly cinderblock walls did wonders for the acoustics. But the best was when it rained, which, in the Pacific Northwest, was ninety percent of the time. I'd park myself in front of my opened window and belt out acoustic versions of my favorite hip hop songs. Even though I haven't been able to play in more than three years, I can't bear to part with my guitar. Maybe one day I'll find a prosthetic arm that isn't a pain in the ass and I can figure out how to attach a guitar pick to it.

For now, Spotify and my KitchenAid mixer are doing the trick. I said in my application that I'd bake cookies if they chose me, so here I am, up to my elbows in flour after an early morning trip to the store for baking supplies. I briefly considered making some laxative cookies for Clay, but given his amount of side-eye yesterday, I'm not sure he eats junk food. He'd probably give the cookies to someone else who'd end up sitting on the pot all day.

No, I'll find another way to exact my revenge.

But the most interesting part about yesterday wasn't Clay's grocery store stunt—which was pretty damn funny. It was his complete lack of concern for my appearance. Sure, he felt like an ass when he thought he offended me, but after that, everything seemed... normal. I saw the way the other customers looked at me. Clay was either oblivious or adept at hiding his thoughts. Regardless, he never asked about my beanie or why I was wearing a jacket in the summer. And it's not that I hate talking about my cancer, it's just not the first thing I want people to know about me.

It's hard to get people to see you as anything else once you're dubbed The Girl With a Disease.

You'd think it would have been the same for losing a limb, but it wasn't. When people looked at me, they saw a woman who survived a Humvee rollover and didn't let physical limitations slow her down. Plus, I had my hair and boobs—two defining parts of any woman's physical identity—so I still looked "*healthy.*" With cancer, there's always a lingering doubt, and doubt is a close cousin to pity and fear. That poor girl. Will it come back? Can she beat it again? *Is she going to die?* And I get it. It's a normal human reaction that I'm probably guilty of myself. But Clay skipped all that and went right to practical jokes and job offers.

And to think, all I wanted when I went to the store was some Fruity Pebbles and cookies.

Kiki said I'd be stupid to say no, and she's right. One of the things I was looking forward to down here was exercising without Mom breathing down my back about over-exerting myself. Now I'll have the perfect place to do that, and I'll get paid.

When the timer beeps, I slide on my Finding Nemo oven mitts and retrieve a sheet of snickerdoodles. The running joke is that my right arm is my lucky fin, so the "mommy and me" set Travis got me for Christmas was hilarious and practical; being able to balance hot bakeware has made a world of difference for me.

Singing my heart out to Drake's *Best I Ever Had*, I transfer the snickerdoodles to a cooling rack and start on a batch of oatmeal raisin. I'm in the middle of creaming together the butter and sugar when two kids burst through the front door.

"Wow, it smells good in here!" A gapped-tooth girl drops an umbrella on the tiled floor and sniffs her way into the kitchen, followed by a little boy with cherub cheeks and matching chestnut hair. She scans the counters, plucks two cookies from the closest plate, and passes one to the boy. "Who are you?"

I turn off the mixer and close out of Spotify before I can damage their innocent ears. "I'm Leilani. I just moved in."

"My mommy lives here," the boy says as he sinks his teeth into his treat. I take pride in the slow smile that spreads across his face until I realize what he's eating.

"Stop!" He bursts into tears and the girl freezes, her hand inches from her mouth. Before I can explain my reaction, I hear a woman's voice coming through the door.

"Not even home two minutes and you're already fighting. That's a record." She shifts the groceries in her arm and drops an overnight bag on the carpet, then looks up. Even with her wet hair clinging to the sides of her face, the woman is nothing short of stunning. And in the span of about three seconds, her face morphs from weary to curious to something bordering on murderous.

Here's the thing about being an amputee... old habits die hard. So when I hold my hands in the air, it's more like one stump and one hand, which isn't exactly how I wanted to meet my new roommate. *Shit.* "Sorry! They grabbed peanut butter cookies and I don't know if they're allergic to nuts."

My plea must work because Mama Bear's expression softens. "No allergies, unless you count their aversion to bad manners. Bristol," she says, raising an eyebrow at the girl, "you should know better."

Crestfallen, the girl mumbles, "Sorry, Mom."

"I'm not the one you need to apologize to." The woman swipes her finger in my direction and resumes her path to the kitchen while the girl repeats the same sad apology to me.

"It's no sweat, kid. Now that I know you guys won't keel over, you're welcome to sample anything as long as your mom says it's okay." Two sets of pleading eyes find their mother, who's putting a bottle of coffee creamer in the fridge.

"You can each have two, but only if you promise not to fight with each other for the next hour."

After a quick glance at each other, the kids shout, "Deal!" and make off to the living room with more cookies.

"Sorry about that. I'm Rebecca," the woman says, extending her hand, "and those monsters are Bristol and Blake."

I twist my left hand, a trick I learned in my Life Skills class, and return her gesture. "Leilani. It's nice to meet you." To her credit, Rebecca says nothing about my awkward handshake. "Do the kids live here too?" The door to the other bedroom was closed when I arrived. Maybe there's a suite behind it?

"No, they live with my parents." She says it matter-of-factly, but her tone and quick glimpse into the living room tell me there's more to the story. Not knowing how to respond, I just nod my head and return to mixing cookie dough while Rebecca stows the rest of her groceries.

When she finishes, she slides onto a barstool and props her elbows on the counter. "In a nutshell, I have a gambling problem and got evicted twice. My parents were ready to send me to a rehab facility in Arizona when they found out about Operation: OklaHOMEa. They have temporary guardianship of my kids while I focus on getting better." She pauses to take a chocolate chip cookie from a nearby plate. "I sleep over every Friday and Saturday night, then bring them here on Sunday afternoons while my parents run their errands."

Whoa.

In my haste to fill out my application, I didn't put much thought into the problems my roommate would be facing. Rebecca might look like a bathing suit model, but she's got a pair of lady balls, too. Something about the way she opened up makes me do the same.

"I lost my arm after an accident in Afghanistan," I say, scooping oatmeal raisin cookies onto a sheet. "I was in a good place mentally after that, but getting breast cancer knocked me on my ass. It's like... why me? Haven't I been through enough?

"And I'm so afraid my twin sister is going to get it. So far, she's in the clear, but the guilt hasn't gone away. And to top it off, my mother pretended I was twelve after my diagnosis and wouldn't let me do anything for myself. Coming here was the best way to get away from her and not get into mounds of debt. Plus, my sister is stationed at Fort Sill." Done with my word vomit, I put the cookies in the oven and set the timer.

"I can already tell you're a thousand times better than the last girl who lived here. I try not to judge people, especially given my current situation, but she played the victim card so bad she carried her own chalk outline. Got on my last damn nerve, that one."

"What happened to her?"

"She took a job in Dallas."

"Well." I lift a snickerdoodle. "Let's toast to good roommates. May our arguments be few and our laughs be many."

"Mom, Blake keeps taking my pillow!"

"Nuh-uh!"

Rebecca rolls her eyes and slumps off the barstool. "What was that about arguments?"

I stroll through the Battles parking lot feeling like a hero. The guys at the auto shop nearly clicked their heels together when I dropped off their cookies this morning. DH, who'd been up since two with his daughter, ate one before I'd even set the container down. "I bet they'll be gone by lunch," I say, holding the front door for Rebecca. With both of us working here, it makes more sense to carpool.

"If I were a betting woman, I'd put twenty down."

I purse my lips and shake my head. "I totally walked into that, didn't I?"

"Right in," she confirms, lightly patting my pixie cut wig. Last night, we discovered we have the same sick sense of humor, and thank God for that. It's nice to have a friend already.

"Good morning, ladies!" Clay pushes out from the reception desk, his jovial expression growing even brighter, and pops out of his seat like a Jack-in-the-box. That is, if Jack was a buff blond with hazel eyes and a five o'clock shadow.

"Is he always this upbeat?" I whisper-shout to Rebecca.

"Pretty much." She takes his place in the black swivel chair and stows her purse in the bottom drawer.

Clay turns his head to me and throws a thumb over his shoulder. "Let's go to my office. We'll take care of your hiring paperwork and then I'll show you around. After lunch, we'll head over to the new facility. I want your take on the space and the budget I'm working with." I nod and follow him past the treadmills and weight benches in the main section of the gym, catching our reflection in the mirrored wall along the way. Clay has nearly a foot on me and probably weighs double what I do, making him look like a Great Dane leading a Chihuahua. Well, maybe a hairless cat would be more accurate.

"This location is geared more toward the twenty-something crowd," he continues over the rock music blasting through the sound system. "We offer a variety of training programs that coincide with counseling sessions, because from my personal experience, sitting on a couch talking about your problems is bullshit." He opens the door to his office, and we're immediately hit with a pungent, chemical smell.

"How many times have I told him?" he grumbles, flipping

on an oscillating fan. "Sorry about that. My office manager likes to build model cars."

Sure enough, there's a truck and a convertible on top of a small bookshelf and what looks like the start to a car from the 1950s on an end table in the corner. That explains the paint thinner smell.

"Anyway." Clay gestures to a worn tweed loveseat beside his desk, so I take a seat. "As a member of Operation: OklaHOMEa, you'll have free access to those services. I have another counselor on staff who works with my employees."

I open my mouth to tell him I don't need them when he holds up a hand. "If you don't want counseling, that's fine. You'll still do monthly progress reports with me to make sure you're setting and reaching your goals while you're here." Clay passes a clipboard and pen to me and takes a seat behind his desk. The first few pages are standard—direct deposit, taxes, and a federal employment verification form. After that, they start getting personal.

"Likes and dislikes? Really?" My brows draw together as I look up at Clay. "What does that have to do with accounting?"

"Not a thing." He eases back in his chair and clasps his hands behind his head, the sleeves of his black Battles polo straining over his biceps. I must have been too hangry yesterday to really appreciate his physique, so I let my eyes linger a few extra seconds. "I like to get to know my employees. It makes spending forty hours a week with them more enjoyable."

I suppose that's fair enough.

Weird, but fair.

I jot down traveling, food, gymnastics, and music for the likes, and cats, cancer, gummy bears, and the smell of tuna fish for the dislikes. The last page is a goal sheet broken down into several categories—financial, occupational, educational, physical, and mental/emotional. There's only one rule, printed in bolded letters at the top: **You must write something in each section.**

"You take this goal thing seriously, don't you?"

Clay pokes his head around the side of the computer. "You have no idea."

"Why?"

"Because a goal gives you purpose, and purpose keeps you moving forward. Ten years ago, I was a fifth of vodka away from drinking myself to death. Goals saved my life." He holds my gaze for several moments, then turns his attention to his monitor.

I glance back down at the paper. The whole thing seems like overkill to me. I rarely drink, and I'm nowhere near suicidal. The only things I want are boobs and the ability to put mascara on with my left hand. Thicker eyelashes would be nice, too. But considering this program is giving me a free place to live and a job without jumping through hoops, I'll play along.

Financial. I tap the pen against my cheek as I think. I don't have many bills. Just my phone, a small balance on one credit card, and my car insurance. *Save money for a trip to Belize.* It's the first country that comes to mind and sounds like a sensible goal.

Occupational. Clearly, I already have a full-time job. What the hell am I supposed to put here? *Don't get fired.* There.

Educational. I have my undergrad, and I don't give a shit about getting a master's degree. *Learn how to make a chocolate soufflé.* That counts as educational, right?

Physical. My first appointment at the VA hospital is in a few weeks, so this one is easy to answer. *Get boobs.*

Mental/emotional. Umm. *To be able to watch Toy Story 3 without crying at the end.*

"Now what?" I ask, securing the packet and pen beneath the metal clip.

"Now you get a Battles shirt and a tour of the gym." He takes my clipboard and pulls a black polo out of the filing cabinet behind his desk. "The women's locker room is around the corner. Just come back here when you're done."

I grab my purse and follow the directions he gave me. One of the reasons I love wearing Travis's old hoodie is because it's baggy enough to hide my mastectomy—and with the way he ended things, I figured I'd earned the right to keep it. But I can't get by with a hoodie and a beanie at work, so a wig and fake boobs it is.

Locking myself in a bathroom stall, I strip off my shirt and slide the polo over my head, careful to not disturb my hair or "boob bags." I opted to wear lightweight microbead breast forms in one of my old bras because all the mastectomy bras I'd tried were more cumbersome than comfortable and the "chicken cutlet" silicone breasts made me sweaty. Wearing a wig makes me sweaty enough. Satisfied with my reflection in the mirror, I stuff my shirt back into my purse and rejoin Clay, who's talking to a guy in his office.

"Leilani, this is Marshall, my office manager. You'll be working with him on our accounts." The other man turns around. He's not as muscular as Clay, but something about him—his black shaggy hair? His bottle-green eyes?—sparks my memory.

"Do I know you?"

He studies me and shakes his head. "I don't think so. I get that a lot though. I guess I just have one of those faces." Marshall offers up an easy grin and claps Clay on the shoulder.

"I'm gonna plug in those new memberships. Let me know if you need anything."

Clay and I retrace our earlier steps through the gym, which is busier than I expected for nine thirty on a Monday morning. "We'll start at the front," he says, rapping his knuckles on the desk. "Rebecca is the receptionist. She handles all calls, keeps my schedule, and stops customers when they try to leave with my towels." His chuckle makes me wonder if he's being serious about that last part.

"Speaking of schedules, your four o'clock canceled. He said he wasn't sure about rescheduling but would call you." The edges of Clay's mouth dip for the briefest of moments before returning to their natural upward curve. It's like his face is programmed to be happy. "And you," Rebecca says, passing me a nametag, "are official."

I unclip the fastener and thread the pin through my shirt... and right into my thumb.

"Ow!"

"Need help?" Clay's voice is calm and uncritical, but it irritates me nonetheless. Just because I can't do something on the first try doesn't mean I can't do it at all.

"I've got it." I start over, and after a few whispered curse words, finally manage to secure my nametag. Who cares if it's slightly lopsided?

Clay ignores my victory smirk and leads me around the gym, pointing out things he wants to keep at the new building and what he plans to change entirely. It's hard not to get caught up in his enthusiasm, and even harder not to get distracted by his upper body. Chemo did a number on my libido, but watching Clay talk with his hands has proven there's still hope in the Land of Promises.

"Um, Leilani? I think you have something… on your…"

I confirm that my hand is still at my side—nowhere near the forearm porn exhibit in front of me. "Huh?"

Clay gestures toward my shirt. "You have…"

I glance down and see tiny white dots clinging to my shirt and the right leg of my yoga pants.

Oh God.

No.

Shit.

Clay

Building Bridges

HER BRONZE SKIN TURNS WHITE. "WHAT'S GOING ON?" She ignores me and tugs on her nametag, choking back a sob when more white specks fly out of her shirt. "Leilani?" Without a word, she pivots and sprints toward the women's locker room with her hand over her chest.

What the fuck?

I chase after her, stopping short when I reach the closed door. I knock three times, but the only response is silence. "Leilani?" Still no answer.

Christ. I scrub a frustrated hand over my face. I know she's in there. Squeezing my eyes shut, I poke my head through the door. "Is anyone other than Leilani in here?" The faint sound of weeping echoes off the walls, but I don't hear any footsteps or running water.

I push through and let the door close behind me, then announce myself again, just in case. "Male in the room! Is anyone else in here?" When no one answers, I pull the "restroom closed for cleaning" sign out of the small janitor closet and place it outside the locker room door. "Leilani?" The sound of her cries leads me to the far shower stall. I move the curtain aside and see her, wig in hand, balled up on the floor.

"Bad hair day, huh?" I press my back against the cool tile and slide into the spot beside her, my legs stretching into the next stall.

"Go away," she pleads into her elbow.

"Nope."

Her sobs grow louder, so I do the only thing I can think of—I reach over and scoop her onto my lap. Breakdowns are part of my job, but something about Leilani falling apart hurts me, too. Maybe it's the soft fuzz on her head where her hair should be. Or the missing hand that can't wipe the tears from her cheeks. Whatever it is, I just want to make it better.

"I think you're more like a hedgehog than a porcupine," I say, trying to lighten the mood.

She sniffs and clears her throat. "Is that so?"

"You're tiny, you curl into a ball when you're in distress, and underneath your prickly outer shell, you're nothing but a softie."

"You already have me figured out, huh?"

I smile. "That's what I do. You figure out numbers, I figure out people." I shift her slightly so I can see her face. "What happened?"

Leilani's tear-filled eyes drop to the wig on the floor beside us. "I... uh... had a wardrobe malfunction, except mine didn't involve boobs, because..."

"Because?" I prompt.

"I had a double mastectomy," she whispers.

Well that explains the wig. "What's the white stuff?"

"The filling from my breast form. My nametag poked a hole in it."

With the basics filled in, I move into problem-solving mode. "Do you want me to take you home so you can change?"

"That's nice of you, but no. I didn't bring any other ones because I'm supposed to be having surgery soon." Her entire body slumps as she releases a defeated sigh.

"Okay." I nod my head, more to myself than to her. That just means we need to fix what she has. "Time for plan B. I'll be right back." I gently deposit her on the floor and stride toward the front desk, scribbling a note for Rebecca, who's on the phone.

Early lunch with Leilani, then going to the new site. Call my cell if you need me.

I make a quick stop at my office for my keys, her purse, and a Battles windbreaker dangling off the rickety coat rack in the corner. When I return to the locker room, I find Leilani at the mirror finger-combing the wig she put back on her head. The short style suits her small, muscular frame, but it's the determined look on her face I find most appealing.

Leilani might have taken a hit this morning, but she licked her wounds and came back swinging. I respect the hell out of people like that. "Here," I say, draping the jacket over her shoulders. It's about eight sizes too big.

"What's this for?"

"It'll hide the evidence." She flashes a relieved smile and slides her arms into the sleeves. I slip her purse onto her right shoulder and lead the way out of the locker room, pausing

34

momentarily to tuck the "restroom closed" sign inside the door.

"Where are we going?" she asks as we turn down a short hallway.

"Out the side exit so you don't have to walk through the lobby."

"I mean after that."

"To see my favorite seamstress."

"Who has a favorite seamstress? And… wait a minute." She glances around when we step outside. "Where's your yellow car?" I laugh once at her simple description of my 1970 Chevrolet Chevelle SS. It's been called many things—a muscle car, a money machine, and a 454 Rat to name a few—but never "my yellow car."

"I only drive that on the weekends." I motion for her to follow me one row over. "Today you get a front-row seat in this beautiful antique." I unlock the passenger door to the Ford Ranger I've had since I was sixteen. The odometer is pushing two hundred sixty thousand miles and the paint has seen better days, but it's still holding on.

Leilani climbs in and fights the sleeves of my jacket to fasten the seatbelt. When it's clear the jacket is winning, I reach over and guide the buckle into the slot.

"Asking for help is not a sign of weakness," I say, my face inches from hers. I don't normally get this close to my clients—or my employees for that matter—but I'm learning that nothing about Leilani and her mile-wide stubborn streak is standard operating procedure.

She juts her chin out. "I don't like it when people assume I can't do something." Her tone sounds more like the woman from the Jeep this weekend than the one from the bathroom only minutes ago.

"And I don't like it when people put words in my mouth. I never said you couldn't buckle your own seatbelt." I close her door with a pointed look and walk to my side, making mental notes on the way. *Competitive. Needs to be in control. Only willing to accept help when it's a situational issue. Questioning her physical abilities is a no-go.*

"For the record," I say, starting the truck, "I will never automatically assume you can't do something because you're an amputee. I used to train a guy who played basketball with one prosthetic leg and he kicked my ass every time." Leilani's sharp expression softens, and her lips turn upward. "That's not even the worst part. The guy was only five-foot-six." She throws her head back and fills my truck with melodic laughter. The sound alone is rewarding enough, but seeing her face light up like that? *Wow.*

"Clay?"

"Yeah?"

"Why are you staring at me like that?"

I lift a shoulder. "My mom always said when you see something beautiful, you should take a moment to admire it. You have an amazing smile."

"Um, thanks." Her cheeks flush a gorgeous shade of bashful, and I spend the ten-minute drive thinking of ways to make her laugh again.

Leilani peers out the windshield as the truck rumbles to a stop in front of a two-story brick house. "Who lives here?"

"The reigning Oklahoma State Fair needlecraft champion."

I jump out and walk around to open Leilani's door. "Before you get any ideas, I do this for all women, not just those missing limbs." I lean forward, cupping my hand like I'm telling her a secret, and whisper, "It's called manners."

She rolls her eyes and lightly smacks me on the chest as she steps out. "Are you sure it's okay that we stop by unannounced?"

"I do it all the time." Not bothering to knock, I lead us inside and hang my keys on a hook in the foyer. "Hello!"

"Back here!"

Leilani shoots a quizzical look at me but follows my path to the living room, where we find my mother in her natural habitat—buried under yards of fabric in her favorite recliner. One of the things I love the most about my mom is that she's never met a stranger. It doesn't matter if she's at the grocery store, the doctor's office, or gardening out front, she has one of those faces that invites people in and makes them feel comfortable. Which is exactly what Leilani needs, given the sensitive nature of her issue. "Hey, Mom." I bend down to kiss her cheek. "Whatcha whipping up today?"

"A baby quilt for DH and Paige since I don't have any grandchildren yet," she teases.

"Sell that sob story to Heather or Danielle. They're the married ones," I say, holding up my hands. Mom never fails to remind us that she's not a grandma, but since my younger sisters live out of state, I'm the one who gets the brunt of her good-natured guilt trips. When she peeks past my shoulder, I instantly know where her mind is going. "Leilani, this is my mom, Beth. Mom, this is Leilani, my new bookkeeper."

I emphasize the last word, hoping it implies *off limits, not dating,* and *don't even think about trying to set us up.* Mom's notorious for that. "Leilani needs some sewing help. I was hoping y'all could work on that while I make lunch."

Mom folds her quilt and sets everything in a cloth-lined basket beside her recliner. "What kind of help do you need?"

"Um…" Leilani's eyes flash with panic. I can only imagine how awkward this is for her, standing in her boss's mom's living room discussing prosthetic breasts. Without hesitation, I throw myself to the wolves to take some of the heat off her.

"She can tell you all about that in your sewing room. And whatever you do, please don't tell her any embarrassing stories about me. I'd like to leave here with my head held high." Sure enough, Mom is off the recliner before I even finish my sentence, and I'd bet money she's figuring out which story to tell first.

I'm so screwed.

We make it a mile down the road before Leilani bursts into laughter. "Did you really want to grow up and be a lobster?" she asks when she finally catches her breath.

I should have known. That's one of Mom's favorites. "In my defense, my parents told me I could be anything I wanted when I grew up." Her shoulders shake with a new round of giggles, and I find myself joining in, even if it is at my expense. It's a small price to pay to see her smiling for more than a few seconds.

"Your mom is really sweet. Thanks for taking me over there this morning."

"Don't mention it." I don't know how Mom fixed Leilani's breast cushion thing, but when they came out of the sewing room, Leilani had ditched the jacket and her clothes were free of white specks.

"How come neither of you have asked about my arm?"

Part of being a counselor is knowing when to push, but Leilani won't ever be my client so the ball's entirely in her court when it comes to personal information. "Well, the fact that you're missing part of it is obvious. The rest of that story is yours to tell when and if you're ready."

She nods, considering my words, then shifts in her seat. "I was on a convoy in Afghanist—"

My cell phone cuts her off. I glance at the display expecting to see Marshall or Rebecca, but the caller ID shows "Unknown" instead. "I'm sorry, I need to take this." I feel bad interrupting her, but unknown numbers are not something I ignore. I'll never make that mistake again. "This is Clay."

"She's fucking cheating on me." The voice makes my stomach drop. Jonathan, my four o'clock that canceled. He spent most of his last appointment talking about his girlfriend and the issues they'd been having. He was hopeful they could put everything behind them and move on. That was two weeks ago. It doesn't sound like it went well.

"Where are you Jonathan? I'd like to meet you so we can talk about this." Leilani sits up, her face mirroring my own concern, and switches the radio off. *Thank you*, I mouth.

"It doesn't matter. I just need you to tell that bitch this is all her fault."

Fuck, where is this guy? "What's her fault, Jonathan?" I pull over until I know what direction I need to be going.

"She said she hoped I'd drop dead, and she's going to get her wish."

No, no, no. My stomach plummets to my toes. "Okay, I'll tell her, but only if you tell me where you are." I mash the volume as loud as it'll go and strain my ears for any clues to his whereabouts. "Jonathan, where are you?"

"On a bridge."

"All right, which one?" There's no telling how many bridges Cleveland County has, if he's even in the county. He lives just south of Norman, but he could be anywhere.

"How the fuck could she do this to me?" he wails, ignoring my question. "I gave her everything she asked for, including that stupid fucking car she just had to have. That's what she used to meet up with that fuck stick. Do you know how much of a slap in the face that is? I'm paying for her slutmobile." He's not slurring his words, so drugs and alcohol don't seem to be a factor.

"I don't know why she did it, man. That's really fucked up. Let's go get a beer and talk about this. What bridge are you at?" His sobs are my only answer, and my anxiety kicks up a few notches. "Jonathan, please. I want to help you, but I can't do that if I don't know where you are."

"The bridge between Lexington and Purcell," he says, his breath hitching. I throw a silent thank you to God for the additional miracle. That bridge recently re-opened after being closed for repairs. Thanks to all the news coverage, I know exactly where it is.

Glancing over my shoulder, I pull a U-turn and race to I-35. "Okay, Jonathan. I'm coming. I'll be there in about thirty minutes. I want you to stay on the phone with me. You don't have to say anything. Just stay on the line."

"Fine, but no cops. Promise me." *Fuck*. I'd feel a hell of a lot more comfortable with them there, but I can't risk doing anything that will break his trust in me and push him past the point of no return.

"I won't call the police as long as you stay on the line." I put the phone on mute and glance over at Leilani. She hasn't said a word since my phone rang. "I'm sorry about this. I don't have time to drop you off at the gym."

"Don't be. This is your job, and from everything that's happened in the last few minutes, it's a very important one. I just hope we make it in time." Worry lines sprout between her brows. "Can I do anything?"

"Pray for no traffic," I say as we merge onto the interstate. Her reaction to Jonathan's call proves my gut instinct in the grocery store. Battles is my baby, and it's important that I have employees who understand the heart of what we do. If this was a test, she'd pass with flying colors.

The drive takes eons, but I finally reach the end of the half-mile long bridge. "Jonathan, I'm here. I'm on the Purcell side and I'm going to drive until I see you, okay?" He doesn't answer, but I hear him clear his throat so I take that as a good sign.

"There," Leilani whispers, pointing to a man standing on the other side of the guardrail a few hundred feet ahead.

"I see you Jonathan. I'm in a dark blue Ford Ranger. I'm going hang up and get out now." I end the call and turn to Leilani. "Stay in the truck. I left some distance between us so he won't see you and feel ambushed." *And so you won't see the fallout if I fail.*

Leilani nods and grabs my hand. She doesn't speak, but her face says everything.

Good luck.

Be safe.

I'll be here waiting.

"Thanks," I whisper. Seeing Jonathan so close to the

edge—literally and figuratively—makes me as angry as it does sad. *Did I miss something in our counseling sessions? Could this have been prevented? Did I have any role in his path to this bridge?* "Hey, man. Thank you for calling me." I do my best to keep my voice neutral; there's enough emotion swirling around without me adding any more to the mix.

His head snaps up, his red-rimmed eyes wide. "Don't worry, I'm not coming any closer right now." I sit down on the road about ten feet from him, partly to emphasize my point but mostly to keep me from pulling a John Wayne-style grab. Those rarely go well for the patient or the negotiator. "Do you want to come sit beside me?"

He shakes his head and focuses on the water beneath the bridge, shifting his feet back and forth along the concrete. My eyes are glued to his hands as if my gaze alone will tighten his grip on the railing. I'm afraid to move or say anything that will give him cause to let go, so I sit for who knows how long reassuring him that I value his life and won't leave him.

"You know what the real pisser is?" he finally says. "Steph wants me to drop dead, but I don't think she'll even care when she finds out I did." His voice is flat. Resigned. And that scares the shit out of me.

"So many other people will care though. Your mom. Your brother. The guys you work with. Me. None of us want you to die." A car slowly passes behind me, but I don't dare turn around.

"They're all going to think I'm a fool for trying to work things out with Steph."

"No, they're going to think she's a fool for walking away from the best thing in her life." I pause, letting my words sink in. "I'm going to stand up now and take a few steps toward you." I rise slowly and wait two full seconds between each step. "I'd really like to see you on the other side of this guardrail, Jonathan. I promise I'll do everything I can to help you through this if you just climb back over."

His brows draw together. "Why do you even care?"

"Because you're important to me. I enjoy the time I spend with you at the gym and I'd like to see you back there." I'm only about four feet from the railing, and Jonathan's at least fifty pounds lighter than me. As long as I get a good grip, I have no doubt I can haul him back over. "I'm going to take two more steps now." He turns his head toward the water, and my stomach lurches. "Please don't jump. Let me help you."

"I'm scared," he confesses. I still can't see his face, but his voice hints at a new round of tears.

"I know you're scared, but you're not alone. I'm going to take another step, okay?" With his back facing me, I open my stride and close the distance between us. "Jonathan, don't do this. Turn around and I'll help you."

I wait for an eternity, but he eventually faces me and nods his head. My arms are around him in an instant, my wrists locking tightly behind his back. I don't let go when his feet hit the concrete and sobs wrack his body. I don't let go when the faint sound of a siren draws near. I don't let go until paramedics approach us with a stretcher. Weak from emotional exhaustion, Jonathan collapses on the gurney and the medical staff takes over. I spend the next fifteen minutes telling the police what happened and who in Jonathan's family they can contact.

"Just curious—who called you?" I ask when I'm done answering their questions.

"A passing motorist who saw you sitting on the ground." I nod and lumber to my truck, desperately trying to keep my emotions in check. That lasts right up until Leilani throws herself into my arms and I give in to an onslaught of post-adrenaline fatigue.

I wrap my trembling hands around her and bury my face in her neck, hoping my embrace tells her everything I feel.

I'm so glad he lived.

I wasn't sure he would.

Thank you for being here.

5

Leilani

Ugly Duckling

A SHRILL RING SLICES THROUGH MY MORNING MUSIC mix. Careful not to roll my eyes too hard, I finish coating my few lashes in black and accept the call.

"Hi, sweetheart!" Mom lifts the phone, giving me a front-row view of her nostrils. We've been FaceTiming once a week since I moved to Oklahoma—her idea—and we go through this every time. You'd think after four weeks I'd learn to look away.

"Hey, Mom." I drop my lip gloss into the middle drawer and unlock Rebecca's side of the Jack-and-Jill bathroom, though I'm not sure why I bother. She's one of those get-up-fifteen-minutes-before-we-leave kind of women, so her busting in on me has never been an issue.

"How are you feeling? When's your doctor's appointment?

Are you going to be okay while we're gone?" Mom's eyes dart around the screen while she analyzes my face. Dad's taking her on a Mediterranean cruise for their anniversary, and although she's excited, it's killing her to be even farther away.

Me? I'm looking forward to not being nagged for ten days.

"I'm fine, this afternoon, and yes." I toss my phone on the bed so I can change. After the fiasco on my first day, Clay ordered embroidered shirts for the entire staff. He didn't want me fighting with a nametag or feeling out of place for being the only person who didn't wear one. And to top it off, he never brought up my meltdown or treated me differently because of it.

"Are you still liking your job?" Mom asks my ceiling.

That's another question I get every week. I think she's hoping I'll hate it and want to come home. "It's great," I say, pulling on my yoga pants. Beats the hell out of business suits at a bank. "We're about three months out from opening Battles 2. I didn't realize how much goes into a project like this, so the whole thing has been a learning experience." I retrieve my phone and flop on my bed. I never told Mom about the call I went on with Clay. She'd have been on the first flight to drag me back to Colorado.

He hasn't talked about it either, other than letting me know Jonathan is making progress at an inpatient treatment program. I've never met anyone who cares about people like Clay does. It's like you're the only one in the room when he's talking to you. It was odd at first, since I couldn't tell if it was genuine or if he was trying to flirt with me. Not that I'd mind if he was—he's dedicated his mind and body to Battles and holy fuck, it shows.

Last Thursday, I stayed late to finalize the budget for the new gym. Clay had an evening training session and must have forgotten I was still working at his desk. When he came back to his office and stripped off his shirt, I nearly fell out of his chair. That man gives "ripped" a whole new meaning. He apologized for startling me, but all I could think about was the eight-pack my fingers were itching to touch.

"Leilani, why are you smiling?"

I blink and focus on my phone again. "Huh?"

"You got this faraway look and started smiling." Mom's eyes narrow. "Are you okay?"

"Yeah, I was just thinking about all the amazing things you'll see on your cruise. Make sure you take pictures of the Sistine Chapel for me. And any hot Italian guys, too." Giving myself a mental high five for quick thinking, I hightail it into the kitchen and prop my phone against a canister of flour so I can pour a bowl of cereal.

Note to self: don't fantasize about your boss, especially while on the phone with your mother.

"No, something's wrong. Your cheeks look flushed. Are you coming down with a fever?"

"Mom, stop," I call from the fridge. "I'm not sick, and my cheeks are normal. See?" I set the milk on the counter and lean toward my phone, giving her an eyeful of my face.

She gives a quiet *hmph*, which, knowing her, translates to *I'm not happy, but I'm sitting in an airport with a three-thou-sand-dollar trip ahead of me, so I can't back out of it.* "Just prom-ise me that if you need someone, you'll call Kiki. She said she'd drop everything and come to Moore if you need her."

"She'll be here this evening. She's coming for the weekend."

That appeases her enough to soften the lines between her brows, giving me one solid second of peace before she's back at it. "You aren't living off of Fruity Pebbles again, are you? That's not good for your body. You need to eat well so you can stay healthy."

If she thinks this is bad, I have two other cabinets full of food that would make her cringe. Dad, on the other hand, would join me for a midnight snack. When I was in high school, I loved hanging out with him after Mom and Kiki went to bed. He's the one who taught me to make s'mores with Nutella instead of milk chocolate and how to fry Oreos in pancake mix. It's a good thing I spent so much time at gymnastics practice. These days, my saving grace is the weight I lost during chemo.

"Mom, it's six thirty in the morning. You realize this is a perfectly acceptable time to be eating cereal, right?"

"Yes, I know that." She sighs, her shoulders slumping forward, reminding me just how hard this year has been on her. Mom would've traded shoes with me in a heartbeat, even at the cost of her own hair and breasts, if it meant I'd never have to experience cancer.

I think that was the worst part about my diagnosis—having to tell my parents. I'll never forget the sound of Mom's guttural sobs or the helpless look on Dad's face. They both deserve a relaxing vacation now that I'm in remission, so I offer a dietary white flag to put Mom's mind at ease.

"Would you feel better if I only had cereal for breakfast and ate a salad every day while you were gone?"

"Really?" She perks up.

"Really." The smile on my lips comes easy this time. Over the past few months, I've forgotten that Mom wasn't always a nutcase. In fact, she was my biggest cheerleader when I was deployed. The people in my platoon loved it when she mailed care packages because she always packed extra snacks. She even sent mini mason jar cakes and cans of frosting for my birthday.

"Thank you. And yes, I'll take pictures of the Sistine Chapel and hot Italian men." She glances to the left and wiggles her eyebrows. "Speaking of, it's about time to board with my Mile High Club partner."

"Gross, Mom!" I clamp my eyes shut, but the damage is done. I'll never be able to look at an airplane bathroom the same way again. "I have to finish getting ready for work. You two disgusting love birds have a safe flight."

"I'll call as soon as we get home. Don't forget to—"

"I love you both. Bye!" I punch the red button, ending the call, and do the heebie-jeebie dance. Parents are so disgusting.

Rebecca's head pops up from her celebrity gossip magazine. "You brought doughnuts to a gym? Isn't that blasphemous?"

Laying my purse on her desk, I open the flimsy cardboard box and wave it in front of her. "Stop acting like you don't want one." We drove separately today because of my doctor's appointment, which meant I had time for a detour.

After thinking about Clay all morning, I realized I never got him back for the diarrhea medicine prank. If I play my cards right, my revenge will be nothing short of epic.

Rebecca scans the sugary contents, her long fingers wiggling with anticipation, and selects a maple bar. "You're such a bad influence on me."

"And it's a badge I wear proudly."

"Did someone say doughnuts?" Marshall ambles toward the reception desk with Clay three steps behind him, both wearing boyish smiles.

"Leilani's in cahoots with the devil this morning. She practically forced me to take part in her calorie-fest." Rebecca attempts a fake pout before giving up and stuffing her face. Getting her to go for the maple bar wasn't hard. She has a sweet tooth that rivals my own and uses at least half a bottle of syrup on her waffles.

"I'm always up for cahooting. May I?" Marshall points at the box.

"Help yourself." *This is too easy.* He wastes no time snagging the apple fritter in the back corner and leans against the desk beside Rebecca. Marshall wasn't hard to peg, either. Every morning, he brings a thermos of steel cut oats with diced apples and cinnamon.

"Clay, care to partake?" I tip the box in his direction and plaster an innocent smile on my face—the same one I practiced all the way from the bakery. He eyes me, then drops his gaze, zeroing in on the Boston cream.

Bingo.

"I feel like I'm setting a bad example," he confesses, lifting his doughnut. "Maybe I should sneak back to my office to hide the evidence."

I set the box on the desk next to Marshall and grab a cruller. "Consider this a team-building exercise among veterans. It only works when there's one hundred percent participation."

"Well, when you put it that way…"

I school my expression as Clay sinks his teeth into the doughnut.

Three.

Two.

One.

"Ugh!" With an Oscar-worthy grimace, he rolls Rebecca's

chair to the side and reaches for the trash can to spit his food out. "What the hell? Is that... toothpaste?" He swipes the back of his hand over his mouth and tosses the rest of his doughnut in the garbage.

I don't bother downplaying my victorious smirk. "Pastries have a ton of sugar. I was just trying to give you a head start on brushing your teeth." Marshall and Rebecca burst into laughter as I seal my lips around my cruller, savoring the first delectable bite just as much as Clay's reaction to my prank. Victory is sweet and delicious.

"I'm impressed, Leilani." My name rolls off his tongue like honey, and for the briefest of moments I indulge in the fantasy of tasting the chocolate lingering on the corner of his mouth. "How'd you know which doughnut I'd choose?"

"I found your stash of Boston cream pudding cups while I was organizing your filing cabinet."

Clay shakes his head and chuckles, accepting his defeat. "Well played. Shall we call a truce?" His brow inches upward as he locks his hazel eyes on me, a playful smile morphing into a smirk that makes it hard for me to swallow.

"Not a chance," I finally say, licking the glaze from my fingers. "I'm just getting warmed up."

Marshall leans toward Rebecca and whispers something, but I can't hear it over the buzzing in my ears. Clay's doing that thing where you're the only person in the room, and right now I wish I was. Accepting this job has officially become the best decision I've ever made.

"Not fair!" Clay glances over my shoulder at the voice behind me and grins. Confused, I spin and see a curvy blonde woman scowling at the box on the desk. "Is this a trick? Are you going to dangle a doughnut in front of me on the treadmill?"

"Hey, Paige." Clay rounds the corner and kisses the woman on the cheek, landing a simultaneous sucker punch to my gut. *Of course he's taken.* Just because he doesn't share his private life with his staff doesn't mean he doesn't have one. "Don't worry—we save the doughnut-dangling trick for the second session."

He shifts and points to me. "This is Leilani, my newest employee. She's whipping my budget into shape before we open Battles 2. That's Rebecca, the one you talked to when you started your membership. And that's Marshall, your trainer. Guys, this is Paige Rhoads."

A wave of relief washes over me when I hear the last name. She's not Clay's girlfriend, she's DH's wife. The one who had a baby a couple months ago.

Marshall pushes off the desk and leans forward to shake her hand. "You're early. I like that."

"These days, I'm either ten minutes early or thirty minutes late." She traps her curls in an elastic band and props her hands on her hips. "Where do we start? I'm tired of feeling like *Snow White and the Seven Post-Partum Dwarfs*."

Rebecca snickers. "The seven *what*?"

"*Post-Partum Dwarfs*. Lumpy, Bumpy, Frumpy, Dumpy, Pimply, Dimply, and Bulge," she replies, ticking the names off her fingertips.

"Come on, Snow White." Marshall throws a thumb over his shoulder. "Let's go consult the mirror on the wall and see what we can do about that."

With Paige in good hands, Clay turns his attention to me. "Are you up for a new project? I cleared my morning schedule, but I could still use your help."

"Sure. What's up?"

"I'm getting new computers delivered next week. I need to

make sure everything is backed up before then."

Translation: Want to sit next to me for the next four hours so you can stare at my arms while making sure I don't delete important files?

Abso-fucking-lutely.

"No prob. I'm leaving at three for my doctor's appointment, but the rest of my day is wide open."

Rebecca catches my eye as I gather my purse and doughnut box, but I ignore her silent questions. We can gossip about my harmless crush later. Right now, I have more important things to do, like stare at Clay's ass all the way to his office. Why can't the hallway be longer?

When we reach the doorway, he pauses to let me in first. "How are you liking it so far?"

His ass? On a scale of one to ten, it's a solid twelve. "It's awesome. I love it."

I'll take Things You Can Say About Your Job and Your Boss's Butt *for six hundred, Alex.*

"Well, you've been a great asset."

"Thanks." I smile and focus on stowing my purse in the filing cabinet to keep from commenting on *his assets.* "You were right about the job—it beats the hell out of working at a bank."

He laughs and rolls an extra chair to his desk. "I'm glad I could save you from long days in stuffy business clothes."

Hmm. Clay in a suit. I'd gladly suffer through pencil skirts and heels if it meant I got to see that every day. Talk about a benefits package.

My eyes drop to his crotch, wondering what else his package has to offer. The loose fabric of his gym shorts doesn't reveal anything, but based on the size of his feet, there's nothing to complain about.

"Do you mind if I turn on the fan before we start? It's a little warm in here."

Muted country music carries through the paper-thin walls, making the one-stalled bathroom look even more depressing. In my haste to forget the last half of the afternoon, I opted for availability—the Angry Buffalo or Bison or whatever it's called has a fully stocked liquor shelf and it's only two miles from my apartment. As soon as Kiki pulled up, I hopped in her 4Runner and told her where to drive.

I'd left Battles on cloud nine. Clay and I had spent all morning side-by-side, and then we got salads for lunch at a place across the street from the gym. Our conversation flowed effortlessly, whether we were talking about payroll documents or the best chow hall food in Afghanistan.

When I'd walked across the parking lot of the doctor's office, I'd thought about how great it would be to finally have boobs again. Then maybe I could have a shot at starting a relationship with Clay, or at the very least, find out if he tastes as good as he smells.

But no.

Thanks to a mind-boggling level of ineptitude, I'd left the doctor's office ten minutes later with a half-hearted "good luck" and more questions than answers. I was supposed to have a consult for a breast reconstruction. That's what my doctor ordered when I saw her two weeks ago. How that changed to a mammogram referral, I'll never know. Who the fuck orders a mammogram for a woman who has no mammies to gram?

The VA hospital, that's who.

Now I get to fight the system, which will take God knows how long.

Bastards.

I twist the faucet on the pedestal sink and wash my hand with a pea-sized glob of soap, then use my jeans as a towel. Now that I've broken the seal, I'll be back in here every fifteen minutes. It's a small price to pay for alcohol-induced amnesia.

Not bothering to look at my reflection in the dingy mirror, I yank the door open to rejoin Kiki and her Coke Zero at our high top. Given everything that happened today, she's gladly playing the role of responsible twin and I love her for it.

I slide my hand along the wall for balance and make my way across the bar, hoping my next Crown and Sprite is waiting on me. What I find is much worse.

Clay. At my table. Laughing with my sister.

The one with deep caramel hair cascading down her back.

The one with perky boobs and a fit body.

The one who has everything I'm missing.

Clay

Lies That Hide the Truth

EASING MY TRUCK TO A STOP BEHIND A SHORT LINE OF cars, I nudge Marshall's knees aside and pull a quart-sized Ziplock bag from my glove box. It doesn't have much—just some granola bars, a five-dollar grocery store gift card, a small tube of toothpaste, and a toothbrush—but for people who have nothing, a small something can mean everything.

"I can't believe you still do this."

"You should try it sometime." I crank my window down and wave to the man holding a cardboard sign. He scuffs his way over, his worn boots clomping with each step.

"What's your name, sir?" I ask.

His stubbly jaw drops an inch, like he can't believe I'm

speaking to him at all, let alone asking his name. "Um, David," he sputters.

"It's nice to meet you, David. I hope this helps." I pass the bag, taking note of his hands. I should add some fingernail clippers to my kits.

David surveys the contents and grins, tears pricking his eyes. "Thank you, sir," he whispers.

"My pleasure. Take care." He steps back as the light turns green.

"You're too trusting," Marshall chides after I close the window. "He's probably not even homeless."

"Based on his appearance, I'd say that's not a concern. And even if he wasn't, I'm only out a few bucks. People waste more money than that in the Starbucks drive-thru."

"So why not give him cash? You afraid he'd spend it on booze?"

I shake my head. "Did you see the look on his face when he realized someone planned ahead? That's why. What matters is making people feel important. It doesn't take a lot of time or money to give someone hope."

Marshall clutches his chest. "Clay Prescott, always the Boy Scout."

I lift a brow. "I seem to remember someone else who benefitted from my compassion."

He chuckles. "Yeah, yeah."

Two years ago, I met Marshall through a mutual friend. He'd just gotten out of the Army and found himself on the wrong end of a bogus job offer. He was in great shape and knew his way around a gym, so I gave him a spot at Battles until he could find something permanent. He ended up being a perfect fit and became a certified personal trainer.

My clients responded well to having another veteran on staff, and I got a break from the boring shit when Marshall volunteered to take over the books. I never cared much for that, especially when it cut into my counseling sessions, but lately it hasn't been so bad. Thanks to Leilani, I'm a few weeks ahead of schedule for the grand opening.

And it doesn't hurt that she's better looking than Marshall.

But more than that, she has a spirit unlike any woman I've ever met. Leilani is a competitor to her core. It doesn't matter if she's on the treadmill, organizing the office, or sneaking junk food when she thinks no one is looking. She's always on a mission to do it better, faster, or stronger. It's that attitude that drove her decision to amputate her injured arm.

Rollovers are dangerous enough, but having a fully loaded ammo box crush the tissue below her elbow meant her chances of regaining full use of her arm were next to nothing. Two months after her accident, she told the doctor to cut it off and didn't look back.

Her cancer, on the other hand, is something she's still coming to terms with. She hasn't had any more breakdowns, but I catch her looking at Rebecca every now and then, no doubt comparing their physical traits.

I just wish she could see how sexy her grit and determination are.

"That reminds me," I say, pulling into the parking lot of the Angry Bison. "I need you to sit down with Leilani next week. I want to make sure she's tracking on what needs to be done while you're on vacation."

Marshall and I staggered our vacation time this summer, starting with my trip to Hawaii next Saturday, but I'd feel better knowing she's up to speed before I leave.

"That reminds you? Last I checked, we were talking about homeless people, not Leilani." He makes no effort to downplay his side-eye.

Shit.

"We were talking about me giving you a job, which made me think of giving her a job. So yes, *that reminds me.*"

His phone rings before he can respond, and I use the diversion to make my escape. "I'll catch you inside." We come here a couple of times a month, and it always goes like this: Marshall bets that he can beat me in a game of pool and then adds another notch to his losing streak. I quit taking his money a few months ago because I felt bad.

"Hey, handsome. What'll it be?" The woman behind the bar smirks and reaches for a highball glass, knowing I habitually order the same thing—Jack and Coke, hold the Jack. I haven't had a drink since the day my parents scraped me off their bathroom floor and dragged me to the emergency room. That was ten years ago.

Once I got clean, I started setting goals, and one of them was to have a normal social life. My therapist wasn't happy. He said putting a recovering alcoholic in a bar is like giving a kid a piece of cake and expecting him not to eat it. It's a valid concern, and one I've shared with my own clients since then. But I'm stubborn, so I left it on my goal sheet.

It took six years to cross it off.

"Have you reconsidered my offer for a date?" she asks, setting my drink on the bar.

"I wouldn't want Mike to kick my ass." At the young age of fifty-eight, Sharon's a shameless flirt and loves coming up with reasons to feel my muscles. It's a good thing her husband has a sense of humor.

"Oh, please. The only thing he's going to kick is the bucket if he doesn't stop throwing money at that hunk of metal on wheels he calls an antique."

"I heard that." The voice echoes from the other end of the bar. I look down and see Mike smiling in our direction.

"So, you can hear me from over there, but not when I ask you to take out the trash from two feet away?"

Mike cups his hand behind his ear. "I'm sorry, what?"

Sharon chuckles and scratches her forehead with her middle finger. Theirs is the kind of relationship I hope to have someday. Romance is great, but so many people forget that having fun with your spouse will last a hell of a lot longer than a bouquet of roses and a backrub. "You see what I have to put up with? If only I had a man with muscles who could whisk me away to a tropical island. You know," she eyes my arm, "these just might work." She makes a show of gripping my bicep and fanning herself with her free hand. "Yes, those would do nicely."

"Quit fondling our customers, dear," Mike teases.

"And here I thought I married someone who would support my dreams." She sighs and wipes the bar with a dishtowel.

"Tell Mike to get a membership at Battles. I'll see what I can do about those muscles." Smiling, I place a five on the bar, grab my drink, and head toward the pool tables in the back. Halfway there, a giggle stops me in my tracks. I peer to the right and see Leilani at a high top. She's wearing a long wig this time. It's nice, but I still prefer the short, spiky one.

She giggles again, reading something on her phone, and reaches for her glass.

With her right arm.

It's not Leilani. My heart plummets until I realize who I'm

staring at.

"Kiki?" She glances at me, surprised to hear her name. I close the distance and extend my hand. "Hi, I'm Clay. Your sister works at my gym."

Her face lights up when she connects the dots. "It's nice to meet you, Clay. I've heard a lot about you."

I want to throw a victorious fist in the air and ask for a detailed list of everything she's heard, but settle for a polite smile instead. "Same here. Is Leilani with you?" I skim the room, hoping I look casual.

"She's in the bathroom, but she should be back any minute. You're welcome to join us." She points to an empty seat across from her.

I peek over my shoulder, confirming Marshall is still on the phone outside, and slide a barstool out. "I'd love to." Both sisters are knockouts, but now that I'm closer, I see the subtle differences between them. Kiki's lips aren't as full as Leilani's. She's also missing the tiny freckle in the center of her collarbone.

"So," she swirls her glass, "Leilani said you're getting ready to open a new location?"

I spend the next couple of minutes bragging about everything she's done at Battles and segue into this morning's prank, which Kiki hadn't heard about yet. In the middle of the story, I see Leilani on the far wall. She's exchanged her yoga pants and Battles polo for low-slung blue jeans and a pink t-shirt that makes her Hawaiian skin look even more tanned than normal. My smile grows wider, but as soon as she recognizes me, her face twists into a grimace and she bolts for the entrance.

"Umm, excuse me." Before Kiki can beat me to it, I hop off my stool and chase after her. "Wait!" She ignores me, moving unsteadily down the cracked sidewalk, muttering to herself about not being drunk enough.

"For what?" I ask, grabbing her shoulder. "Where are you going?"

She swats my hand away and continues weaving a path across the small parking lot. "Just go back to the bar. I hear the scenery's better there."

Huh?

"What are you talking about?"

"Don't be stupid, Clay. It's insulting." The bite to her voice isn't unfamiliar, but it's the first time I've heard it when she's not hangry.

"I'm not being stupid. You're just confusing the hell out of me." She's about twenty feet from the road. Traffic isn't heavy right now, but I'd rather not bear witness to a sunset game of tipsy chicken. "You're gonna get yourself killed if you keep going."

"Didn't you hear?" she calls over her shoulder. "I don't die. I just lose body parts."

"Last chance, Leilani." She lifts her left hand and extends her middle finger.

That does it.

I sweep her into my arms and do an about-face while she hollers like a petulant toddler.

"Put me down right fucking now!"

Make that a petulant toddler with a potty mouth. I resist the urge to laugh, knowing that will only piss her off more. Something tells me now's not the right time to push her buttons, and as much as I'd like to sit her down and figure out why she's so upset, it looks like Kiki has other plans. She joins us outside, two purses dangling from her arm, and points to an SUV.

"Sorry, Lei. They just announced last call. Why don't we head home and raid your junk food cabinet?" Kiki catches my eye, cluing me in on her fib. The Angry Bison doesn't close for another few hours.

"Last call? It's only…" She examines her watch, blinking several times. "Oh hell. I don't know. That's what I get for coming to a lame-ass country bar." Kiki opens the passenger door, and I lift Leilani inside, then reach for her seatbelt. As expected, she protests immediately.

"Why are you always trying to save me? You're so annoying." She's damn cute when she scowls.

"Take it up with my mom. She's the one who taught me my manners." I click the buckle, shut the door, and walk Kiki to the driver's side. "You need any help getting her home?" Half of me wishes she'd say yes.

"Nah, she's only had a few." She reaches for her handle, but pauses, tipping her head slightly. "Leilani was right about you, you know."

"About what?"

"You're a good guy."

I keep my smile to myself until her car rounds the corner and grin like a lunatic all the way back to the Angry Bison. The moment my hand hits the door, my phone buzzes with a text from Marshall. In the excitement of the last ten minutes, I'd forgotten about him.

Something came up. Sorry to ditch you.

I tap out a quick "it's cool," and head for my truck without putting anymore thought into what happened. He's a grown man who's never had problems taking care of himself. Besides, I have more important things on my mind.

Leilani thinks I'm a good guy.

My bullshit meter has been in overdrive since a quarter to eight this morning when Rebecca came in by herself saying Leilani had a migraine. I'd wanted to stop by her apartment this weekend, but Dad's last-minute deck expansion project kept me home. Mom needed more space for her wood pallet garden, and I couldn't say no, considering they let me live in the cottage on the back edge of their property. It was my grandpa's before he died, and when I got serious about school and opening a gym, they gave me the keys so I wouldn't have to worry about rent and utilities.

It's just as well. Kiki would have been at Leilani's, and I'd rather talk to her alone.

Like she'd be right now.

Marshall glances at me as I approach the reception desk, keys in hand, and shifts his feet to increase the distance between him and Rebecca. "Where are you going?"

"Dropping off some donations during my lunch break." The lie slips past my lips with ease. "I'll be back before my two o'clock."

Marshall holds his hand up as I start for the door. "Before you leave, I've been thinking about what you said." He pauses and grips the back of his neck. "I've seen a few homeless people not too far from the gym. One lady even has a kid with her. What if I invited them to come here and shower?"

My eyes go wide, and Rebecca's hand muffles her, "*Awww.*"

"Um, yeah. That sounds like a great idea." I try hiding the surprise in my voice, but it's no use. Of all the things I expected him to say, that's not even on the list.

"Okay." He nods and rubs his hands together. "Well, have fun with your donations."

"Thanks." I push open the front door to the sound of Rebecca cooing over how sweet Marshall is and hop in my truck, praying for nothing but green lights down Archer Highway. The logical side of me says I'm making an unnecessary trip, but the optimistic counselor can't resist the chance to help someone.

It has nothing to do with the funny feeling sliding around in my chest.

"Nothing at all," I mutter, cranking the radio.

Another lie.

Leilani

Purgatory

WHO NEEDS THERAPY WHEN YOU HAVE A SWEAR word coloring book, Eminem's *The Way I Am* blasting through your Bose speakers, and a noisy auto shop below the apartment that doesn't care about the volume? Call me a chicken all you want, but facing Clay is the last thing I wanted to do today. It was hard enough getting the third degree from Kiki when I woke up yesterday morning.

I've never been jealous of her—we each grew up with our own strengths, and even after my accident, I never felt "less than." But watching Clay smile at her hours after I'd learned I was no closer to having surgery made me see green, and then red, and that just created one shitty pile of brown.

I hate brown.

Except for chocolate, which I wish I had more of. I killed off the last of my stash yesterday after Kiki drove back to Fort Sill. Since I'd never told mom what types of salad I'd have while she was gone, a fruit version made with Granny Smith apples, chunks of Snickers, and Cool Whip sounded like a decent dinner. Rebecca's kids pushed cubes of pork chops around their plate while eyeing my food, so I sacrificed my last Snickers bar to make their dessert.

Being dubbed the best person in the world as they left with their grandparents was worth it.

Finishing the last of my coloring page, I lean back in my wooden chair and admire my work, briefly considering the ramifications of sending it to the VA hospital. *Go fuck yourself* seems like a message they should hear today. I even used patriotic colors.

My mind is halfway made up when Eminem ends, leaving just enough time to hear a knock at the door before the first notes of Big Sean's *I Don't Fuck With You* fill the room. Guess I was wrong about the shop not hearing my music.

I press the mute button, slide a Colorado Rockies ball cap on my head, and swing the door open, hoping my apologetic smile buys me brownie points. "I'm sorr—"

The word fades into silence as my body reacts to the man standing on the welcome mat.

Heart and lungs? *Stopped.*

Stomach? *Dropped.*

Nervous system? *On high alert.*

Clay's lips curve into their usual upward position. "I'm impressed. You rapped that song with such conviction." He lowers his face to the screen and whispers, "I think my favorite part was when you talked about grabbing your balls."

Fire ignites on the tips of my ears, blazing across my cheeks and down my neck. Why is he here? Does he visit every employee who calls out sick? "Uh, hi. I was just..." About to get fired, probably.

"May I?" He points to the black aluminum handle and I nod, still unable to form complete sentences. Clay steps inside and surveys the kitchen and living room, his eyes moving from the box of Fruity Pebbles on the counter to my coloring book on the table before settling on my hoodie draped over the back of the couch. Oh, God.

I glance down at my fitted black tank top wishing I would have put on a bra today. There was no need because it was just me. But now... *Shit*. My arms instinctively move to a defensive position across my boyish chest, but even that fails thanks to my missing limb. *Double shit.*

"Stop." Clay's voice is gentle but firm.

"Stop what?" I rub my right shoulder like I caught a sudden chill and casually retrieve my hoodie.

"Overthinking."

My fingers fumble on the zipper. "I wasn't."

He shoots a pointed look at me. "Just like you weren't hiding from me today?"

"I wasn't," I lie again, dropping into a ball with my back against the arm of the couch. "Why are you here, anyway?"

"Ah, there she is." Clay ignores my question and sits on the opposite end, squaring an ankle over his knee like he doesn't have a care in the world.

"There who is?"

"My favorite hedgehog."

My jaw drops. "I'm not a hedgehog!"

"No?" he teases. "When faced with an uncomfortable

situation, you immediately curled up and activated your prickly outer shell."

"You're so annoying," I mumble, plucking invisible lint from the knee of my yoga pants. Why can't he just sit there and look pretty?

Undeterred, Clay shifts, draping his arm across the back of the couch. "What happened Friday night?"

I lift a shoulder and analyze the chipped red polish on my toes. "Nothing."

"Bullshit. You were pissed off about something and took it out on me. And," he holds up a finger, "before you say something about not remembering, I know you weren't *that* drunk." He taps the bill of my ball cap to emphasize his point.

I swat his hand away and readjust my hat. "It doesn't matter. There's nothing you can do about it."

"Maybe. But keeping it to yourself won't fix anything either." He meets my narrowed gaze with a cool smirk and whispers, "It's okay to admit I'm right."

I remain silent on principle, toying with a stray thread on my hoodie, when I feel him tip my hat up. "Leave my—"

"Your hair's growing back," he murmurs. I sit frozen as Clay removes it completely, revealing a fresh crop of dark strands covering my head. "It looks good. Why are you still wearing your wig to work?"

God knows I wouldn't sweat as much if I left it off, but it's become a weird security blanket. Right now, I feel naked. I swallow twice, trying to force moisture back into my mouth. "It's still a little short," I finally eke out, running my hand over the back.

"Nah, it just looks like you got a haircut." He smooshes the hat back down, making my head bobble like a plastic sports figure. "Was it long before?"

I nod. "Longer than Kiki's."

"It was weird seeing her at the bar. I don't know how anyone gets you two confused."

I raise my right arm. "That hasn't happened in a few years," I say, my wry smile causing us both to chuckle.

"That's not what I meant. Your faces are different."

"Our faces?" My brows draw together. "Clay, we're identical."

It's his turn to nod. "I know."

"So, what's different?"

He fidgets with the edge of the cushion, keeping his eyes away from mine. This can't be good. My nails make crescent-shaped indentations in my left palm as I brace for something like "she's prettier than you."

"Um… your lips. They're… fuller. Nicer."

Oh. The temperature in the room shoots up a dozen degrees as I absorb his words. *He thinks I have nice lips?* This is good. This is so very, very good. I relax my fist and release an inaudible sigh of relief.

Clearing the gravel from his throat, Clay glances at me, his cheeks looking as pink as mine feel. He's no stranger to giving compliments. I can't count how many times he's praised the staff for the work we do or cheered his clients as they hit a new record in the gym.

But this is different. These words are electric, charged with the hope that maybe my feelings aren't as one-sided as I thought. The right side of my mouth inches up. "Thanks."

"Of course, your personalities are different, too. Kiki doesn't seem to be nearly as stubborn as you."

He flashes a devilish grin and I narrow my eyes in mock indignation. "Jerk." I smack his shoulder for effect, but he catches my wrist before I can pull away. His hand is strong, but gentle, and his fingers overlap just above my pulse point. I will my heart rate to keep my feelings toward Clay a secret.

"What happened on Friday?" he asks again, his playful expression gone.

Talking about my crush-induced outburst isn't an option, so that leaves one alternative. "I can't get my reconstruction."

Clay releases me, but leans forward. "What? Why?"

"I'm not sure yet. I tried calling the VA this morning. In the span of an hour and a half, I was disconnected twice, transferred four times, and given a bullshit song and dance from every person I actually spoke to. Hence, the loud music and swear word coloring."

"Okay, what's your plan?"

"What do you mean? I just told you. No one knows anything. At this point, I'm not even sure I can get an appointment with my primary care doctor." I rub the furrow sprouting between my brows while silently cursing the VA for ruining my chance to look like a woman again.

"I asked what your *plan* is, not what the problems are." Clay and his damn goals and plans.

I shrug. "Keep calling, I guess."

"Nope. Not good enough." His face turns resolute. "Tomorrow morning, you're driving to the VA to talk to the patient advocate."

Bless his heart, sometimes he can be so dense. "I have to work tomorrow."

His lips, never far from a smile, turn up. "It's a good thing you have a great supervisor. Don't come to work until you're done at the VA."

I open my mouth to say it won't do any good when he takes

my chin with his thumb and index finger. "That's a great idea, Clay," he says, moving my mouth while he imitates me. "Thank you so much for giving me the morning off." He drops his hand, lowers his voice, and continues. "You're welcome, Leilani. I'm always glad to help." Pleased with my forced agreement, he rises and heads for the door.

My disappointment over his departure is made marginally better by my view as I trail behind him. What's that saying? *I hate seeing him go, but I love watching him leave.*

"One more thing." With his hand on the knob, he turns, and I shift my gaze from his ass to his face a millisecond before I'm busted.

"Yes?"

"The pink shirt you wore Friday night? You should wear it more often." His honey eyes hold mine for an extra beat, and then he's gone. A small part of my brain registers the sound of his truck driving away, but the larger part is occupied with a single thought: Clay has touched me more times in thirty minutes than he has in thirty days, and I already want more.

Thirteen years of Sunday School taught me that hell is nothing but fire and brimstone. The last forty-seven minutes of my life confirmed hell is actually the parking lot at the VA hospital. Even at 9 a.m., the Oklahoma sun is trying its best to burn everything, and the dumpster on the back edge of the lot reeks of rotten eggs.

I'm so grateful to find a spot that I almost don't mind parking next to it.

Almost.

The hospital directory seems straightforward—the patient advocate is in Zone F and I'm in Zone C. That means I need to take two lefts, three rights, and a final left to reach the office. Easy enough, until I factor in the motorized scooters, hospital beds, crash carts, and elderly patients walking at a snail's pace.

Maneuvering through the hallways becomes a live version of Tetris with me pretzeling myself in empty spaces to avoid getting run over. I'm doing well until yellow tape and plastic sheeting force me to stop.

Come on.

"Closed for construction?" I groan, reading the paper hanging from the sheeting. The detour information posted on the wall is less than helpful, considering half of it has been ripped away. Defeated, I retreat to the previous hall and consider my options. Logic says I need to keep moving toward the back of the hospital, but the restricted access sign at the end of the corridor makes that impossible.

"Pardon me, miss." I feel a tap on my shoulder and spin around. "Are you a damsel in distress?" The gentleman's wide smile separates his handlebar moustache and chest-length beard. He smells of aftershave and pipe tobacco and has at least fifteen years on my dad.

"That depends. Are you a knight in shining armor?

He lifts his left pant leg and whacks his prosthetic with an American flag cane. "Titanium, actually."

A chuckle slips past my lips. "Impressive."

"But wait, there's more," he says in a dramatic voice. The man drops his pant leg, tosses his cane to his other hand and strikes his right side, just above his shoe. The fabric muffles the *ping*.

"Now you're just showing off," I tease.

"Guilty as charged. Where are you headed?"

I glance at the restricted access sign again. "I'm trying to find the patient advocate's office."

He nods. "They've had this half of the hospital blocked for months. Supposed to be a new radiology clinic, but I'll probably be dead before it opens." Not missing a beat, the man crosses in front of me and holds out his elbow. "Right this way." I slide my hand through the crook of his arm and follow him out a side door. "What's your name?"

"Leilani. Yours?"

"Tripod." He guides me around a clump of small trees and down a grassy path.

"Are you a photographer?"

His deep baritone laugh reminds me of flannel shirts and fireplaces. "No, just a double bologna with a cane."

I shoot a quizzical look to my left. "A double bologna?"

"My amputations. They're both below the knee. Bologna. Add my cane and I make one hell of a tripod." He steers me around the corner of another building while I dissolve into a fit of giggles. I can't wait to tell Dad I was escorted by a man who could pass as Wilfred Brimley's little brother.

"How long have you been coming here?" I ask.

He moves the fingers on his free hand while he silently counts. "Probably since you've been in diapers."

"No wonder you know your way around." He nudges me to a set of wooden steps leading to a row of single-wide trailers. "Am I keeping you from an appointment?"

"Nope. I just got done seeing my doctor. My Betty won't be done with her physical therapy for another half hour."

"Who's Betty?"

"The sweetest lady this side of the Mississippi." Tripod beams with pride. "She was my consolation prize from Vietnam. I lost

SAVED

my legs but I found the love of my life. Her friends were worried that it was the Florence Nightingale effect. They finally quit fussing about that twenty years ago." He winks and stops in front of the second trailer. "Here you go. Door-to-door service."

I smile and untangle my arm from his. "Thanks for the escort. It was nice meeting you."

"The pleasure's all mine." Tripod salutes me with the tip of his cane and retraces his steps toward the main hospital while I take a moment to assess where I'm at. I may need to draw on my land navigation skills to find my Jeep, but that's the least of my worries right now.

The aluminum door squeaks open, revealing a small waiting area littered with old magazines. Three chairs have already been claimed and judging by the expressions on the occupants' faces, they're just as unhappy about something as I am. I sign in and take a seat in the fourth chair.

The air conditioning unit in the window to my right rattles and hums just loud enough to make small talk impossible. Instead, I focus on the line of posters on the wall across from me, each bearing a word and an inspirational quote.

Change. "Embrace change. True success can be defined by your ability to adapt to changing circumstances."—Connie Sky

Patience. "A jug fills drop by drop."—Buddha

Perseverance. "Perseverance is not a long race; it is many short races one after another."—Walter Elliot

Achievement. "Without failure there is no achievement."—John C. Maxwell

Integrity. "Honor your commitments with integrity."—Les Brown

The irony is overwhelming. Some poor sap displayed these images as a literary pep talk for life's challenges, when really, they all apply to VA health care—or the lack thereof—in one way or another.

The person in the first chair gets called back twenty minutes later, but they stay in the patient advocate's office twice as long. By the time the third customer stands up, my ass is numb, my cell phone battery is at nine percent from playing games, and I'm in desperate need of anything with sugar as the first ingredient. If hell is the VA parking lot, then purgatory is this waiting room.

I lean my head against the wall and think of the flavors on the Sonic Blast menu. Bits of candy bar in a sea of ice cream sounds heavenly right about now. I'm debating between Snickers and Butterfinger when I hear my name.

Finally.

"I'm sorry," the woman says. "The office is closing for lunch."

I shoot out of my chair. "What? But I've been here since nine thirty!"

"I know." Her remorseful expression does nothing to lessen the blow. "You're welcome to come back tomorrow, though."

"Tomorrow? Why can't I come back when you re-open?"

"We only take appointments in the afternoon."

Bullshit. Bullshit. Bullshit. I take a calming breath. I need this woman's help, which means I need to keep my temper reasonably contained. "Okay, can I make an appointment?" I politely seethe.

"Absolutely." I follow her down the hall to a makeshift office.

"Let's see." She logs into the computer and brings up her calendar. "It looks like my next available is… 2 p.m. on August seventeenth."

My stomach drops. "That's five weeks away."

She nods. "We fill up quickly. Would you like me to put you down, or do you want to try again during our walk-in hours?"

I don't expect Clay to give me another morning off, and even if he did, there's still no guarantee I'd be seen. That means I have another month of no answers, and God knows how long after that to find out what's going on. It looks like I'll never have my surgery. Angry tears prick my eyes as I accept my reality.

"I'll take it."

Clay

Goals and Gratitude

"SPECIAL DELIVERY." A TINY WOMAN WALKS INTO MY office, and my face lights up when I see what she's carrying.

"Rosa, you never cease to amaze me. I'm surprised you didn't have a line of people following you down the hall." I take the plate of tamales and bend down to kiss her cheek. "How's Eduardo?"

The news that he'd collapsed last month while teaching a summer school algebra class at Lawson High was devastating.

"He's feeling better. He has one more week of restricted activity and hates that I'm holding him to it. I told him if he went for his mid-day walk while I was gone, I would sell his gun collection on eBay."

We chuckle. "I hope for his sake he follows directions."

"He probably won't. He'll pretend he was watching TV the whole time and I'll pretend I don't see his shoes in the bedroom. I swear that man is going to turn the rest of my hair gray."

"Do you need to take more time off?"

She pats my arm. "No, *mijo*. You've been very generous, but I'm looking forward to coming back to work. After a month at home, there's nothing left in my house to clean." We visit for a few more minutes before she turns to leave, saying Eduardo should have had enough time to lie down and look innocent.

As soon as she clears the door, I grab a fork out of my desk and tear into my tamales with little regard for the extra miles I'll need to log tonight. I've inhaled three by the time Leilani stomps into my office, flings her purse into the filing cabinet behind my desk, and plops on the chair in the corner. I take full credit for the ball cap she's wearing today, but given the murderous look on her face, that's the last thing she wants me to bring up.

"Grocery store out of Fruity Pebbles? I hate when that happens," I say, hiding my smile behind my napkin.

Leilani's brows bump together in a scowl. "You're so annoying."

"You've mentioned that. How'd it go at the VA?"

"It didn't."

"What happened?"

She rolls her eyes. "I got lost. Someone escorted me to the patient advocate's office. I signed in. I wasted two hours of my life. They closed for lunch. I stopped to get a milkshake but the stupid machine was broken. I came to work. Happy?"

Her logic when she's hangry is laughable at best—I don't know anyone else who would forego food because they couldn't eat dessert first. I grab my plate, load my fork, and wheel my chair toward her. "Open your mouth."

"No." She sets her jaw.

"So help me God, open your damn mouth."

"You can't—"

Seeing an opportunity, I slip the fork past her lips. Her nostrils flare once before her taste buds turn her protest into a satisfied sigh. No one can resist Rosa's cooking. "Now tell me why you're not at the VA talking to the patient advocate."

"They only take appointments in the afternoon." She gazes longingly at my food, though I know she'd rather eat her foot than ask for another bite.

"Did you make one?"

"Yes, but it's not for another five weeks."

I nod. "On the bright side, at least you made some progress today."

"Easy for you to say. Your boobs are bigger than mine." She cocks a brow and steals my tamales.

"First," I say, leaning forward in my chair, "I don't have boobs. And second, you didn't say please." I snatch the plate back and take a victorious bite, enjoying the hell out of the daggers she's shooting at me.

"You're so mean!"

"Maybe." I wave the dish in front of her face. "I'm also the one with the food. If you ask nicely, I'll share." She says nothing, as expected, so I grab her chin. "Clay, I'm too stubborn for my own good. Can I please have some lunch before my stomach shrivels up?" She keeps her narrowed eyes on me as I answer my own question. "No problem, Sonic. You know I'm always happy to help."

"Sonic?"

"The Hedgehog."

"Ass," she mutters.

Not bothering to hide my smirk, I pass my plate and grab her employee folder from the filing cabinet. "Time for the next order of business."

"Which is?" she asks around a mouthful of food.

"Going over your goals. We were supposed to do this last week, but I got sidetracked." I remove the paper from her packet and scan the answers.

"Belize?" I chuckle. "I didn't realize you had such an interest in Central America. Or chocolate soufflés. How are the cooking lessons going?" She pauses mid-chew. "What about *Toy Story 3*? Have you watched that recently?" Her head turns back and forth. "Well, we already know about the status of your surgery, so it looks like the only goal you met last month was not getting fired. You're one for five."

Leilani swallows and sets the plate on my desk. "Funny, aside from keeping my job, surgery was the one thing I thought I'd actually accomplish. Or at least have scheduled by now."

"I can only imagine how frustrated you are, but you still have a lot to be grateful for."

"Like what? Stellar health care? Half-off on manicures? Saving money on shampoo? How about a boyfriend who dumped me because I got cancer? I get that you're Mr. Sunshine, but gratitude doesn't fix anything."

I comb through her questions, zeroing in on the last one. "Wait, your boyfriend dumped you because you were sick?"

She flashes a wry smile. "Nice of him, huh?"

I can't imagine letting go of a woman like Leilani. In the short time we've known each other, she's become one of my favorite people. Work is never boring when she's around, and she's already come up with a bunch of different advertising ideas for Battles 2. "That's really shitty."

"Yeah, well, I'm good at losing things." She leans back, resting her hand on the top of her ball cap.

"I know it sounds hokey, but there's truth to the power of positive thinking. I promise if you start looking for the good in situations, you'll realize things aren't quite as bad as they seem."

"Clay, seeing the good isn't going to make the VA do their job properly. I'm just sick of looking like a boy."

Her honesty is as appreciated as it is alarming—getting the truth out of my clients can take months, but what Leilani sees as the truth is completely distorted. I maneuver my chair in front of hers, trapping her between my knees and the wall.

"Hey." With a heavy sigh, she drops her hand and drags her gaze to mine. "You could wear a three-piece business suit with a football helmet and a pair of construction boots and still look like a woman."

She grins. "Or a very confused man."

"Also that." Her giggles fill the space between us. It's a sound I've heard many times before, but never while I've had a front-row seat to her smile, and especially not while I've imagined what her lips would feel like pressed against mine. "Come to Hawaii with me."

Two things happen the moment those words leave my mouth: Leilani's eyes turn to saucers and my brain launches into damage control to craft an explanation for my semi-out-landish request—preferably one that doesn't include my desire to see her in a bathing suit or put sunscreen on her back. I start by rolling my chair to my desk. I can't not look like a creeper if our knees are still touching.

"Every summer, I do some sort of fundraiser to help a

non-profit. Last year, I hosted a bachelor auction for VETSports, and this year I teamed up with a few people to participate in a summer camp sponsored by Helping Hawaii. But instead of just raising money, we're lending our services, too. I'm leaving on Saturday with two doctors from Barton Memorial, an art teacher from Hawthorne Elementary, and an executive chef from the Rolling Thunder Casino."

Leilani tilts her head. "What's Helping Hawaii, and why do you want me to go?"

"It's an organization that helps children affected by homelessness and poverty. Fifty kids between the ages of twelve and seventeen will be split into groups of ten, and they'll rotate each day. Local companies have sponsored trips to the Honolulu Zoo and a day of water activities, and the Battles team will cover the remaining three days at the community center. The doctors will spend the week at the hospital—one in the pediatric clinic and the other in surgery."

Remembering the stash in my filing cabinet, I retrieve two Boston cream pudding cups and plastic spoons. I'm not above bribery. "I want you to go because your story will resonate with these kids. They've had it hard their entire life. You're a great example of how to overcome challenges. And on the flip side, you could benefit from the trip, too." I peel off the lid to the pudding cup and plunk the spoon inside, then roll toward Leilani.

"How would I benefit?" She accepts the container without arguing about me helping her. It's a small victory, but I'll take it.

"It'll give you some perspective. I know you're pissed about your surgery, and that's completely understandable, but that's the *only* shitty thing you're dealing with right now. These kids aren't even close to being that lucky." I open my own container and lick the lid before dropping it in the trash.

"I see where you're going with this, but I never got my Belize travel fund off the ground. I don't have enough money to buy a ticket to Hawaii four days from now."

I grin, knowing she's already convinced. Now it's just a matter of hashing out the logistics. "I've got it covered."

She cuts a glance at me. "I'm supposed to believe you have thousands of dollars to spare on someone else's flight?"

"Dollars, no. Every spare cent to my name is tied up in the new gym. But I do have a shit ton of airline points from my credit card."

"Where would I—"

"Sleep?" I finish, scraping the inside of my pudding cup. "Volunteers are staying at a hotel right down the road from the community center. It's not a five-star resort, but it's clean and safe."

She finishes her last bite and purses her lips in thought. The only thing we haven't covered is her work schedule, which won't matter because I had this trip planned long before she came to Battles. Leilani nods when I tell her that.

"You realize this is crazy, right? Normal bosses don't invite their employees on last-minute jaunts to Hawaii."

I point my finger at her. "Let's get one thing straight. I never claimed to be a normal boss. And this is no jaunt. It'll be a working vacation. From 8 a.m. to 6 p.m., we'll be up to our eyeballs in kids, sports equipment, and fitness challenges. In fact, if we're both there, we can do some team competitions. That is, if you're not too afraid of losing in front of everyone."

With a smug smile playing on her lips, Leilani wheels her chair to my desk and tosses her trash in the metal can. "I can't wait to prove you wrong."

I give myself a mental high five for the Herculean task of

containing my excitement. "Excellent. I'll take care of your flight when I'm done with my afternoon sessions."

"Do you need my information for the ticket?"

"I have it right here." I hold up her paperwork before tucking it inside her folder.

"I guess I should apologize about the goal thing. Do you want me to think of some new ones?"

I study her face as I consider her question. If it was anyone else, I'd say yes; working toward something is a great way to stay motivated. But Leilani needs a project that will shift her focus from goals to gratitude. One thing I've learned over the years is the simple notion that by helping others, I help myself. I want that for her.

"We're going to do something different. For the next month, you'll perform random acts of kindness. I'll write down one word for each day and you'll have to incorporate that in some way."

She scrunches her face. "What do you mean?"

"Let's say your word is 'book.' You could read to a child or write something encouraging and slip it inside a book."

"What about buying a book for someone?"

"You could do that too, but the purpose of this project isn't about spending money. It's to get you thinking of creative ways to do something nice for other people."

Leilani tilts her head. "So, this takes the place of my goal sheet? I just have to do one nice thing every day for the next month?"

"That's it."

She nods and collects Rosa's plate but pauses when she reaches the doorway. "Thanks for lunch and dessert. You've made my afternoon a hell of a lot better than my morning was."

"My pleasure." We exchange smiles, and then she's gone, leaving me to add up the calories I need to burn during tonight's run. I already know I'll spend my entire route thinking about how good her ass looks in those yoga pants. I'll wait until my shower to think about how good she'd look out of them.

9

Leilani

Robin Hood

FRESH AND CLEAN AFTER A THREE-MILE RUN, I GRAB MY laptop and sink into the sofa next to Rebecca, who's on a video call with her mom.

"I'm so proud of you, sweetheart." From my position, I see her mom dab a tissue at the corners of her eyes.

"You should hang it on the fridge, Grandma!" Bristol shouts as she twirls behind Mrs. Perry.

"That's a great idea, dear." She chuckles and pats the chair beside her. "Come say goodnight to your mom while I help Grandpa tuck Blake in."

Bristol sits in front of the screen and launches into a story about the next-door neighbor's dog who got out of the fence and pooped on the Perry's front porch.

"No way!" Rebecca wrinkles her nose.

"Yes way! Grandpa had to get the hose to wash it off. Hey, do you think we could get a dog when you live with us again? I could train it to poop in the backyard."

She hides her sadness behind an overly enthusiastic smile. "I can't promise we'll get one, but I promise to think about it, okay?"

Bristol nods, and after a volley of blown kisses, Rebecca ends the FaceTime call.

"She's right," I say, pointing at the Wells Fargo bank statement. "You should put that on the fridge."

My roommate stares at the paper, her face a mixture of disbelief and pride. "I know a thousand dollars isn't much, but I never thought I'd see that number in my savings account. I guess that's what happens when I don't blow it at the casino," she jokes before shifting her attention to my laptop. "Are you buying boobs on Amazon Prime?"

"Yup. And a bathing suit to go with them."

"For what?"

"For my trip to Hawaii." I click on an image of a nautical one-piece to confirm the top has pockets for my breast forms, then add it to my cart along with a matching cover up.

"You went from being screwed over by the VA to going on a trip to Hawaii?"

I nod. "It's been a strange Tuesday."

"So, when are you leaving?"

"In four days."

Rebecca raises an eyebrow. "Interesting. I'm aware of someone else who's leaving for Hawaii on Saturday. Would you happen know anything about that?"

The corners of my mouth tip up. "Maybe."

She shrieks and smacks the couch cushion. "Spill it!"

"It's not as sexy as it sounds," I say, holding up a cautionary hand. "I'm just helping him with the summer camp." I repeat the words in my head as a reminder that while it's nice to fantasize, I don't need to get carried away. This is strictly a business trip—one I likely wouldn't be on if I wasn't an amputee or had taken my goal sheet seriously.

"Not as sexy, my ass. The man you have a massive crush on made an excuse to bring you to Hawaii, where there's a one-hundred-percent chance he'll see you wearing—" She grimaces when she looks at my shopping cart. "Why are you buying a muumuu?"

"It's a cover up!"

"That covers you from your neck to your knees. And a one-piece? Really?" She shoots a playful side eye at me.

"I don't want to worry about my boobs falling out."

Rebecca commandeers my laptop and types *mastectomy bikini* in the search bar. "See? They do exist. And with that body, you'd be a fool to pass up a chance to make Clay's tongue wag."

"I appreciate your vote of confidence, but I'm playing it safe." I reclaim my computer and click the checkout button before she gets any ideas about adding stuff to my order.

Clay walks into his office wearing a faded "I did it all for the cookie" t-shirt, complete with Cookie Monster wearing a red ball cap, and heads straight for the package of water bottles on top of his filing cabinet. With a twist of his wrist, he opens the lid, downs half of it, and collapses onto the chair in the corner.

"Clients kicking your ass this morning?" I tease.

"It's my fault for scheduling two milestone sessions back-to-back, especially when one of them was Dustin." I've never heard of a trainer turning the tables on himself, but Clay has discovered how motivating that opportunity can be. When his clients reach a milestone in the gym—be it a personal record or a breakthrough in counseling—Clay rewards them by switching roles.

"What'd you have to do?"

"Two hundred sit-ups for Elisa and the Murph Challenge for Dustin."

I wince knowing how taxing that workout can be. My amputation has prevented me from doing the prescribed one hundred pull-ups and two hundred push-ups, but I have done the remaining steps—a one-mile run, three hundred squats, and another one-mile run, all while wearing the required twenty pounds of body armor.

"Maybe I should re-think my goal sheet. I could get on board with making you sweat." *Oh God.* Heat floods my cheeks as I realize the double meaning behind my words. "Um, in the gym, not..." Clay chuckles while I stare at the floor wishing I could get a do-over for the last ten seconds of my life.

"I'll make you a deal. If you get through my random acts of kindness challenge, I'll do anything you want."

My gaze shifts from the worn carpet to his face. I already agreed to participate, so I'm not sure why he'd offer me a milestone workout, or why he'd say he'd do anything I want. Is this him playing to the competitor in me because he thinks I'll fail otherwise? Or does he know I have feelings for him? His eyes don't offer any hints either way, so I clear my throat and steer the conversation back into safe territory. "Okay. What random acts you come up with, anyway?"

Clay hops out of the chair and nudges me back so he can open his top drawer. "I wrote down the first thirty words that came to mind." He passes me a sheet of paper from a Battles notepad and sits on the corner of his desk. The first several seem easy enough—wheels, red, and flower—but numbers ten, seventeen, and twenty-four turn my cheeks pink all over again.

Wet, sticky, and dirty.

What was he thinking about?

Before I have time to speculate, he raises his brows and says, "I called the airline last night. Please tell me you don't have any plans on Friday."

"Just packing, why?"

He lets out a relieved sigh. "Thank God. They didn't have any available seats on Saturday, and we can't travel on Sunday because we have orientation. I sort of assumed you didn't have anything going on and booked us on a Friday morning flight instead." A sheepish smile plays at his lips.

"I almost never have weekend plans. My life basically consists of working, eating junk food, and exercising." I pause. "It sounds so sad when I say it out loud."

"I know how to cheer you up," he says, voice low and eyes sparkling.

Why yes, a strip tease would *be nice right about now.* "How?"

He tips his head toward me. "Ask me where we're sitting on Friday."

"Where are we sitting?"

"First class."

My mouth falls open. "Are you sure? Those seats aren't cheap."

"Airline points, remember? It didn't cost me a dime." Clay uncaps his bottle, leans back, and chugs the rest of his water as Marshall enters the office. Per usual, I'm hit with the same wave of familiarity. We've talked about our time in the military over the past month, but thanks to chemo brain, I've yet to pinpoint where I might've seen him before. It's so annoying.

"You survived!" Laughing, he claps Clay on the back and slides the empty chair to the desk, turning his attention to me. "You ready to rock and roll, Short Stuff?" Marshall set some time aside this morning to help me get our new computers up and running. The system he's used for the last couple of years is more complicated than it needs to be, but I suppose that's expected from someone who was never formally trained.

"I'm just about done." His wide-eyed expression makes me grin. "I've already transferred the employee profiles to the new computer and created the financial spreadsheets for Battles 2. I just need your help with a few more things."

"I'll leave y'all to it." Clay gives us a quick wave and heads for the door while I pull up the program we use for tracking our hours. I've just started my questions for Marshall when Clay peeks his head back in. "Hey. I'm heading out tonight to grab a few things for the trip. Want to come with me?"

My traitorous cheeks threaten to turn crimson again, so I pretend it's my dad at the door asking if I want to join him for a round of golf. "Sure," I say, proud of my calm voice.

"Great. Pick you up at six?"

"Sounds good." The corners of my mouth find a happy median between casually pleased and *hell-yes-can-we-leave-now-instead*. When Clay disappears again, I turn my attention back to Marshall, trying to focus on what he's saying.

Too bad it doesn't work.

I'm ready fifteen minutes early. With Rebecca at Bristol's ballet recital, I pass the time by rotating between peering through the wood blinds, going pee, and checking my reflection in the mirror. Tonight, I'm leaving the house without anything covering my head, a first since I lost my hair. Forget butterflies in my stomach—these are dueling pelicans.

I'm at the pantry shoving a granola bar into my purse when I hear Clay's engine rumble to a stop outside. To make it look like I haven't been stalking my window, I toss my bag on the table, scurry around the couch, and turn the TV on, then wait a slow count of eight before I answer his knock.

"Hey," I say, slightly breathless, my eyes raking over his body. He's traded his gym gear for jeans and a simple dark green t-shirt—a combination I could see on any department store mannequin, none of which would turn my head like the man on my doorstep.

"Wow. You look… *wow*," he says, the ever-present smile curving even higher, chasing away the unwanted creatures flapping around my insides. "You ready?"

"Yeah, let me grab my purse and turn off the TV." I spin on my heels and hear him chuckling behind me. "What's so funny?" I call over my shoulder.

"What are you watching?"

I glance at the entertainment center and, to my utter embarrassment, hear two characters speaking Spanish to each other. I haven't Español'ed since my junior year of high school. The only thing I remember from that class is how to twirl a pencil between my fingers, but even that skill is useless because I don't have that hand anymore.

"Research for my Belize trip. I decided maybe that goal wasn't so bad after all."

He smirks. "You sure about that?"

"Of course." With feigned smugness, I click the remote, lock the deadbolt, and follow Clay down the stairs. "The yellow car? What's the occasion?" We reach for the handle at the same time and our fingers tangle behind the strip of metal.

"Manners, not inability," he says with a gentle undertone.

"Right." I step back to give him room to open the door, but mostly to keep my hand from touching the blond stubble covering the lower half of his face. He's always been clean-shaven at work. This new development adds one more entry onto my reasons-my-boss-is-freaking-hot list.

He waits until we're both tucked inside to answer my question. "I won't get to drive it while we're gone, so I'm making up for it tonight."

"Aw, you're going to miss Buttercup?"

Clay turns his head, arching a brow. "Buttercup?"

"Don't men pick girly names for their cars?"

He chuckles at the sweet smile I send his way. "Some do, yes. I was thinking of something more masculine though." His fingers tap a beat against the steering wheel. "What about Bumblebee?"

"The fuzzy thing that flies?"

"Clearly, you've never seen *Transformers*."

"Big Bird?" I offer. "He's a dude who can fly, at least in theory."

"Wolverine," he counters, drawing the name out for emphasis.

I shake my head. "How about Princess Consuela Bananahammock?"

Clay barks out a laugh. "Princess *what*?"

"Clearly, you've never seen *Friends*." We continue tossing names back and forth, each more ludicrous than the last, while picking up jump ropes, wrist bands, collapsible water bottles, and tote bags for the kids. When we're done, I tip my head at the small mountain of shopping bags in the backseat. "How are you going to get all this to Hawaii?"

"I'm paying for another checked suitcase. It was cheaper and quicker to do it that way." Clay reverses out of the parking space but stops short at the end of the lot. "Want to grab a bite before I take you home?"

Nestled in a small table near the back of Cattlemen's Steakhouse, I tell Clay about my first and only trip to Hawaii while we wait for our food. "My sister and I were five or six, and my mom told us we were going there to bury my grandpa. All the relatives wore white the day of the funeral, which is common for Hawaiians. Apparently, that confused Kiki because when it came time to leave for the ceremony, she threw a fit and said she wouldn't go."

Clay leans forward on his elbows. "Was she close with your grandpa?"

"No, we hardly knew him. Kiki just thought we were dressed in white because everyone was *marrying* Grandpa and she refused to kiss a dead guy."

His laugh pours over the table as the waitress delivers our

meals, causing her to chuckle along with us. Once my plate is in front of me, it's all I can do to stifle my moan. We both ordered the Hawaiian chicken breast, and even though it doesn't look like anything my mom's ever made, it smells amazing.

"Was it hard to re-learn stuff like that after your surgery?" Clay nods at my stump, which is holding the end of my fork upright while I cut my dinner.

"Some things. Tying my shoes was a pain in the ass. I had to—"

"I didn't know it was cripple night at Cattlemen's."

My face and neck prickle with heated awareness. I don't need to look at the table to my left to know the man is talking about me, his not-so-subtle barb piercing the easy atmosphere in the dining room. It's not the first time this has happened since my accident, but it never gets any easier.

"How about you put that thing away? Some of us are trying to eat," his friend adds. The venom-laced words hit their mark again. My shoulders, my head, my heart—they all fall, until I'm staring at a ceramic plate of rice pilaf wishing I was anywhere else.

"Can we go?" I whisper to Clay. When he doesn't respond, I look up. The muscles in his jaw flex and strain as he works to control the fury in his eyes, and then, with a careful swallow and a deep breath, he replaces the fire with an icy calm and rises.

"Good evening." He grips the edge of their table, his voice low and steely. "You have exactly five seconds to apologize to my date, get up, and quietly walk out of here or you won't be able to take a solid shit for a month, and when you finally do, you'll see the tread from my boots stamped in every nugget that your sorry asses drop into the toilet."

The man on the right shifts in his seat. "We were just—"

"Four."

The one on the left glances at me and back to Clay, whose expression has shifted from angry to lethal.

"Three." He forces the word through his teeth.

"Two." Finally realizing Clay is serious, the men scoot their chairs out, toss a halfhearted "sorry" over their shoulders, and speed-walk to the front door, their cowardly tails tucked between their legs.

Who knew Dr. Jekyll would turn into Mr. Hyde on my behalf?

That's something Travis never would've done, because it's bad PR for a radio deejay to get into a public brawl. Not that he could've handled a two-on-one fight in the first place.

My heart maintains its runaway rhythm, thanks in part to Clay calling me his date, as he returns to his seat. "You didn't have to do that, but thank you."

"They were *not* getting away with disrespecting you like that. I'm kind of sorry they left before I got to 'one,' though." He hatches a mischievous smile and picks up his fork. "So finish telling me your story about tying your shoes?"

"No way!" Rebecca's mouth falls when I tell her about the near-fight at the restaurant.

"Yup! And then Clay had the waitress put their food in to-go containers and gave them to some homeless people on the way home."

"He's like a brawny Robin Hood."

"Aaand now I'm picturing him in tights," I giggle, grabbing the remote so we can catch up on the last episode of *Big Brother.*

When the screen comes on, she arches a brown in my direction. "Were you watching the Spanish channel?" I explain what happened before Clay arrived while I pull up the DVR menu. "Leilani, I hate to break it to you, but the national language of Belize is English."

"Oh God," I cringe. "No wonder he smirked."

Clay

Starfish

THAT PINK SHIRT. THE ONE I TOLD HER I LIKED.

Did she wear it for me? Did she think about me when she got dressed? Christ, did she think about me *before* she got dressed? And what about not wearing her hat? Was that because I said I thought her hair looked good?

These questions have hamster-wheeled inside my head all damn day—my early morning workout, back-to-back sessions in the gym, even during the worst game of pool I've ever played at the Angry Bison.

I can't believe Marshall won.

Still, I wonder if—

Mom clears her throat, reminding me that she's waiting on my muscles. "I ran into Anna today at the grocery store. She asked about you." I make a noncommittal grunt and twist the jar of peaches open with a satisfying *pop*, then pass it to her. "She read the article in the paper about your new location and said she was proud of you for following your dream."

"The one she hated in the first place?" The only thing Anna enjoyed in our six-month relationship was hanging on my arm at community events. She spent the rest of the time complaining about the hours I logged with my clients at the gym. Anna never understood the work I do, and shortly before Christmas when I told her I planned on opening Battles 2, she flat-out accused me of making my business a bigger priority than her.

I agreed. Aside from several tear-filled voicemails and an awkward visit to my office right after New Year's, I haven't heard from her since we broke up.

Marshall thought I was an idiot for giving up a prime piece of ass—his words, not mine. When I called him a dick for making a comment like that, he laughed and said that's how he knew I made the right decision; if I actually loved her, I'd have kicked his ass instead.

"She also gave me her phone number in case you don't have it anymore and said she'd love to catch up with you." Mom lifts an eyebrow as she preheats the oven.

I ignore her comment and tip my head toward the new cookbook on the counter. "Another one?" She always loved cooking and baking, but she's taken it up a few notches now that Dad is on the road for a week every month. Retirement from the military didn't sit well with him, and having him underfoot all the time didn't sit well with her. A part-time trucking job was the perfect solution for them both.

"I won it at bingo last week. It has more than a thousand five-star reviews online."

My eyes scan over the cover. *Pearl's Heavenly Desserts—Saving lives, one sweet tooth at a time.* "Huh. Did you see this?" I point to the text on the bottom, where it says all profits benefit Thrive + Blossom, an organization for domestic violence survivors.

"I thought you'd like that part." She gives me a warm smile as she opens the book to a cobbler recipe. "You ready for your trip?"

Grateful she's dropped the conversation about Anna, I lean my hip against the counter. "Yup. Just have to pack a few more things tomorrow morning. And thanks for the last-minute embroidering."

When I showed her the stuff Leilani and I bought last night, she came up with the idea of adding "Face Your Battles" to the wristbands. The motto for my gym has multiple meanings—not running away from your problems, not backing down from challenges, and, in the case of the kids I'll be working with next week, understanding that we can't always *choose* our battles. Sometimes life chooses them for us. All we can do is turn and face them head-on.

I'm glad they'll have a tangible reminder after I leave. With what I already know about their conditions, they're going to need it.

"Are we ignoring the elephant in the room?" Mom asks, mixing the fruit with a blend of sugar and spices.

I glance around the kitchen. "Huh?"

"Leilani?"

"What about her?"

She pours the peach mixture into a baking dish and pops it in the oven. "You've had this Hawaii trip fine-tuned for months. Any particular reason you added a wild card less than a week before you leave?"

Christ. It's like she went from Rachael Ray to Dr. Phil. I move to a barstool on the other side of the countertop to get some space from her questions. "She's not a wild card. I just figured with everything she's overcome, she'd be a great addition. I texted the rest of the team to explain my idea and they agreed." And thank God for that, seeing as I didn't ask for their input until after I invited Leilani.

Mom levels a scoop of flour and drops it into the mixing bowl. "So, this has nothing to do with your feelings for her?"

"My what?" My pitch increases an octave on the last word. "Mom, no. She's my employee." My very hot, very intelligent, very *single* employee, not that I've shared those thoughts with anyone. Not even my two closest friends. DH is out because he's her landlord, and I'd rather not discuss it with Marshall. Knowing him, he'd make some idiot remark that would piss me off, and I don't condone violence in the workplace.

"You go ahead and keep telling yourself that." Mom smiles as she combines the remaining ingredients for the cobbler.

"I have no idea what you're talking about." I cross my arms for good measure.

"Mm hmm. Just like no one knew what I was talking about when I said Heather was taking a job in New York City or Danielle was going to marry Shawn."

I think back to Mom's predictions about my sisters several years ago. Still, I refuse to admit Mom's right about this.

She retrieves the baking dish from the oven and carefully spreads dollops of batter over the peaches. "Has she mentioned what her plans are after she's done with Operation: OklaHOMEa?"

"Not particularly." I haven't discussed it with her. Haven't really *wanted* to discuss it with her.

"Just be careful, son. I'd hate to see you get even more attached to someone who has no roots here." With that, Mom places the dessert back in the oven and sets the timer.

As I watch the numbers drop, I think about how many months Leilani has left and whether I can convince her to stay after December 1st. Then I wonder if I should be freaked out at how easily that thought slipped in.

Leilani's phone dings three times in the short elevator ride to our floor. "I told you Kiki would freak!" Her latest message, a series of heart-eyed emojis, follows a jaw-drop gif and the words SO GORGEOUS.

"All that over a picture of our pilot?" I ask, shaking my head as I maneuver the luggage cart down the hall.

Leilani flashes a grin. "He looked exactly like Nick Bateman."

"Who's that?"

"Model. Actor. Martial arts extraordinaire." Leaning toward me, she whisper-shouts, "You should see what he can do with a bo staff."

A model twirling a stick? *That's* what impresses her? Hmph. I bet he can't bench three hundred pounds or do the Murph Challenge in twenty-six minutes.

Bo staff, my ass.

Leilani slides the key card into the lock and holds the door of our suite open. John and Kristin, the doctors from Barton Memorial, are married, so they'll be in their own room. It made more sense for the rest of the team to split a suite. I'm sharing a room with Brandon, the art teacher, and Leilani will bunk with Quinn, the chef.

The only problem is they won't get here until tomorrow evening, which means for one torturous night, it'll just be me, Leilani, and a thirty-foot no trespassing zone in the living room. Yeah, I knew the circumstances before we left home, but damn, this is like being on a diet and having a sleepover at a bakery. My only hope now is an afternoon of physical exertion that will guarantee I fall asleep quickly tonight.

"Feel like sightseeing?" I ask, making a quick detour to drop her luggage in the room on the left.

She tips her head and wrinkles her nose. "Hmm, you're sort of old. Do you think you can keep up with me?"

Oh hell no. "Old?" I close the space between us, my mischievous smile matching hers. "I think you vastly underestimate my physical abilities."

"Is that so?"

I nod, never breaking eye contact.

"Maybe you should bring your medical info, just in case." She brushes past me, throwing a smirk over her shoulder, and disappears behind her door.

I allow myself a few moments to think about the curve of her lips, then grab my bags and shuffle to my room to change. Except the second my cargo shorts hit the floor, Leilani belts out what can only be described as a war cry. Instinct has me racing toward her, but the fabric around my ankles has other ideas. My left hip and elbow engage in an intimate relationship with the carpet before I'm on my feet again, rocketing across the living room.

"Leilani?" I holler, pounding on her door.

"I'm fine! Everything's okay. I'm just going to kill—" She

swings the door open, her jaw falling slack as she gets an eyeful of my boxer briefs. Thank God I didn't go commando today.

"What are you killing?" I step around her to sweep the room for critters or nefarious stowaways. Instead, I see the contents of her suitcase scattered over the bed along with the outline of a small rectangular box. "Is that…" I lift a shirt, confirming my guess. "You brought Fruity Pebbles to Hawaii?"

"You said to bring the essentials."

A low chuckle rumbles through my chest. Thus far, she's managed to keep her gaze above my neck, but the noise makes her eyes hopscotch from my torso to the wall beside me.

"Can you put on some clothes?" she asks the standard-issue hotel painting.

My laughter increases. "I was working on that before you went all Braveheart." Ever the problem solver, I snag a towel from the bathroom and wrap it around my waist. "There. Is that better?" She rocks back on her heels and mutters something that sounds like *sweet Jesus*, which makes me feel damn good given our earlier conversation about Rick Bateman.

Take that, ninja pilot.

"So, what are you killing?" I continue.

"Rebecca. She played personal shopper without consulting me."

"And that means?"

Leilani sighs, pinching the bridge of her nose. "She took the bathing suit I ordered and replaced it with a different one."

Despite my underwear situation, I slip into counselor mode with ease. The outcome could mean the difference between sightseeing together or watching her brood all afternoon.

Ain't nobody got time for hedgehogs in paradise.

"Do you think she was trying to sabotage you?"

She pulls in a deep breath and lets it out slowly. "No."

"Neither do I. Now, let's look at your options. You can wear the one she bought," I hold up a finger, "buy something else," I add another finger, "or not go swimming while we're here." I raise one more and wiggle all three.

"Clay, this is Hawaii. I'm not staying out of the water."

"Excellent." I lower that finger.

She sits on the bed, careful to avoid her cereal. "And I can't just buy *any* bathing suit, so it doesn't make sense to go shopping."

"Good point. Can you wear the one Rebecca packed?"

"Mm hmm."

I drop my middle finger. "Well, there you have it."

"It's not that simple." She falls back, her arms spread across her clothes. The image reminds me of the story about the boy who rescued stranded starfish at the beach. Although he couldn't save them all, he made a difference for each one he threw back into the water.

That's always been my approach to counseling—to save the ones I can. But for some reason, I want to make a difference for this starfish *and* keep her, too.

"Can I give you some advice?" Leilani lifts her head toward me. "Don't overthink it. I'm going to finish getting dressed. I'll be in the living room when you're ready."

This time, I manage to put my clothes on without harming myself and check my email while I wait.

Clay,
You still good with letting people shower here? I have a few more that could use one.
Marshall

Huh. I expected his idea of helping the homeless to fade. Community service has never been his thing, and I honestly thought he was just trying to score bonus points with Rebecca. He's mentioned a few times that he wants to take her out but hasn't asked her yet, possibly because I told him if he screwed up and she quit, he'd have hell to pay.

No prob. Thanks for handling things while I'm gone.
–C

Leilani cracks her door as I empty my junk folder. "Clay?" She hesitates and my heart plummets. "Can you come here?" I rise and cross the room, bracing myself for the news that she's staying at the hotel. Instead, my eyes and mouth mimic the door as she toes it open.

Wide.

Wider.

Holy fuck.

Whoever said it wasn't polite to stare has never seen Leilani Moretti in a red bikini.

A. Red. Fucking. Bikini.

All thoughts of sightseeing on the North Shore have just detoured to the bed three feet behind her. My hands and lips beg to forge trails down her neck and over her shoulders. To explore the soft skin on her stomach and traverse the gentle curves of her hips. To get lost inside her with no hope of ever being found.

In one instant, she's become my favorite destination.

"Um, will you tie me?" The soft question anchors me in her room again, and I realize she's holding her triangle-shaped top in place with her hand. Now her war cry makes sense. Not only did Rebecca choose a two-piece for Leilani, she got one that forced her to ask for help.

A slow smile spreads across my face.

Rebecca is so getting a raise.

Leilani

What Goes Up

HAVING CANCER IS AN INVITATION TO BE TOUCHED. Doctors. Nurses. Sympathetic friends. An overbearing mother. For months, I dreaded having someone else's hands on my body.

But now? Now I crave it. Especially with Clay staring at me like I'm the only one who can quench his thirst. I'd gladly be his water. The glass. Hell, I'd even be the ice cubes if he'd give me a few hours and a freezer.

"Um, will you tie me?" I give myself ten bonus points—five for speaking coherently and five for omitting the word "up" at the end.

He steps behind me, and my skin prickles in anticipation. Even my goose bumps want to be as close to him as possible.

But none of that compares to the second his fingers brush the skin on my shoulders. I officially take back every curse word I aimed at Rebecca when I opened my suitcase.

I'm baking her a cake as soon as I get home.

"Is that too tight?" Clay's voice is deeper, huskier, and damn if that's not the sexiest thing I've heard in… ever. I want to say yes, so he'll have to start over, but a girl only has so much self-control. He'd probably say something like "how do you want it?" and then I'd turn around and hump his leg because I'm all about hands-on demonstrations.

"It's perfect."

"Great. I'll double-knot it so you can just slip it over your head next time."

I'd be sad if it wasn't for the light squeeze he gives my neck when he's done. Committing that feeling to memory, I pull a tank top over my head and slide my feet into my sneakers, shoving all thoughts of molesting Clay out of my mind. "Where do you want to go first?"

"Shouldn't I be asking *you* that?" The edges of his mouth tip up.

"Yeah, yeah, I'm the world's worst Hawaiian." I shoot playful daggers at him.

"Hey, you said it, not me." He holds his palms out, proclaiming his innocence. "Thankfully, one of us came prepared. I was thinking of a short hike and then maybe some paddle boarding."

It's my turn to lift a hand. "The hike sounds fine, but one of us did not come prepared for paddle boarding. Unless you don't mind going in circles." His eyes crinkle as I simulate rowing with my stump.

"Don't worry, this place has two-person paddle boards." He

pulls the keys to our rental Jeep from his pocket and twirls the ring around his finger. "Ready?"

Clay plops down beside me and taps his water bottle against mine. The hike to the top of the Ehukai Pillbox Trail was short and full of goading on both sides, making the trek equal parts entertaining and intense.

"Can you believe this is real?" Our vantage point from the second pillbox provides an epic view of the North Shore. The water is a blend of blues and greens that, up until this trip, I'd only seen in a crayon box. With the sun on my shoulders and a slight breeze on my face, I whisper a silent thank you to the universe for the ineptitude of the VA hospital. I wouldn't be here if it wasn't for the patient advocate fiasco on Tuesday. God, was that only three days ago?

"I always wanted to be stationed in Hawaii," he says. "It's too bad the palm trees in Baghdad didn't come with the same sense of relaxation."

"You don't talk about that deployment." It's as much a statement as a question. All the stories I've heard Clay share about his time in combat have been from his first deployment to Afghanistan.

He props his arms on his knees, his trademark smile looking more like a balloon with half its helium. "I was part of a 26-man convoy security team. In eleven months, we logged more than a million miles in Iraq."

"That's impressive, but I thought you said you were a parachute rigger?"

"I was. Most of the guys on our team were. The Army wasn't doing airborne operations, so they tasked us with other missions. We got to Camp Victory in the summer of 2005. It was hotter than anything I'd ever experienced and had this powder-fine sand that got into everything. All my clothes from that deployment were stained light brown."

He takes a long pull from his water bottle and continues. "Our vehicles had 'Mad Max' armor, which was nothing more than steel plates they added on in Camp Buehring, Kuwait. My mom freaked when she found out I was on a convoy team. I spent most of my deployment reassuring her that being in the last position meant my truck was the safest."

"Was it?"

"Every vehicle is the most unsafe, and whichever one you're in is always the one they want to blow up. It didn't help that I was the gunner. We drove around with a target on our heads for a year."

"Since you're still here, it looks like they had terrible aim." Instead of smiling at my lame joke, he drops his head and releases a breath through his nose.

Oh shit.

"There were seven other security teams on our base. We always lined up our trucks when we came back from a mission to make it easier the next time we left. Whoever got back first parked first. One night, our team was delayed several miles from base. When we finally made it to our gate, we were right behind the guys from Fort Lewis so we parked behind them."

He pauses for another drink of water. "We rolled out the next morning the same way we'd done hundreds of times. The Lewis team was about a mile ahead of us when we heard an IED go off. Turns out, it hit the last truck. The gunner took shrapnel to his neck and upper thigh and died before we got there. If we hadn't been delayed the night before, that would have been my team. My truck. My position. That was just a few months before we came home."

I want to say something, *anything* to erase the pained expression on his face, but I don't dare open my mouth for fear that the words "I'm so glad it wasn't you" would tumble out.

"Anyway," he rubs his forehead, "that fucked with me for a long time. It's one of the biggest reasons I started drinking like I did."

"But you having PTSD and drinking is what led you to start Battles, right?"

This time he smiles and looks at me like I've just solved world peace.

"What?"

"You get it. Making something good out of the bad."

His praise turns my cheeks pink. "Thanks."

"For the record, it took me years to see that." He salutes me with his bottle and downs the rest of his water.

"I'm sorry for bringing it up," I say, wrinkling my nose.

"It wasn't all bad. One of these days I'll have to tell you about using Saddam's golden toilets. I even have some action shots." Our laughter chases away the remaining tension of the moment, but I still have one more question.

"Why'd you tell me all of this?"

Clay leans over, tapping the bow he tied behind my neck. "Because you did something brave this afternoon. Figure I'd do the same." He rises and offers me a hand up. A month ago, I would have swatted it away and grumbled about doing it myself. Today, I'm smarter.

Much, much smarter.

Quinn's high-pitched laughter on the other side of the door adds one more knot to the growing collection in my stomach. I want to leave. I want to get up, walk outside, and let the salty air carry my worries away. Instead, I'm forced to settle for the soft breeze from the AC vent as I contemplate why humans aren't equipped with tiny antennae to alert us of impending disaster.

The morning of my Humvee accident three years ago, I'd taken a PT test. Push-ups, sit-ups, and a two-mile run were never difficult, not after years of gymnastics. Still, I'd been surprised at my score—only nine points away from a perfect three hundred. I had no idea those would be the last push-ups I would ever complete.

On Valentine's morning five months ago, Travis sent a dozen red roses to my bank. For eight hours, I stared at the most beautiful, fragrant flowers I'd ever seen while the other women complained about forgetful husbands and backrubs that led to mediocre sex. I counted down the hours until our date that night, not realizing it would become the moment my life split into BC and AD. Before Cancer, After Diagnosis.

You'd think after two monumental events in my twenty-seven years, I'd be able to sense what was coming. That I'd feel a certain vibration in the ground or notice a shift in the universe. *Something*.

But when the sun rose this morning, nothing was out of place. The air was warm and sweet, and the water beckoned us, so Clay and I ventured down to Sharks Cove, a rocky slice of heaven nestled in the North Shore. He put a waterproof case on his phone and must have taken a hundred pictures between snorkeling and wading in the tide pools. I'm disappointed I didn't think of the same idea. I had the glory of looking at his semi-naked body and only had the mental images to show for it.

He even got a picture of me being photobombed by a smiling sea turtle. I didn't believe it myself until he showed me the photo. Do you know how hard it is to say, "No way!" around a mouthpiece without ingesting water?

When our rumbling bellies finally led us back to land, we ate shrimp platters from the North Shore Shrimp Truck and had dessert at Anahulu's Shave Ice. The concept is similar to a snow cone, but shave ice is powder-soft instead of crunchy and comes atop a scoop of vanilla ice cream.

Basically, heaven in a cup.

The best part of our perfect afternoon, though, was the artwork on the side of Anahulu's—a larger-than-life-sized set of angel wings painted with a medley of white, magenta, blue, and purple. Clay grabbed his phone, capturing me in a series of silly poses as he tossed out questions like the paparazzi.

"Miss Moretti, who are you wearing? Can you tell us about the upcoming movie? Are the rumors about you and Chris Hemsworth true?" The last one made me laugh. Even with the sexy accent, I'd pick Clay over him any day.

When we left for dinner that evening, I was famished and ready to meet the rest of the team. They'd texted Clay to say they were starving, too, and would meet us at the restaurant instead of stopping by the hotel first. After a quick round of handshakes with Quinn Phelps, Brandon Allbaugh, and Kristin and John Simmons, we'd eagerly followed our hostess to a rectangular table in the back of the dining room.

As the smallest in the group, I'd taken the chair in the corner, expecting Clay to sit beside me, or even across from me. Instead, Kristin and John flanked me on my right and Brandon took the chair opposite me, with Quinn to his left and Clay beside her.

And, just like my previous two catastrophes, I had no idea everything was about to go down in flames.

It started innocently enough. Quinn leaning toward Clay as she pointed at various items on the menu. Complimenting him on organizing an event like this thousands of miles from home. Laughing half a second before anyone else when he said something funny.

Then came the stories. *Remember when you bet my brother you could bench press him? Remember our picnic on the dock? Remember all the things that have nothing to do with Leilani?* By the time the waiter brought our food, it all made sense.

Quinn wasn't just here to cook for homeless kids.

I'd tried consoling myself with the knowledge that Clay never mentioned having a relationship with her. I'd heard about Anna and a couple of girls before her, but nothing about the chef he invited to Hawaii. And it's not like I could have asked him right then, anyway. His ankle was too far away to kick, and I didn't know Morse code for *WTF*.

Instead, I'd spent the duration of our meal staring at the rivulets of condensation on my glass, the interwoven squares of my palm leaf placemat, and the mostly uneaten food on my plate. Anywhere but the train wreck across the table.

When Kristin asked me if I was okay, I'd told her I had a headache from too much sun and excused myself to the restroom to splash water on my face. And because the universe clearly had it out for me today, Quinn popped out of her chair and declared she was joining me.

Her drivel about the scenery turned into the number of times Clay brushed his knee against hers during dinner (six) and how she was glad he wasn't intimidated by cougars (wink, wink).

I was pretty sure cougar status required more than a few years on the man, but I'd kept my mouth shut. The other alternative—that Quinn was actually in her forties and didn't look it—wasn't one I'd wanted to admit to anyone, let alone to the devil herself.

After we returned to our hotel, Clay, in his permanent role as Mr. Congeniality, had taken her suitcases up to our suite. John and Kristin headed to their room one floor down, and Brandon stayed up long enough to run some ideas past the rest of us before going to bed himself.

That's when things had gone from awful to disastrous.

Clay had made an off-handed remark about tweaking his shoulder when he lifted Quinn's suitcase, and she took that as an invitation, swooping in like a vulture on a fresh kill. *You poor thing! Let me help!* I watched with horror as she kneaded his neck and upper back while reminiscing about the day they met.

I couldn't do it anymore. I couldn't sit there while a woman with a head full of hair and two hands rubbed all over the man who'd taken up residence in my heart, so I retreated to my room. The only flaw in my plan? Having no escape route.

For the last hour, I've been a prisoner.

Waiting.

Wishing.

Crumbling.

I'm torn between wanting to press my ear against the door to decipher their mumbled voices and locking myself in the bathroom to keep from hearing them at all. If Kiki were here, she'd tell me life is too short to watch the things you want pass you by.

Maybe she's right.

Maybe, like Clay, I've been guilty of being too nice today.

With renewed determination, I pull myself off the bed and take several fortifying breaths. There's nothing special about Quinn Phelps. Sure, she's known Clay longer and has a few body parts I don't, but she lacks the deep connection he and I share. It's time she realizes that.

I twist the doorknob, ready to stake my claim, and find Clay standing in the middle of the living room. My eyes instinctively track to his lips.

The ones I could draw from memory.

That smiled at me all day.

That I've longed to feel on mine.

On hers, instead.

Clay

All or Nothing

A FRESH WAVE OF REGRET WASHES OVER ME AS I THUMB through the photos on my phone. Leilani sleeping on the plane. Posing like Rocky on top of the pillbox. Pointing at a fish swimming past her at Sharks Cove. I scan them all, stopping at the last image of her in front of the angel wings, arms at her sides, one knee bent, and her head tilted slightly to the right. She's relaxed. Happy.

And I'd destroyed that in less than five seconds.

Well, Quinn destroyed that, but I take full responsibility for putting manners before boundaries. Sagging against the bathroom wall, I dial DH, the only person I know with enough experience in the doghouse to help me out of a situation like this.

He picks up after the third ring. "What's up man?"

"I need your advice."

"Aren't you in Hawaii? What time is it there?"

"A little after three a.m."

"Shit. Are you in jail? Hang on, let me grab a pen."

"Dude, I'm not in jail. Why would you even… never mind," I sigh, scrubbing a hand over my face. "I have a situation involving two women."

"Ah, say no more. In my experience, you can't convince someone to do a threesome if they're not ready. I learned that the hard way. Killed the whole mood."

"Christ, DH! That's… *No.*" I'd bang my forehead against the wall if it wouldn't wake Brandon up. "I don't know why I thought it was a good idea to call you."

"Because no one is as good as I am at fixing shit they've messed up. Now lean your head on my shoulder and tell me what's wrong."

The smile in his voice replaces some of my lost hope. "Woman A kissed me, and Woman B saw it and got upset."

"She probably just felt bad for interrupting. I wouldn't worry about it too much."

"It's not as simple as that." Exhaustion lures me to the floor as I recall the look on Leilani's face for the millionth time.

"Why not?"

"Because feelings are involved with Woman B," I mumble, tracing the tiny square tiles beside me.

"On her part or yours?"

I think about all the times I would glance over at her, only to catch her already looking at me. "Um. Both, maybe?"

"So why were you kissing the first chick?"

"You don't listen for shit. I told you, *she* kissed *me.*"

"And how did that make you feel?"

SAVED

"Terr—" DH laughs the moment I realize he's throwing one of my counselor questions back in my face. "You're such a dick."

"Yeah, yeah." His laughter grows, ending in a pronounced cough. "Let's get back to the crisis at hand. Woman A kissed you, and now Leilani's upset and you need help to fix everything."

"Exactly." A relieved breath whooshes past my lips. Now maybe we can get on with figuring out how to—*Motherfucker.* "You knew? How?"

"Did you forget I have a membership to your gym? You stare at her like a love-struck teenager every time she walks by. It's kind of pathetic, really."

"For the record, I hate you so fucking bad."

He fills my phone with even more laughter, still at my expense. "What was it you used to tell me? *You don't hate me. You just hate it when I'm right.*"

"I also used to help you figure out what to do. Think we can skip the ridicule and get to that part?"

"Fine," he says, drawing the word out. "You can't just tell her you're sorry. You have to show her."

I wait for the rest of his advice but nothing comes. "That's it? That's all you got?" For a man who pissed off most of the women in central Oklahoma before he got married, I figured he'd have something more eloquent than that.

"Yup. Now if you'll excuse me, I have a breakfast date with a hot blonde."

I thank him—for what, I don't know—and end the call with a heavy sigh. How the fuck am I supposed to show her I'm sorry when we're stuck in a hotel with no hope of privacy?

Silently praying no one screams, I twist the knob and open the door. Entering a woman's room without permission goes against everything my father taught me, but even he would make an exception this morning.

Once my eyes adjust to the darkness, I close the distance to Leilani's bed and gently nudge her foot. "Hey," I whisper.

She stirs but stays asleep, so I do it again. "Clay?" she yawns, pushing herself to a sitting position.

"Shh." Making sure Quinn is still sleeping, I take a few more steps and bend down, placing my mouth just above Leilani's ear. "Can I take you somewhere?" I resist the urge to brush my lips against her cheek as I pull away.

Please don't tell me to go fuck myself.

Pleeeeease don't tell me to go fuck myself.

I mean, she has every right to, but still.

She taps the button on her phone to check the time. "It's four fifteen! Have you lost your mind?"

I swallow and wipe my palms against my cargo shorts. "It's possible."

She stares at me for several seconds and releases a breath through her nose. "Let me get dressed."

Leilani spends the hour-long trip across the island curled up like a hedgehog with her feet propped on the dash, while I white-knuckle the steering wheel and analyze all the ways my plan can fail. My only comfort is the contents of the bag behind my seat. I've never put more thought or hope into an idea, so if I crash and burn, at least I can say I tried.

"Where are we?" she asks as I pull into a parking space and turn off the engine.

"Kailua Beach."

She says nothing, but unbuckles her seatbelt, so I take that as a good sign and hop out of the Jeep. I retrieve my bag and the blanket I stole off my bed. According to Google, Kailua is one of the best places on Oahu to watch the sunrise. The moment our feet hit the sand it's easy to see why. The horizon goes on forever, accented by two tiny islands to the east that will serve as the perfect stage for nature's upcoming performance.

But first, apologies.

I spread the blanket on the sand and settle next to Leilani, propping my arms on my knees to keep from touching her. "Yesterday didn't end the way I wanted it to. I'm sorry for what you saw in the living room."

She keeps her focus on an old couple and their cocker spaniel walking in ankle-deep water. "You don't have to explain yourself, Clay. What you do and who you do it with is none of my business." Her flat tone and icy words create a wall of invisible bricks between us.

Fuck, this is not going the way it's supposed to. A little jealousy is good, but this much means I've lost the race before I've left the gate.

"That's not what I meant." Scrubbing a hand over my face, I take a deep breath and start over. "I don't like Quinn. I didn't want to sit next to her or have her massage me, and I damn sure didn't want her to kiss me."

"Funny, I didn't hear you complaining or telling her to stop."

Guilt pulls my head down. "You're right. I didn't want to be rude and cause tension on the first day, so I just kept hoping she'd get the hint. After you went to bed, I grabbed my laptop to get some work done. Marshall screwed up a purchase order with one of my suppliers and I needed to fix it. Quinn kept trying to talk to me, which was as annoying as it was distracting, so it took twice as long. When I stood up and turned around to walk to my bedroom, she made sure I walked into her instead. *She* kissed *me*, not the other way around."

I twist my head toward Leilani. "I'm sorry I didn't do more to prevent that from happening. All night, I kept picturing you standing in the doorway and it killed me." My chest aches as I relive that memory. I wish they made Listerine for the brain.

"Why are you telling me this?"

"Because I hurt you and I want to make it better."

Her eyes slowly meet mine. The sadness is still there, but her brows have become two imploring arcs. "*Why?*" she whispers.

I brought her here to apologize, but I can't explain why I'm sorry without telling her how I feel. They go hand-in-hand. All or nothing. With a heaping dose of brilliance or stupidity, I reach over and scoop her sideways onto my lap, lifting her chin so she can't look away. "You're the most incredible woman I've ever met, and the fact that I made you feel anything less than that is unacceptable. I'm sorry."

My thumb grazes the skin beneath the swell of her bottom lip while I search her face for any hint of what her verdict will be.

A small eternity passes before she tilts her head. "Does this mean you like me?"

I stifle a laugh and release her chin, letting my hand fall to her hip. "Yeah. It means I like you." Saying it out loud feels good, but seeing the corners of her mouth curve up feels even better.

"Well, I'd hate to waste a beautiful sunrise." She glances at the deep reds, oranges, and yellows in the sky. "So I guess I can accept your apology." When she looks at me again, I see no traces of the shadows from last night. Relief and gratitude are my new best friends.

"You guess, huh?" I tease, wrapping my arms around her,

pulling her to my chest.

Leilani giggles. "Your heart's racing."

"I'm nervous."

She pulls back, slack-mouthed. "*I* make you nervous?"

"You make me a lot of things." My gravelly confession charges the air between us. Kissing her wasn't part of my plan, but now it's all I can think of. Her breath catches as I slide my hands up to her shoulders and run my thumbs along her collarbone. Her neck. Her jaw. "I've wanted to do this for so long," I murmur.

She trails her fingers up my arm, gripping my bicep to pull me closer. "Same," she whispers.

I take her face in my hands and—

"Intruder alert! Intruder alert!"

"Dammit!" she groans.

"What's going on?" I look around for the source of the alarm.

"My mother's impeccable timing is what's going on." Leilani slides off my lap and pulls her phone out of her purse. "Hi, Mom." She rolls her eyes and mouths a string of curse words, but keeps her tone polite. "I'm glad you made it home, but now's not a good time. Can I call you later?"

The muffled voice on the other end of the line fires off a volley of questions. "Mom. Mom! Stop! I'm right in the middle of something. I promise to call you tonight, okay? Love you too." She tosses the phone on the blanket and scowls. "Sorry. It's like she has a damn radar pointed at me."

Though I share her frustration, I can't help but smile. Leilani is fucking adorable when she pouts. "I have something that might cheer you up."

"A time machine?"

"Even better. Close your eyes." She studies me for a moment

before lowering her lashes. "Are you peeking?"

She smiles. "No."

"You sure?" I slowly unzip the bag I brought with me.

She makes an X over her chest. "Cross my heart, now hurry up!"

"Bossy, bossy," I joke, arranging the contents on the blanket. "Okay, open."

She dissolves into a fit of giggles when she sees the setup in front of her. "Fruity Pebbles?"

"This morning was important. I wasn't above bribery." I pour cereal into each of our paper bowls and add milk from a metal thermos. It's not gourmet by any means, but her reaction makes me feel like a million fucking dollars.

"When did you plan all of this?" She balances her bowl on her lap and takes a bite.

"I spent all night thinking about what I could do and came up with this around three thirty."

"You didn't sleep?"

"I couldn't. I kept seeing your face in the doorway. And then knowing you were sharing a room with her..." I blow out a breath. "No, I didn't sleep."

"I wonder what she'll do now that... umm..." She drops her gaze to her bowl.

"Now that?" I prod, enjoying the hell out of teasing her. When she doesn't finish, I take her chin and move her bottom lip, imitating her voice. "Now that I'm dating the hottest guy on the planet."

She laughs and swats my hand. "Let's not get carried away."

"What?" I clutch my injured heart. "You mean all those times you stared at my abs, you were *faking*?"

Her jaw drops. "All those times? What about the times I

caught you appreciating my yoga pants?" She pops a brow and points her spoon at me. Her sassy side is so fucking sexy, and I've just been cursed to a life of boners every time I think of plastic cutlery.

"They're *great* pants," I say.

"Well, I guess your abs are okay... if you're into the eight-pack look."

It's my turn to raise a brow. "How do you know what I'm packing?" I catch her quick assessment of my shorts and bark out a laugh as her face skips every shade of pink, moving straight to scarlet.

"Anywaaaay," she rolls her eyes, "you never did answer my question. You think Quinn will be upset?"

"It won't matter. She's not staying."

Leilani wrinkles her forehead. "She already talked to you?"

"No, I'm telling her when we get back. Battles is my baby and this project is a direct reflection of its mission. I need people who are here for the right reasons."

And I don't want Leilani feeling uncomfortable all week, but that's irrelevant at this point.

"It just sucks because now I'm down a chef."

She sets her bowl aside. "What kind of stuff was Quinn going to do in the kitchen?"

"Cooking lessons with the kids. So many of them are responsible for younger siblings, so she was going to teach them easy meals. I'll have to get with the Helping Hawaii staff before orientation to see if we can get someone local to step in. The kids shouldn't suffer because Quinn screwed up."

"I'll do it."

"You'll cook?"

Leilani nods. "You, Marshall, and Rebecca might tease me

for my love affair with junk food, but I know my way around a kitchen. I can get some recipes from my mom when I talk to her later today. That might help take the sting out of telling her I'm in Hawaii, now that I think about it."

Logistically speaking, it's the perfect idea. I had my events planned before I invited Leilani, so her moving to another area won't be a problem. She'll do more good there anyway. I can't think of a better way to teach these kids that physical injuries don't have to be a barrier in life.

My brain wants to say something like "thank you" or "that'd be perfect," but my heart is standing by with "I love you" and "will you marry me right fucking now." For safety's sake, I shovel more cereal in my mouth until I can trust myself to speak.

"Remind me to send your mom a thank you card," I say several bites later.

"For the recipes?"

"For annoying the shit out of you so you'd move to Oklahoma." Setting my bowl next to hers, I rise and pull her into my arms. "I know I said it earlier, but you really are the most incredible woman I've ever met."

She tips her head up and treats me to a slow smile. "I should volunteer to be a chef more often."

Exhaling a soft laugh, I lower my mouth to hers, one beautiful, torturous millimeter at a time, until there's no space for words or air or anything but lips and tongues and unspoken promises. She's not the first woman I've kissed, but fuck if she's not the first one I've wanted to be my last.

Leilani

The Bright Side

CLAY RAISES HIS WATER GLASS. "JOHN AND KRISTIN, thank you for dinner tonight, and to everyone, thank you for taking time out of your lives to come here. What started as a crazy idea one year ago turned into a week of exhaustion, but the looks on those kids' faces made it all worth it." His eyes move around the table and land on me. "And a special thanks to Leilani for stepping up and kicking ass in the kitchen. I heard from several people that you made one-handed cooking with fifty teenagers look easy."

Motivation can come from anywhere. In this case, it was a desire to represent Battles to the best of my ability. Making sure no one could say Quinn would have done a better job was just a bonus. She planned breakfast, lunch, and a dinner the kids could take back to their families, so naturally, I added dessert, too. I might have also let them eat it before dinner. I clink my glass against Clay's. "Years of elite and collegiate gymnastics taught me how to excel under pressure."

"Was it hard to give that up after your accident?" Brandon asks.

"Not really. I closed that door before I joined the Army, so I never felt like I didn't get to finish something I loved. It just meant I couldn't take anyone else's money when they bet on how many back handsprings I could do."

Clay chuckles and shakes his head. "Why does that not surprise me?" I stick my tongue out at him, and his wink makes me want to show him how flexible I still am.

"What do you miss the most about having two hands?" Brandon continues.

After dreaming about Clay in a white towel last night, I'd have to go with pinching my nipple and playing with my clit at the same time. None of the brochures, support groups, or online forums had said a word about missing out on *that*. "Playing my guitar. It was one of my favorite things to do."

"Would a prosthetic arm help?" That question is from John, who has been a surgeon for almost twenty years.

"I had one, but it's too clunky and made my back hurt. I feel less like an amputee without it, as odd as that sounds. Thanks to my Life Skills class and a hefty dose of stubbornness, I figured out how to do just about everything."

"What's Life Skills?" Kristin asks.

"A class that teaches logistical stuff like tying my shoes, buttoning pants, cooking, eating, putting on jewelry. But for me, the hardest part was developing habits for the little things no one ever thinks about."

"Like what?"

"Did you notice where the toilet paper was in the bathroom?"

She glances up at the ceiling in thought. "No. I just know the shower was on the left and the sink was straight ahead."

"Exactly. You've never had a reason to pay attention to that. But when you're held hostage in the restroom because you can't reach the toilet paper with your only hand…" One by one, they connect the dots, their expressions a mix of horror and humor that lift the corners of my lips.

"Well that's a shitty situation."

"Oh, God." Kristen facepalms at John's joke. "We'd better leave or he'll stay here all night doing this."

Her husband leans forward, cupping his hand beside his mouth, and fake-whispers, "She's such a party pooper."

"Check please!" she groans.

Undeterred, John points to the dessert menu. "Hon, didn't you want to try the apple pie à la commode? Urine for a real treat." She fights to keep a straight face but fails, giving in to a resigned smile that makes John pump his fist in victory.

I'm going to miss this group and our nightly dinners. Maybe it's the soldier in me, but there's something about people from different backgrounds joining together for a common cause that makes me feel like I have a purpose.

That's not to say I wasn't overwhelmed this week. During orientation, we learned some staggering statistics about poverty in Hawaii that made our mission of helping fifty teenagers seem pointless. Clay drew a quarter-sized starfish on the inside of my wrist to remind me that while we couldn't save everyone, we could help some very deserving kids—and in typical Clay fashion, he retraced his drawing every morning so I'd have a boost of inspiration any time I needed it.

I love that he thinks of unique ways to help people, even when he's not at work. And the best part is he doesn't realize he's doing it. It just happens. It's as natural for him as breathing, which is probably why Battles has been so successful.

Well, that and he's a walking billboard for health and fitness. Nothing says, "get a membership to my gym" like a man with muscles like his.

"What are you smiling about?" Clay asks, his lips an inch from my ear. Jesus, his voice should be classified as a deadly weapon.

Warning: May cause spontaneous orgasm.

"Oh, just a hot co-worker."

"Hmm. How hot are we talking?"

With a wicked gleam, I lift my hand and move my thumb and pointer finger an inch a part.

"That's it?" he challenges. "You sure it's not something more like this?" He props his elbow on the table and places his fingers between mine, pushing them farther apart.

"I don't know, that's pretty hot. I'll have to check and get back with you."

"Why don't we—"

"Ahem." Clay and I turn our heads to find John, Kristin, and Brandon staring at us, each wearing an amused expression. "You two ready?" John asks.

"One sec." I grab the black check folder and scribble a message to the waitress on the back of our receipt, then follow the team outside.

"What was that?" Clay asks, helping me into the Jeep.

"Today's random act of Clayness."

He lifts a brow.

"Kindness, Clayness. Same thing." I tap the screen on my phone and show him a picture of the list he wrote. "Day nine is paper, so I wrote her a note."

"You've been keeping up with that?"

"Every day."

He opens his mouth like he's going to say something, but instead kisses my cheek and mumbles the word "incredible" as he shuts my door. We cruise along the curves of Kamehameha Highway in comfortable silence until he passes the road to the hotel.

"You missed the turn."

"We're not going back yet."

"Oh?"

He smirks but remains quiet, driving several more miles until we reach Sunset Beach. We came here last Friday after we finished paddle boarding. I've heard people use the phrase "breathtaking sunset" before, but I'd never experienced it until that day. I'm glad we get to see it again before we leave, to end our trip the way it began.

Clay retrieves a bag from the glove box and leads us down to the water as the sun begins its final descent. I will my brain to memorize every detail, but there's too much to take in. The warmth. The breeze. The sand. The man sitting next to me, brushing his thumb over the faded starfish on my wrist. Everything about this moment is perfect.

And as the next wave washes ashore, it suddenly hits me.

This week—hell, this summer—never would have happened if I didn't lose my arm and get cancer.

I wouldn't have met fifty incredible teenagers who will think about the lessons they learned at camp every time they make loco moco or macaroni salad.

I wouldn't have met Clay.

I'm here in this little piece of paradise, not in spite of everything that has happened to me, but because of it.

Because of it.

Gratitude surges through me, washing away the bitterness and anger I've clung to for years. I don't realize I'm crying until Clay wipes my cheeks. "Sorry," I mumble.

"You don't need to apologize."

He repositions himself behind me and pulls my back into his chest, wrapping his arms around my shoulders. I could live a thousand lifetimes and never get tired of the way this feels. "How did you know I needed this? I didn't even know."

"You do numbers, I do people, remember?" He said the same thing in the bathroom on my first day of work. God, that feels like forever ago. "Still," he continues, "there was no guarantee you'd figure out my secret."

"Which is...?"

He brings his mouth to my ear and whispers, "It's easier to see the bright side when you let go of the dark."

Mostly ignoring the crop of goose bumps on my arms, I consider his words. They're not too far off from our conversation last Friday on top of the pillbox. "Why didn't you tell me this secret when we went hiking? Isn't making something good out of the bad the same thing?"

"It's close, but no. It's like the difference between being content and happy. You can have one without having the other."

"I don't get it."

"When you moved to Oklahoma, you weren't at peace with what happened to you, but when you ate junk food, you were happy. Contentment is long-term. Happiness is fleeting."

"So how does that relate to our hiking conversation and

your secret today?"

"You saw how I let go of my darkness but you didn't realize you were still holding on to your own."

His truth hits me in the most beautiful, unexpected way. "That's some pretty deep shit, Clay Prescott. I feel like I should be taking notes."

He laughs softly, pressing a kiss to my neck. "It's good to know all those years of school paid off."

"Should I expect a bill for this session?"

"Nope. In fact, I have something for you." He releases my shoulders and grabs the bag from the glove box, holding it in front of me.

"That looks a little small for Fruity Pebbles."

"Hopefully you're not too disappointed."

I lift the tissue paper and burst into giggles the second I see what's inside. This is way better than cereal.

"Brandon let me use some of his craft supplies. I felt a little nerdy playing with a hot glue gun, but I have to say, it's a spitting image of you."

One of Brandon's activities during the summer camp was making something beautiful out of something broken. It was his way of getting the kids to look at situations differently. For my present, Clay took a starfish with one arm partially missing and added a coffee bean bra and a tiny grass skirt made from bits of a palm frond.

"This gives a whole new meaning to 'perky boobs.'"

Laughter rumbles through his chest as he hugs me from behind. "I don't think I'll ever look at a cup of coffee the same way again."

When it's time to pack, I wrap the starfish in four shirts and tuck it in my carryon to keep it safe on the flight home.

A screaming baby lures me from Clay's office to the main gym, where I see Paige beside a treadmill holding her daughter. "Poppy, please. I'll buy you a pony. Or a unicorn. One that poops Skittles and farts rainbows. Just please stop."

To Paige's dismay, Poppy wails louder.

"I'm can relate. I'm not a fan of the treadmill either."

She tosses a weary smile my way while she readjusts the burp cloth on her shoulder. "My mom normally watches her, but she woke up this morning with a migraine. DH is at work and I didn't want to bail on Marshall. I figured I could just bring her with me because she usually sleeps for a couple of hours in the afternoon. Except today." She sighs. "It's a good thing she's cute."

"I'll take her. We can hang out here on the bench while you work out."

Paige looks at me like I sprouted two heads. "Are you sure?"

I hold my arms out. "Positive."

She carefully passes the baby to me. "Here's her pacifier, and her bottle is in her car seat. I couldn't get her to take either one of them."

"We'll be fine."

"Thanks!"

Paige puts in her earbuds and I settle Poppy in the crook of my right arm. She's a tiny thing with as much hair on her head as me and an attitude to match. I like her already. "When I'm upset, there's one thing that always puts me in a better mood," I tell her. "Well, two things, but you can't use swear word coloring books yet." Hooking her tiny hand on my finger, I introduce Poppy to a G-rated version of Post Malone's *Rockstar*. Her wails turn to whimpers by the second verse and by the end, she's quiet.

"You like that, huh? What should we do next? Maybe some French Montana?" She doesn't object, so I continue with our baby hip hop session, rocking her back and forth to the beat until her eyelids droop and her breathing falls into a steady rhythm.

"Remind me to add 'baby whisperer' to your list of accomplishments," Clay says, joining us on the bench for a break between clients. He's been playing catch-up all week, which means I haven't seen him much. "How'd you get her to stop?"

"We rapped."

"You rapped to a two-month-old?"

"Lullabies are for nerds. Cool chicks like us need good music."

"If you say so." He laughs and shakes his head. "How's your day going?"

"Not bad. I posted the job ads for Battles 2 on every website on our list and in the newspaper. I noticed several positions had a certified inclusive fitness trainer requirement." It's a statement and a question rolled into one. I saw the drafts for the job announcements when I started working here, and that qualification wasn't on the list.

"I wondered if you'd catch that." He smiles and rubs the back of his neck. God, he's adorable. "Seeing you in the gym after work made me realize I'm missing out on the chance to help an entire demographic, so I'm creating an adaptive program for Battles 2. The trainers, equipment, and space will be specialized for clients with physical disabilities."

I made him do... *what*? "How did you do this? I've worked the budget report. There's nothing in there about adaptive equipment."

His sheepish look is back. "I might have had Marshall order everything while we were in Hawaii and tweak a few things to hide it. I wanted to surprise you once everything was delivered, but it turns out you're a hell of a lot more observant than I thought."

Oh God. This is it. I'm going to melt into a puddle of goo while holding another woman's baby. "I don't even know what to say. That's..." I scrunch my eyes. "Thank you. This is the coolest thing anyone has ever done for me. I'm sorry I spoiled your surprise though."

"You didn't spoil anything." He glances at his watch and rises. "I've got to meet my next client. We're still on for tonight?"

I nod. Mystery date with Clay? Hell yes.

"Excellent. I'll catch you two beautiful ladies later."

"Did you hear that, Poppy?" I whisper after Clay leaves. "He thinks we're beautiful."

Staring at my reflection in the bathroom mirror, I alternate holding tubes of lipstick against my mouth. "Which one? Crimson Kiss or Scarlet Devil?"

"I read an article a while ago that the best shade of lipstick is the color of your nipples," Rebecca calls from her closet.

I poke my head around the corner. "So... concealer?"

She crosses the room with a wry smile and brings both tubes to my lips. "This one. It'll look better on Clay." She hands me Scarlet Devil and goes back to tossing clothes in her week-end bag. "Where are you going tonight?"

"He still hasn't said. I just know there's food involved."

Rebecca laughs. "That's probably for his own protection."

"Ha ha," I say with a healthy dose of side-eye. I refuse to admit she's right.

"Seriously though." She leans against the doorjamb of the bathroom. "You look amazing."

"Aw, thanks Bec." My heart leaps when I hear three quick knocks at the front door. Whether it's because it startled me or because of who's behind it is anyone's guess. I check my reflection one more time and shoot my roommate a nervous smile. "I'll see you Sunday."

I grab my purse off the table and open the door. The logical side of me knows this is how a date works. He asks. He picks her up. They depart together. But I need a few milliseconds to process the fact that Clay Prescott is standing on my front step looking like sex on a damn stick and he's here for *me*.

I follow him down to his truck and collect a kiss before he starts the engine. "Where are we going?"

"It's a surprise."

"You're already giving me my own corner of a gym. It's going to be pretty hard to top that."

His laughter fills the truck. "I should have started out with flowers, huh? Parts of a building are more like a second date kind of thing."

"Well, we're already dressed and on our way. I can make an exception this one time."

"That's mighty kind of you." Clay links his fingers with mine at a red light. That alone is enough to make me sigh, but when he lifts my hand to press a kiss on the back of it? Yeah.

Total goner.

Another truck rumbles to a stop beside us. The tires are almost as tall as me, and there's enough chrome on the body to qualify as a multi-angle mirror. "I wonder if he knows that's the international sign for 'I have a small dick.'"

"Is that so?"

"Yup. The bigger the truck, the smaller the junk."

He leans over the console with a devilish smirk. "I guess it's a good thing I have a tiny truck."

14

Clay

Losing My Senses

I notice two things when I pull into the parking lot of Rhoads Auto Shop—my girlfriend trying to cheat death, and how amazing her ass looks in those tiny jean shorts while she's doing it. Rather than continue around to the back of the building, I leave my car in the main lot and saunter toward the aluminum ladder she's perched on. "At the risk of asking an obvious question, what are you doing?"

Leilani smiles down at me beneath a Battles ball cap she stole from my office last week. "My random act of Clayness."

I love knowing that she's taking the list I made her seriously. "What's today?"

"Dirty." She smirks and goes back to cleaning the shop windows. If I didn't know her better, I'd be concerned that a

141

one-armed woman was fifteen feet off the ground with a squee-gee in her hand and a bottle of glass cleaner dangling off a tool belt.

Since I'm not, I take a seat on the curb and enjoy the view while she finishes the last two panels.

"I can feel you staring at my ass," she says a minute later. Maybe it's the angle of the late afternoon sun playing tricks on my eyes, but I swear she pops her butt out even more.

I glance around to make sure no one else is ogling her. "Is that my punishment for showing up early?"

She stops mid-swipe and sends a wicked grin over her shoulder. "Maybe it's your reward."

Christ almighty. After a week of fourteen-hour days while Marshall's been on vacation, I'd love nothing more than to spend the evening collecting on that. I rise to make room for the growing bulge in my pants. "You about done?"

Laughter is her only reply, but she descends the ladder and greets me with a kiss. "I'll grab my purse and be out in a few."

My dick perks up again. If she followed my instructions, her red bikini will be in that purse. If she didn't… well, I'll be okay with that, too.

We're going swimming at my house either way. She loved our date last weekend to Alberto's, but we're both looking forward to a relaxing night in.

"Hey!" Kurt wipes his hands on a grease rag as he ambles out of the bay. "I was beginning to think you lived at the gym."

"Most days I do." We trade handshakes and easy smiles. He knows more than anyone how hard it is to stay away from the business you've grown from the ground up.

"You ready to sell yet? I'll give you forty-seven." Kurt's made it no secret that he's in love with my Chevelle. He knows exactly what it's worth and isn't afraid to sweeten the pot. Last time, he offered forty-five thousand and free oil changes for my truck.

"It's tempting," I lie, "but I'm not ready to part with her just yet." Or ever. Nothing will make me sell my dream car.

He sighs. "Didn't think so, but it was worth a shot." He slings the rag over his shoulder and folds his arms across his chest. "How's the new gym coming along?"

"Good. I think we'll open in another few months. I still need to sit down with Leilani and get that planned." Between catching up after our trip to Hawaii and taking some of Marshall's clients while he's been out, I haven't had much time to think about Battles 2.

"I'll be sad when she moves out."

"Why's that?"

"She bakes us stuff every Saturday. It's one of the reasons I don't mind being here on my day off." He pats his stomach like a jolly garage Santa.

"Is that why I've seen you around on the weekends?" Leilani says, joining us outside. "You should have said something. I can bring treats to your office during the week instead."

Kurt leans in, clapping my back. "Take some advice from an old man. You might want to keep this one around."

We share a chuckle while Leilani blushes, but I keep my reply to myself—it's not the first time I've thought about that.

Leilani peruses the pictures in my living room while I load our plates into the dishwasher. We've gone out to eat plenty of times, but there's something intimate about cooking beside her.

The way she sways her hips as she chops vegetables and sings while she stirs. It's foreplay for all five senses. The only thing better than that was being in the pool with her. We'd be out there again if it wasn't for the thunder rumbling in the distance. Damn Mother Nature and her shitty timing.

Leilani moves to the frames on top of the bookshelf, pointing at the gangly eighteen-year-old version of me the day I shipped out for basic training. I weighed one-twenty soaking wet and hadn't grown into my nose. "You were cute back then," she says, tossing a smile my way.

"And now?" I approach her from behind, pulling the towel she wrapped around herself to the floor.

"Eh, you're okay."

"Just okay?" I brush my lips along the skin between her shoulder and neck. "You sure about that?"

She sucks in a breath. "Yup."

"Then why do you stare at me every time I have my shirt off?" I murmur just below her ear. I fucking love this spot. Maybe coming inside wasn't so bad after all.

"I do not."

Her words would be a hell of a lot more convincing if her knees didn't buckle when she said them. I spin her around and back her into the bookshelf. "Liar."

She lifts her chin, challenging my heated gaze with her own. "Says the man who stares at me every time I wear a red bikini."

"Wrong again. I stare at you all the time, no matter what you're wearing." My feet inch forward like they're taking instructions from my dick to get as close as possible. This is the first time I've been alone with her since we kissed in Hawaii, and I have a lot of catching up to do.

The slow staccato of fat raindrops falling against the house

SAVED

turns into a downpour. Leilani smiles against my mouth and says, "I heard driving during a storm isn't safe. I guess we'll have to stay here until it's over."

Her velvety voice intensifies the bulge in my shorts. "What if it lasts all night?"

She peers at me through black lashes and snakes her arms around my waist. "I'm okay with that." It's all the invitation I need.

I cup her ass, lift her up, and maneuver down the hallway while I feast on her neck, pausing at the threshold of my room long enough to flip on the light switch with my elbow. Three steps later, my thighs meet my mattress, and I lay her down. She keeps her ankles locked behind my back and lifts her hips, moaning when my cock slides over the slick fabric between her legs.

It's the sexiest noise she's ever made. I rock back into her just to hear it again, this time adding a circular motion that turns her throaty purr into a cry of pleasure. It's the sound men scale Everest for. Fight bulls for. And she did it before our clothes are even off. I won't pretend I don't get a little ego boost from that.

I gently nudge her up the comforter until she's resting on my pillow, hair slightly damp, lips red and plump, wearing that goddamn bikini.

No one has ever looked as sexy on my bed as she does right now.

Settling half on top of her, I trace the curve of her collarbone, first with my thumb and then my mouth. She's soft. Sweet. Every taste has me wanting more, especially when she melts into me and drags her nails along my back.

Fuck, that feels good.

But as I skim the side of her chest and stomach, she freezes.

145

It's brief—barely enough time for my brain to register the pause in the rhythmic movements of her fingers before she starts up again—but it's one second too long. "What's wrong?" I ask, shifting my weight off her.

"Nothing."

"Not buying it."

Her eyes dart to the flash of silver-blue outside my bedroom window. "Just a little nervous."

That's plausible. A few jitters aren't out of the realm of possibility when you're with someone for the first time, but that's not it. She was as ready to go as I was until…

Shit.

How could I have been so stupid?

"Are you nervous because you don't want to do this, or because of what I'll think about you?"

She studies my stomach as a war plays out across her face. Is this is what she looked like when she opened her suitcase in Hawaii and saw the wrong bathing suit? "I want to," she finally says, "but it's sort of like bungee jumping. Knowing what's going to happen before you climb up there is one thing. Actually standing on the ledge is something different."

Okay. That's good. That's something I can fix.

"First, sex is a two-person game. Being in my bedroom doesn't mean it's a given. Second—" I roll off the bed and curl my finger at her. She tips her head in curiosity, but joins me on the floor. "You don't need to worry about what I think." I undo my button and kick my shorts somewhere near my dresser, taking pride in the way her eyes turn to saucers when she sees my cock, hard and ready.

"This," I fist my length, "is because of you. This is the effect you have on me."

She draws a breath and nods.

"Do you trust me?"

She nods again.

"Close your eyes." As soon as she does, I grab a condom from the nightstand and toss it by my pillow. "Are you peeking?"

"No." She bites her bottom lip.

"You'd better not." I draw my curtains, quietly shut the door, and turn off the light, plunging my room into complete darkness.

"What are you doing?"

"Patience." I retrace my steps and take her face in my hands. "What do you hear?" She angles her head toward the window, giving me the perfect chance to lay a row of kisses on her throat.

"Rain and thunder."

"Mm hmm." I step around her to continue my assault on the back of her neck. "What do you feel?"

"You."

My fingers dig into her waist as I pull her against me. "More specific."

"Lips. Stubble. Muscle. Cock."

"Very good." I grab her ass because I'd be stupid to pass up an opportunity to do that, then crawl onto my bed. "Last thing. Open your eyes and tell me what you see."

She gasps. "Nothing."

"Which means you have nothing to worry about. Now get up here. I have plans involving my tongue and your body."

Quiet giggles float through the air. "What if I had plans with my tongue and your body?"

"I'm flexible."

"That's supposed to be my line."

Christ Jesus. "You're going to be the damn death of me, you know that? And why aren't you up here yet?"

"Patience," she teases, parroting my earlier comment, and I can't help but smile.

"You know, this scenario isn't too far off from what happened in my room last Saturday night."

"Which was…?"

"Me lying here, picturing you naked."

Leilani trails her fingers from my ankle to my thigh as she comes around the side of the bed, then places one knee on the mattress and swings her other leg over me. "You mean like this?"

I let out a hiss. She's warm and wet and straddling me about four inches above where I need her most. Continuing her torture, she leans her body forward and rocks her hips back just enough to brush the top of my cock with her ass.

"Holy fuck, woman. Keep that up and you're going to pay."

"Kind of sounds like a win-win to me." I hear the sultry smile in her voice before she does it again.

"How did I know you'd see that as a contest?" I groan.

"Me? Competitive?" She lowers her lips to my neck. "Never." Alternating between kisses and gentle bites, she works her way down my chest to my abs, her hum of approval making me grateful for every hour I've ever spent in the gym. "Besides, you have the advantage, anyway."

"How so?"

"You have two hands."

"I don't need *any* hands to make you come."

She sits up. "I don't believe you."

Whether it's a true statement or a thinly-veiled challenge is irrelevant. All I see is an opportunity. "When are you going to learn not to underestimate me?" She yelps when I flip us over, caging her between my arms and legs and settling my dick at the top of her thighs. That spot feels like it was made for me and judging from the way her hips respond to mine, she agrees. It's tempting, so fucking tempting, to slide into her wetness right now. God knows it's better than anything I imagined while I rubbed one out last weekend. But I'm a man of my word, and like Leilani said, our little contest is win-win.

As promised, I keep my hands on the bed. The darkness of my room was supposed to keep her from overthinking like she tends to do, but the unexpected benefit is my heightened awareness. I guess what they say about hearing things better when you lose your sight is true.

Her breaths, slow and measured while we kissed, stutter the moment my mouth reaches the lower half of her body. The half I haven't been able to explore because doing that at work or in restaurants would be awkward to say the least. I don't need light to know I've reached the tan line she earned in Hawaii. It's a line men would beg to cross and I'm the lucky bastard who gets to do it.

When my lips graze the slope just inside her hip bone, she moans and parts her legs. I meant what I said about having no expectations when we came in my room but holy shit I'm glad she's on board. I feel like a teenager trying not to blow his load thirty seconds in, so I do what I always do when I need to calm down.

I take a deep breath.

Wrong answer. Wrong fucking answer. The soft scent of her arousal amplifies my pubescent problems until I feel like a man who's about to overdose on Viagra. The only thing worse than coming when you're eating a woman out is coming before your mouth ever touches her.

I issue myself a new, unspoken challenge of making Leilani come in less than three minutes because that's about all the time I have before my dick will take over.

I move my hands down the bed, propping myself on my elbows, and trail my lips along the inside of her thigh until I reach her folds. I don't bother holding in my groan when I dip my tongue inside her and slide it up to her clit, trading long strokes and quick flicks.

"*Mmmm fuck.*" She rakes her fingers through my hair and when I add light suction, her moans turn to vowels.

Bingo.

I quicken my pace as her pitch climbs higher, kicking myself for restricting the use of my hands. But do fingers really qualify as hands? Probably not, right? Otherwise, they'd have a different name, like "handers."

Though at this point, I doubt Leilani would begrudge me using my handers either.

Feeling fully justified, I bury two fingers inside, and she bucks off the bed. In a matter of seconds, I feel her walls tighten and then she's screaming.

I've heard variations of my name all my life. First name for most people, first and middle when I got in trouble, and last name for anyone who served with me.

But it's never sounded better than it does right now, echoing in the darkness of my room. Thank God my parents wanted to give my grandpa some privacy when they built his cottage. Any closer than the back edge of the property would have alerted them and the rest of the neighborhood that I, Clay Prescott, just gave my girlfriend the best orgasm of her life.

Her legs tremble as I slow my tongue, coaxing her down from her peak. I'm not sure if that was under three minutes. All

I know is she came and I didn't and that's a miracle.

"You... I... never... *holy fuck.*"

With a low chuckle rumbling in my chest, I reach for the condom I tossed by my pillow. "Do you still want to—"

"Yes. Now."

I laugh harder. "Well, when you ask nicely like that..."

Leilani

The Hero and the Bad Guy

"I S IT SAFE?"

I drag my eyes from my computer to Clay's office door expecting to see him. Instead, all I see is a doughnut with something sticking out of the top. "Is that a..."

He inches around the door, a mischievous grin on his face, and presents a Boston cream with a makeshift white flag on a toothpick. My stomach doesn't know whether to growl in appreciation of the carbs or flip in response to the man who brought them. "How'd you get this? I thought you said your schedule was full today."

"I called DH and asked him to grab one on his way to the gym. Figured you could use it after the morning you had."

He's right. Between spilling my last bowl of Fruity Pebbles

before I could take a bite and almost getting rear ended on the way to work, my Monday was off to a fantastic start. That's only part of it, though.

Marshall was sitting in my chair when I got into the office. He must have broken something because I can't fix it, which means my feet have been swinging like a kindergartener all morning. And let's not forget the stench of his damn model car supplies. What person in their right mind thinks it's okay to use paint thinner in a room with no windows?

But the final nail in my shitty Monday coffin came when I logged in. The simple task of reconciling purchase orders turned into a quest to unfuck everything Marshall touched in the past few weeks. It's like he forgot to pull his head out of his ass before he turned on the computer.

Clay came in mid-rant. When he asked what was wrong, I played up the idiot driver and my despair over having to eat Kix in lieu of my favorite cereal. I don't want to cause any tension between him and Marshall. I fixed it on my own and planned to reward myself with one of Clay's Boston cream pudding cups when I finished, but the real deal is infinitely better.

I smile as I remove the white flag. "Nice touch."

"That was Rebecca's idea. She used a blank mailing label and said if all else failed, to tell you I was coming in peace."

"She makes me sound like a lunatic."

"Well, you *do* take your Fruity Pebbles seriously. I don't know anyone else who travels with them." He sets the dough-nut on my desk and checks the door before bending down and sealing his lips over mine. Not much has changed between us at work. Even though the staff know we're dating, we keep physical affection to a minimum—at least until we're alone.

"Thanks for the special delivery."

"Just a random act of kindness for a beautiful lady. Speaking of…" The mischievous grin he wore moments ago has turned downright wicked. "Your challenge ends this Friday. Have you thought about what you want me to do when you finish?"

"I feel like I should say something respectable like, 'Help me bring donations to the animal shelter.'"

His hazel eyes darken. "What do you want to say instead?"

"How 'bout a repeat of Saturday night?" It's a bit forward, especially for ten thirty in the morning, but it's better than, "Let me have your babies. Is this afternoon good for you?"

He either likes my answer or doesn't care about puppies today, because his mouth is on mine again. Our first kiss was quick and sweet. This one is full of need—specifically, the need to have him naked and on top of me… or behind me. "So that's a yes?" I ask when we finally break apart.

He chuckles and adjusts his shorts as best as he can before retreating to the door. "Enjoy your doughnut."

I do, partly because it's fucking delicious but mostly because *he's* fucking delicious. I need this week to be over *now*.

Licking the last of the filling from my thumb, I turn my attention to the computer, ready to make these purchase orders my bitch. Halfway through the next document, my phone pings. It's easy to ignore the first one, but the following two draw my attention. All three texts are from Kiki.

I tagged you in something on Facebook.
Are you watching it?
LEI??

I let her know I'm checking it now and launch my app, where the top notification is a link to an afternoon radio show.

"This can't be good." I mutter, clicking the link. Ten seconds into the broadcast, I confirm my suspicion.

The video, recorded from a camera mounted in the corner of a studio, shows two deejays. The one on the left is Bubba. I once joked that he should have chosen a nickname that wasn't so cliché. When he showed me his driver's license proving it was his real name, I felt like an ass. Turns out he was born in a rural town in southwest Kentucky and has a brother named Jimbo. Thankfully he's a nice guy and didn't hold it against me.

But the guy on the right? That's the other half of *Bubba and Trav in the Afternoon*. The position of his chair only gives me access to one side of his face, but I can tell he's grown a beard, and he's either wearing a shirt that shrunk or he's been spending more time in the gym. Regardless, his physical appearance has zero effect on me now. I just wish I could say the same for his voice.

That, unfortunately, is just as sexy as I remember.

The clip starts with him on the mic. "If you're just joining us, we've been talking about Russ Robinson's new song, *All Your Stupid Reasons*, which a lot of people think is about his recent split from Celeste Martin. We asked listeners to share their break up stories, and first up is line three. Heather in Denver, you're on *Bubba and Trav in the Afternoon*."

"First, I want to say I love you guys. I listen every day and you make my drive home so much better."

"Thank you, we appreciate that."

"To go back to your question, a guy I dated in college dumped me because I wouldn't have sex with him in the library. He ended up getting caught with another girl the next semester, and both of them lost their scholarships."

"Gives a whole new meaning to 'hitting the books,' doesn't it?" Travis chuckles at his own joke while I roll my eyes. "All right, let's move to Pete in Boulder. It says here you gave your ex a dumb reason to cover up something else?"

"Yeah. She was hot as fuck and we got along great, but the tip of her nose moved when she talked. I didn't even notice it until a friend pointed it out and it was one of those things I couldn't unsee. Every time she talked to me, I stared at her nose."

"So what did you tell her?" Travis asks.

"I didn't want to hurt her feelings because it's not something she can help, so I told her I got a job in another city and didn't want a long-distance relationship."

"I feel like that's the male equivalent of a woman washing her hair," Bubba says. "Did she take the bait?"

"Yeah, thankfully. I've dated a few girls since then, and one of the first things I do is watch them talk."

Bubba thanks him for calling in and then puts Travis in the hot seat. "What about you, Trav? Do you have any stupid break up stories?"

He scratches the back of his neck and shifts uncomfortably in his chair. I know that move well. It's the one he makes when he's about to say something like, *I'm sorry, Leilani, but I can't do this.* "Yeah, my last relationship, actually."

Oh shit.

"What happened?"

"I kind of panicked when she had a health scare and broke up with her." Bubba raises his eyebrows. I guess Travis never shared that tidbit at work. "I still feel bad about it. She's an amazing girl."

"Sounds like you're still hung up on her."

"Are you fucking serious?" I ask the screen.

"About what?" I jump as Marshall strides into Clay's office, folder in hand.

"Umm, nothing." *Why can't I silence this damn—*I breathe a

sigh of relief when my thumb finally finds the lock button.

He quirks his head at me like I'm up to no good, which is ironic considering its his shit I've been fixing all morning. My lips flatten to a thin line, the last of my doughnut-and-Clay-induced high fading.

Marshall steps around my broken chair and tucks the folder into a filing cabinet, giving me a perfect view of what looks like a new watch. It's the kind that tells you the time, your heart rate, and whether you're out of ketchup, and it's around six hundred bucks. The only reason I know that is because Mom got Dad a similar style last Christmas. Too bad it doesn't help with purchase orders, too.

"So, you and Clay are still a thing, huh?" He nudges the drawer closed and returns to the front of the desk.

I repeat his words in my head in case I heard them wrong. "Yeah, why wouldn't we be?"

"Look, I love the guy like a brother, but I wouldn't expect it to last long if I were you."

The muscle beneath my right eye starts twitching. "Excuse me?"

"It's nothing personal." He holds his hands up in surrender, like that dulls the sting of his words. "Clay's just extremely dedicated to Battles. In the two years I've known him, he's only had one semi-serious girlfriend. If Anna couldn't keep him around, well…" He pops a shoulder.

"What are you implying, Marshall?" Part of me wishes he'd say it. That if a woman with two arms, boobs, and a head full of hair didn't hold Clay's interest, there's zero hope for me. Then I'd have an excuse to high five his face with my keyboard.

"I'm not implying anything. I just don't want to see you get hurt." With that, he spins on his heel and returns to the main gym while I take a series of deep breaths and concentrate on not getting fired for workplace violence.

My phone chimes on the way to the checkout.

Rebecca: Where are you?

Me: In line at register 8

She joins me moments later, along with Bristol and Blake, who are devouring their free chocolate chip cookie from the bakery. Clay got a call from a client while we were in the bread aisle shopping for our staff barbecue this afternoon. He left after confirming Rebecca could pick me up and said he'd meet us at the park instead. I've never swooned over a man while holding hot dog buns, but I guess there's a first time for everything.

"Who called him?"

"I'm not sure. I think it was Stephen, though. I saw him Tuesday morning and he said the anniversary of the crash was a few days away." We've gotten to know several of the regulars at the gym, including Stephen, a burly firefighter with a booming laugh. During his weekly visits, I've learned he's a sucker for fried chicken and his miniature pinscher, Charlie, and that two summers ago he responded to a collision only to discover his wife and daughter were the victims. Healing from something like that seems impossible, but he said he's come a long way, thanks to Battles.

"Aw, Benjaley broke up."

"Who?"

Rebecca gestures at the gossip magazine above the checkout counter while we unload the contents of the cart. "Benjamin

Danner and Ashley Strumm? The couple who starred in *One More Promise* last summer?"

I shrug. Movies aren't my thing, so her sad news is lost on me. "Who comes up with those names, anyway? *Benjaley*?"

"I think it's cute. Oh! We should make one for you and Clay."

"That's not necessary."

"What are we making, Mommy?" Bristol asks.

"A special nickname for Leilani and Clay."

She scrunches her brow and then says, "I know! They can be 'The Workouts!'"

"That's good, but I was thinking something more like..." Rebecca snaps her fingers. "Claylani."

"Oh my God, are you serious?"

"It's genius! You two should get married and make fitness videos. You could call it 'Killing Calories with Claylani.'"

"Don't you think you're getting a little ahead of yourself?"

"Absolutely not. Clay's the one who's all about goals. I bet if I ran it past him, he'd give me a gold star for planning ahead."

I point a two-pack of sausage in her direction. "If you do that, I'll tell him you haven't started looking for a place to live yet."

Her mouth opens, then closes as she accepts defeat. With a month and a half left in Operation: OklaHOMEa, she's supposed to have a list of potential houses already. "You're evil," she says, scratching her nose with her middle finger.

"And yet you love me." Three short warning sirens from my back pocket interrupt our banter. "Oh, sweet Jesus," I mutter, pulling out my phone.

Mom: Are you going to be home tonight?
Me: Yes
Mom: Good

Me: ??

Mom: Special delivery.

I tap the thumbs up emoji. Knowing her, she's probably sending an industrial-sized box of bubble wrap to protect me from the hazards of life.

"Have you told your mom about Clay yet?"

"Hell no! It's bad enough getting the third degree about my health every week. I don't need her meddling in my love life, too."

Rebecca nods in sympathy. She's heard enough of Mom's interrogations to know what that would entail. "You'll have to tell her eventually… unless you plan on going home after your time's up here?"

It's easy to catch the hidden message. Kiki asked me the same thing a few days ago. Some of my civilian friends back home thought I was nuts for choosing to move to a place without knowing anyone, let alone stay there for good. In their world, they have plenty of time to make friends and develop relationships, but we don't have that luxury in the military. We eat fast, march fast, and skip all the introductory bullshit that comes with meeting new people. We jump right into the deep end because our world doesn't have any room for the shallow side.

I don't hide my smile when I answer her. "If I go home, it'll just be for a visit."

"Eek!" Rebecca's entire face lights up while we cross the parking lot. "You two are so getting married."

For a split second, I indulge her fantasy. Clay and I have only been together or a few weeks, but it might as well have been all summer. It took my parents far less time to realize they'd met their match, and they've been married for more than thirty years now.

Bristol glances up at me with an expression that mirrors her mom's. "You're getting married, Leilani? Can I be the flower girl?"

"No, your mom's just being silly."

"I bet you twenty bucks I'm right."

I whip my head toward Rebecca, ready to talk her down, when I catch her smirk. "Jeez, the girl with the gambling addiction makes one joke…"

"He's gonna get meee!" The combination of Bristol's shrieks and giggles when Marshall hoists her over his head proves she's not the least bit upset about being captured. With the two of them distracted, Blake positions himself at the top of a rocket-shaped jungle gym and aims his water gun, blasting them both with a steady stream. He belts out a pint-sized evil laugh and escapes down a slide.

Rebecca smiles, tipping her chin toward the playground. "It's hard to tell who's having more fun out there."

I nod. I'm happy the kids are having fun—that was the point of doing this barbecue before we got wrapped up in final preparations for Battles 2—but being around Marshall still makes my eye twitch. He hasn't said anything else about my relationship with Clay since our conversation on Monday. In fact, he's gone out of his way to be complimentary. I know he's being fake, but it's hard to explain to other people why you don't like someone who's telling you how great your eye makeup looks.

Today, he made a big show of helping Rebecca and me unload her trunk, saying shit like, "Oh, wow! You got my favorite sausage!" and "This fruit salad looks delicious." I should have gotten a trophy for only rolling my eyes once and not tripping him while he was carrying the food.

"What's that grin for?" Rebecca asks.

Oh, just thinking about Marshall face-planting into the baked beans. "Clay's on his way." Which is also true. He texted me while she was fixing Blake's sandal a few minutes ago.

"So…" Rebecca glances around our picnic table ensuring we're alone. "You know how Marshall pulled me aside after we set up the food?"

"Mm hmm."

"He asked me out again."

"What's this, the seventh time?" I scoff. She's always turned him down because she wanted to focus on her fresh start with Operation: OklaHOMEa. Sadly, I think it only encouraged him. Men like Marshall don't like hearing the word no.

"I said yes."

My first reaction is to check her for a fever. I blame that on Mom. "You sure that's a good—"

"He's picking me up tonight at my parents' after the kids go to bed."

Wait, she went from being nowhere near the dating train to driving the damn thing? "Why so soon?" *Or ever*? I silently add.

She fiddles with the tab on her Dr. Pepper can while choosing her words. "Hearing Bristol ask about being the flower girl made me realize I won't ever find someone if I don't start dating again. It's hard enough to meet a guy who's okay with me having kids. Meeting one who can also hold down a decent job is even harder. Marshall has a check in both boxes, plus he's fucking hot. Why shouldn't I date him?"

I could list a few things right now, starting with *because he's*

162

an ass, but this requires a more rational approach. "He doesn't seem like a good fit for you. I mean, have you ever noticed who the majority of his clients are? Women. He doesn't strike me as the kind of guy who wants to be exclusive."

Her brows pull together. "Why does it sound like you're trying to talk me out of this?"

"I'm not. I'm just concerned."

"About a man who's been nothing but nice to you?" She rises from the bench. "Of all the people in the world, I thought you'd be happy for me. Guess I was wrong." She strides toward the playground, leaving me in an alternate universe where Marshall's the hero and I'm the bad guy.

By the time the barbecue ends, my head is throbbing and my loins are giving me the middle finger because there's no way I can collect on my random acts of kindness reward tonight. I blame Marshall, which only amplifies my animosity toward him.

"I'm sorry," I repeat as Clay drives around the auto shop to my apartment.

"You have nothing to be sorry about." He links his fingers with mine and lifts the back of my hand to his lips, but pauses midway, squinting out the windshield. "Is that…?"

His headlights illuminate the passenger side of a red Camaro.

Oh God.

Mom's special delivery.

Clay unclips a key from his keyring and unlocks the glove box. "Stay here." He's halfway out of the car when I realize what's in his hand.

"Clay, no! Don't shoot him. I know who it is."

"Him?" His voice is low, teetering somewhere between murderous and accusatory.

I nod. "Travis."

Clay

Jackass Number Nine

SWEAT STINGS MY EYES AS I START MY NEXT SET OF alternating hammer curls. This time I pretend it's Travis's neck I'm gripping instead of my dumbbells.

It's hard to say what I hated more—not being allowed to kick his ass for thinking he still had a chance with her, or knowing he was there because Leilani hasn't told her parents about us. I didn't expect her to make some grand proclamation to them, but damn, wasn't I at least worth a passing mention?

I figured she'd tell that cock-juggling thundercunt to leave but instead, she mumbled something about listening to what he had to say.

I left her apartment about three minutes after I pulled up

SAVED

because I was dangerously close to getting arrested for battery. Thank Christ for Battles being closed and the extra gear I keep in my office. After a couple of hours of bench presses, flys, pull ups, and rows, I'm finally feeling less homicidal.

On my last curl, my phone lights up with Marshall's name. I hit the speaker button and wipe the bottom of my shirt across my face. "Hey, man."

"Hey, I saw you called earlier."

"Wanted to see if you were up for a game of pool or something. I ended up coming to Battles instead."

"Sorry, I just got back from a date. You okay? I thought you had plans with Leilani tonight."

"They changed."

"You sound pissed."

"We… had an argument." Not exactly, but that's the easiest way to sum up our short exchange of words before I left.

"About her moving back to Colorado?"

I stare at the phone trying to make sense of what he said. "What are you talking about?"

"Oh. Uhh." He pauses. "I overheard her on the phone with someone a few days ago. She said something about going home as soon as her lease was up."

My lips press into a thin line. So this is all a joke to her? A way to pass the fucking time while she's down here?

"Maybe I'm wrong though," Marshall quickly adds.

"Maybe," I echo, wishing I believed it. So much for being a good judge of character. "I've gotta go, man. I'll see you on Monday."

"Later."

I toss my cell on the bench and attempt to focus on my last set of hammer curls.

165

Lift, exhale.
Lower, inhale.
Lift, exhale.
Lower, inhale.

Marshall's words flood my head again. Moving back to fucking Colorado? Is that why the taint licker drove here? I should've thrown him off the staircase when I had the chance.

With a new surge of anger fueling my arms, I abandon my counting and curl the dumbbells until my form turns to shit and my muscles beg for mercy. I curse his name all the way back to the weight rack, then collapse on the rubber mat, palms upward, too exhausted to do anything but breathe.

A knock on the glass door interrupts my break. It's as irritating as it is surprising.

"Done playing catch-up with Travvy-wavvy?" I ask, twisting the deadbolt with more force than necessary when Leilani steps inside.

Her brows draw together. "You act like I had something to do with him showing up on my doorstep."

How she can stand there and act like she's innocent is beyond me. I stride past her, stopping at the first leg machine I come to and count the number of forty-five pound plates on either end of the barbell.

Two. Four. Six. Seven.

Not enough—not nearly enough—but my upper body is too smoked to sling more weights around.

I adjust the seat and position my shoes on the footplate, then flip the safety catch and relish the burn in my quads each time my knees bend.

"He left. He's staying at a hotel tonight and driving back tomorrow."

I'd love to see that pansyass press this. He'd probably shit himself.

"Jesus Christ, Clay. You communicate for a living. Will you quit acting like a caveman and talk to me?"

Fuck that. I lock the safety and spring off the seat. "You want to talk about cavemen? He came down here to piss on your leg and drag you home!"

She stomps toward me. "And you assumed I was going to run back to him! Does our relationship really mean that little to you?"

My body instinctively wants to lean in and wrap my arms around her, so I step back and run my hands through my hair instead. "Our relationship? You mean the one you were planning to throw away in three months?"

"What?"

"You're going home as soon as you're done here! Maybe *that's* why you never told your parents about us." Saying it out loud is another sucker punch straight to the gut. I can't believe I was dumb enough to get involved with her.

"What makes you think I'm going home?"

"Marshall heard you say it."

"*Marshall*?" Her nostrils flare like a bull ready to charge. "You're pissed off because of some shit he told you?"

My arms fly out from my sides. "At least he told me! It's more than you did."

She narrows her eyes to thin slits and jabs her finger in my chest. "First of all, Marshall has no idea what he's talking about. I'm not going anywhere. Second, I had a very specific reason for not telling my parents about you. And third," she jabs me again, pushing harder this time, "screw you for assuming the worst about me without even fucking asking me."

167

We stand there, toe-to-toe, chests heaving, while I wait for her to look away. To cue the water works. To give me any sign that she's full of shit so I can be done with this once and for all.

Five seconds.

Ten.

Fifteen.

She still hasn't moved.

Oh. Shit.

"You're not moving back to Colorado."

She shakes her head an inch to each side.

"And you and Travis aren't…"

Another shake.

"Fuck." I let out a ragged breath as regret and remorse become my new best friends. "I'm sorry, Lei. I just…" I lift my shoulders, unable to find the right words to say how badly I fucked up.

"Turned into a jealous Neanderthal?" she suggests.

I nod, knowing it's on the nicer end of the names I deserve to be called.

"Well now that I've had some ibuprofen and you've pulled your head out of your ass, we need to discuss a few things." She arches a brow and points to a weight bench a few feet away. Leilani's almost a foot shorter than me and weighs about a hundred pounds less, and right now she holds all the power. My stomach lurches as I take a seat beside her.

"I am going home after my lease ends, but only for a week. My mom didn't like the idea of me moving down here for good. I talked her off the ledge with a promise to *visit* them when Operation: OklaHOMEa is over."

For good. She's moving here for fucking good. I don't know who's more stupid—Marshall for running a seventh-grade gossip mill or me for believing it.

"And the reason I didn't tell them we're dating had nothing to do with Travis or me not taking our relationship seriously. Up until tonight, you were *mine*. You weren't another topic on the list of things my mom interrogates me about. I wasn't ready to give that up."

Although that makes perfect sense, I can't help but zero in on one phrase. I grip the edge of the padded bench and ask, "What does 'up until tonight' mean?"

"It means you have a FaceTime date with my mom tomorrow afternoon."

"Thank God." My breath comes out in one giant, relieved whoosh.

She scrunches her face. "You're happy about that?"

"I'm happy you're not breaking up with me for being the world's biggest jackass."

"You're more like the ninth biggest jackass," she says, the corners of her mouth curving up. "We have to save room for the people who kick puppies and illegally park in handicap spaces."

I return her smile. "We can't forget about them. But seriously… how much groveling does Jackass Number Nine have to do? Asking for a friend."

Leilani throws her head back in a fit of laughter. "I'll give you a get-out-of-jail-free card because you're usually the rational one and you're kind of cute when you're jealous."

I turn sideways, straddling the bench, and pull her onto my lap. "You think I'm cute?"

"And modest, too," she jokes, wrapping her legs around my back. I lace my fingers across her ass and lower my forehead to hers, appreciating everything about this moment more than I ever have before.

"I'm really, really sorry."

"I know. I wouldn't be here if you weren't."

She brings up an interesting point. "Speaking of, how'd you know where I'd be? You never called."

"I saw the way you looked when you got in your car. There was no way you were going home." Her tone isn't accusatory, but I still feel like shit for the way I acted.

"Can I blame tonight on temporary insanity from being crazy about you?"

Her eyes flicker with mischief, but before I can ask what she's up to, she grinds against me in a slow, torturous circle. "You're crazy about me, huh?"

"A little." I fight to keep my hands in place, which becomes increasingly difficult when she repeats the motion with more pressure.

"How about now?"

My fingers dig into her hips to keep her from moving, but she does it again, this time raking her nails up the back of my head.

"Lei," I whisper, half warning, half plea.

"Security cameras?" Her breath is hot against my neck and I instinctively tilt my head to give her better access.

"Just outside."

With a wicked grin, she stands up and drops her shorts to the floor. "Good. It's time to collect on my random act of Clayness prize."

Leilani scoops another glob of coconut oil from the jar and rubs it across my upper chest. Her silky touch would be a hell of a lot more enjoyable if we were in my bed and not the middle of my gym. Desperate to stop the telltale tightening in my balls, I think of as many cities in Oklahoma as possible.

Tulsa.

Norman.

Bixby.

"It's times like this I really wish I had two hands."

"Why's that?"

Mustang.

Holdenville.

Seminole.

"It's a damn shame I can't feel this twice over." She helps herself to more oil and slides her palm down my torso.

"You're not helping right now," I say through clenched teeth.

She laughs. "Aww, is someone having a hard time?"

"Someone is trying *not* to have a hard time. These pictures are for promo, not porno." I shoot her a side-eyed smirk and go back to my list.

Muskogee.

Chickasha.

Enid.

Christ, that feels good.

Lawton.

Broken Arrow.

Checotah.

"There." She wipes her hand on a gym towel slung over her shoulder.

I glance down. Every inch of bare skin below my neck is coated in a sheen. "I feel like one of those greased pigs at the rodeo."

"And you smell like a piña colada."

"The only thing that matters is the way you look." Jesse double checks Leilani's handiwork and unsnaps the lens cap. "Those muscles on a couple of billboards will pay your electric bill for months."

Leilani makes a show of checking me out. "I agree. Your abs will bring all the girls to the gym." She launches into her own version of *Milkshake* while I roll the barbell into place on the mat. I know it's only been a few months, but it's hard to remember what Battles was like before she got here.

I've never had an employee fit in so seamlessly before. For that matter, I've never had that in my personal life, either. It's refreshing not worrying about how many hours I've spent at work or whether she understands the mission.

Her kick-ass advertising plan for Battles 2 is just a bonus. Over the next few weeks, I'll have a segment on News 9, a feature article in *The Oklahoman*, and a radio spot on 101.9, which she assured me was part of a well-rounded media blitz and had nothing to do with Captain Fuckface. Once we open in October, we'll get some footage for a commercial, too.

And if that wasn't enough, she has some great ideas for ways to bring Battles to veterans who can't come here on their own. It took me ten years to build this program, and in a matter of weeks, she figured out how to increase our outreach by about ten thousand percent.

Fuck, I need to stop thinking about that or I really will get a chub.

"You ready?" Jesse asks.

I nod and position my hands in a wide grip on the barbell.

"Remember, just hold it a couple of inches off the ground."

I do as I'm told for the next hour as we move through a

series of photos that Leilani said would be perfect for the website, flyers, and her bedroom wall. She didn't look like she was kidding about the last one. That led to a joke about me being hung that left her red-cheeked for five solid minutes.

I love embarrassing that girl.

In fact...

"Hey Jesse, I just had a great idea."

He looks up from his laptop.

"You know how we were talking about the adaptive equipment at the new gym? I think we should get some promo stuff for that, too."

"Sounds good."

"And I have the perfect model." I shift my gaze to Leilani, who looks horrified.

"Uh-uh." She moves her head back and forth, but I'm not fazed.

"Oh yes. This is happening." I saunter toward her and unleash a smile I know damn good and well she can't say no to.

"Nope." She takes a step back and points a finger at me. "You don't get to come over here all sexy like that. It won't work."

I cross my arms. "You sure about that?" She tries to scowl, but her eyes keep dipping down. From what she's said, I'm the Ron Jeremy of forearm porn.

"Now you're fighting dirty."

"I thought you liked it when I was dirty," I say, my voice just loud enough for her to hear, "but, I understand if you're scared."

"I never said I was *scared.*"

Bingo. One thing I can always count on is Leilani's competitive side. As long as it's not morally wrong, the quickest way to get her to do something is to imply she can't.

"So what's the problem?"

"I'm not all…" She waves her hand up and down my body.

"Covered in oil? I can fix that."

"No, you're the guy with the bulging muscles. I'm just a regular person."

I take two steps into her personal space. "You look like you belong in a gym. You're toned and healthy. You have an ass that women would kill to have. Your skin is flawless. Sounds like the perfect model to me."

"You're biased."

"Hey Jess?" I call out, keeping my eyes locked on Leilani.

"Yeah?"

"Do you think my girlfriend is hot?"

He pauses. "Can I answer that honestly without you punching me in the face?"

"Yep."

"She's smokin' hot, bro."

I lift a brow. "Told you."

"You're relentless."

"It's one of my best qualities." I lean in and tip her chin up. "Are you convinced yet?"

She smiles slowly. "On one condition. You have to do them with me."

"Fine, but I get to oil you down."

That makes her giggle. "I don't know if I just lost or won."

"I'd say we both won." I press a kiss to her cheek and turn back toward Jesse. "Looks like you've got yourself two models."

He nods and scans the area around his setup. "Before y'all get ready, why don't you help me move that weight bench over here." I choke back a laugh when he points at the same one Leilani and I christened last weekend.

So much for not having a boner in these pictures.

"A Jack-less Coke for the hunk at seat number four." Sharon adds a maraschino cherry and a paper umbrella and sets my drink on the bar. "Where have you been? We haven't seen you in a while."

"Working my ass off."

"Oh, no!" She clutches her chest. "Stand up."

Confused, I push my barstool back and rise.

"Turn around."

The moment I do, she heaves a sigh of relief. "Thank God. It's still there and looking just as firm as ever."

My shoulders bounce with laughter as I take my seat again. "I can't believe I just fell for that."

"But I'm so glad you did," she says, wiggling her brows. "Where's your partner in crime?"

I take my phone out of my back pocket and tap the home button. Marshall should have been here fifteen minutes ago. "Running late, I guess."

"And who's that?" Sharon points to my background image of Leilani in front of the angel wings at Haleiwa. Of all the pictures I have of her, this one is still my favorite. "You're going to tell me she's your girlfriend and shatter my dreams, aren't you?"

I give her my most apologetic smile. "I'm afraid so."

"Dammit." She jokingly hangs her head, then demands to see the rest of my photos of her. We spend the next half hour talking about my trip to Hawaii and all the plans Leilani and I have for Battles 2.

When my phone finally rings, I expect to see Marshall's

name since the fucker still hasn't showed. Instead, John's pops up.

"What's up, dude?"

"Just got back from a conference in Tulsa. Did Leilani ever get a surgery date?"

"Not yet. The patient advocate figured out where they screwed up the paperwork, but she has to start at the beginning again. She has an appointment next month to get her referral going. Why?"

"I met up with one of my plastic surgeon buddies at the conference. We got to talking about the VA and how they screwed her over and he offered to do her reconstruction for free if she doesn't mind driving to Tulsa."

My jaw drops. "He *what*? Why?"

"His dad was a Vietnam vet who never got the medical care he needed before he died. I guess this is his way of giving back to help other people."

"I'll be damned."

"It's worth a consult, at least. I'll text you his info."

"Thanks, man. I'll keep you updated." I toss a ten on the bar, tell Sharon bye, and smile all the way to Leilani's apartment.

"Lei, you have a visitor," Rebecca calls over her shoulder.

"I swear to God if it's that asstwat again…" The murderous look on her face dissolves the second she clears her bedroom door and sees me. "Hey! What are you doing here?"

"Remember John from our Hawaii trip?"

Her brows pull together. "The surgeon?"

"Yup. He called and said he has a friend who offered to cover the cost of your reconstruction." I pull up the information he texted me after I left the Angry Bison. "His name is Dr. Anderson. He said he'd do it all—the expanders, the fills, and the implants. We just have to drive to Tulsa for your appointments."

Her hand flies to her mouth. "Everything?"

I nod.

"For free?"

I nod again.

"Holy shit."

With tears in her eyes, she walks into the kitchen and collapses on the counter, covering her head with a nearby towel.

Rebecca and I exchange a confused look. "Why are you hiding under a dishtowel?" she asks.

"Because I'm an ugly crier," Leilani wails, which makes us chuckle.

I join her in the kitchen and remove the towel so I can pull her into my arms. "I hope those are happy tears."

She tilts her chin up and gives me a watery smile. "Very happy tears. Thank you for this."

"I'm just the messenger, but you're welcome."

According to my sixty-second internet search before I drove here, she won't be done with her reconstruction until January or February. My next goal is to convince her to stay with me while she recovers, but I'll save that for another day.

"Clay?"

"Hmm?"

"You think they'll give me star-shaped nipples?"

I toss my head back and bark out a laugh. Holy fuck, I think I love this girl.

Leilani

Flying and Falling

KIKI SMIRKS AND SHAKES HER HEAD AS SHE LOADS MORE paint on her roller. "You're hopeless."

"It's not *my* fault," I say, jerking my chin over my shoulder. "He's the one who refuses to put a shirt on." Not that I'm complaining. Watching the muscles in Clay's arms and back has made seven hours of painting completely worth it.

Rosa bringing tamales for lunch helped too, but it was mostly his muscles. They're incredible. Delectable. And, judging by the puddle of paint I'm wiping up, really damn distracting. Thank God Clay had the foresight to get the walls done before the flooring guy comes in.

While I'm on the subject, I should also thank the good Lord for the truck Marshall bought today—more specifically, for it being at some dealership two hours away. Not even Clay's muscles would have made up for spending a Saturday at Battles 2 with that witless cocksplat.

He keeps doing petty, passive-aggressive shit like taking the pens out of Clay's desk or leaving the speaker volume on full blast. Last week, he hid the refills for the stapler. It wouldn't have been a big deal if I wasn't trying to get my month's end paperwork done. Although we still aren't speaking outside of basic office pleasantries, I know he's behind this nonsense. But rather than give him the satisfaction of hearing me bitch about it, I got my revenge in a different way.

I put an ad on Craigslist for two free goats and listed Marshall's number in the contact information along with, "Se habla Español." The last part was a spur-of-the-moment idea, and thanks to Marshall's lack of brain cells, it ended up casting all suspicion away from me. Every time someone called, I heard him curse *the ignorant asshole who can't get his numbers right in his own fucking Craigslist ad.*

That wasn't even the best part, though. He was still trying to finalize the details of his truck purchase—the one he picked up today—which meant he couldn't turn his phone off because he didn't want to miss a call from the dealer. I celebrated my victory with a doughnut.

Sticks and stones may break my bones, but goats will never fail me. I should put that on a bumper sticker and slap it on his tailgate.

"Sooo," Kiki starts, dropping beside me to roll her brush in the tray, "we get a four-day weekend for Columbus Day."

"And?"

"I thought I'd come for another visit and celebrate the grand opening with you guys." Her innocent smile might fool everyone else, but I'm not buying it for a second.

"And by 'celebrate the grand opening,' you mean seeing if Alex is still single and interested in dating a hot soldier?"

She juts out a hip. "Can't a girl support the hard work her sister has done all summer?"

"Sure." I tuck my tongue in my cheek and wipe up the last of the paint I spilled. Kiki got to Battles late yesterday afternoon, just as Clay and I were finishing up the hiring paperwork for one of our new personal trainers. Alex Browning is thirty-two, has two bachelor's degrees, and just moved here from Amarillo, Texas.

Kiki, in her sneaky journalistic glory, spotted his bare ring finger and asked how his family was settling in. When he said it was just him, her eyes lit up like a kid in a candy store.

Their flirty exchange was a welcome palette cleanser after the squabble Clay and Marshall had right before Alex's interview. Instead of helping, Marshall made last-minute plans with some friend who was only in town that evening. I could practically taste victory when Clay said, "What the fuck, man? Skipping this *and* going out of town tomorrow?"

But no. Marshall gave a lame-ass apology, and rather than fire him for flaking out on his responsibilities, Clay just reminded him that he was a key member in the Battles team and that we needed him.

I don't know about that "we" part. I need Marshall as much as I need a hemorrhoid.

"Hell yes!" Kiki abandons her roller in the paint tray and bounds over to the speakers, cranking the volume as the first few notes of Flo Rida's *Low* fill the empty gym. In an instant, I'm whisked back to the summer before my senior year in college. Me and a bunch of girls I trained with were bored and made up a floor routine to this song. It's one of my favorite memories from gymnastics. No judges. No costumes. Just six athletes doing what we did best for the fun of it. Kiki never made it past a basic tumbling class when we were kids, but she hung out with us when she wasn't training for track. That day, she became the videographer.

"What do you say?" She grins widely, taking her phone out of her back pocket. I haven't done this routine in years—certainly not since my Humvee accident—but we used to do one-handed stuff in the gym all the time. It shouldn't be too hard to adjust for my missing arm and rusty skills.

"I say challenge accepted." Finding enough space isn't difficult, considering the only furniture in the building are the chairs we brought to stand on while we painted. I glance over at Clay, who's eying us from his section on the far wall. Aside from watching me do an aerial cartwheel while we were in Hawaii, he's never seen me in action.

I give him an air-kiss, take my place, and count down the beats to the opening hook. When it starts, I launch into a power hurdle for a round-off, back handspring and trade my double Arabian for a simple back tuck to gauge how my body responds.

I'd forgotten how good it feels to soar through the air, and now that I have a little taste, I want more.

I split-leap and twirl across the gym and move into a series of dance elements that are more fitting for a club than a competition, but that doesn't seem to bother Clay as I slide up to him, rolling my hips lower and lower in time to the lyrics. He groans, and I laugh before bounding to the other side of the room.

My second tumbling pass adds to my high. Coach used to say, "You can take the girl out of gymnastics, but you can't take gymnastics out of the girl." She was right.

Kiki cheers as I sail past her on my way to the corner to set up for the final pass—a round-off, back handspring, double whip, back handspring, full twist. With the adjustments I've made to the first two passes, I know she expects me to change the last one too. Logically, I should, and I almost do… until I get my feet in position and lift my head. Clay's standing about fifty feet in front of me wearing an expression I've never seen. It's a mix of pride and reverence that has me flying, flipping, and spinning toward him. I land with a small hop to the right, a pounding heart, and a grin glued to my face.

It takes him a few seconds to pull his jaw off the floor. "That was fucking incredible."

I nod, not because I'm cocky, but because he's right. That was the best routine of my life in all the areas that matter most—I challenged myself, believed in myself, and had so much fun doing it.

Kiki pockets her phone and high-fives me as DH, Paige, and DH's cousin, Eric, join us.

"I don't want to brag or anything, but I can trip over my own two feet on a flat surface," Paige teases.

"Sometimes it only takes one foot, babe." DH punctuates his jab with a kiss on the top of her head.

"Don't be jealous," she says, swatting him in the stomach. "Seriously though, I've never seen anything like that before."

"Me neither," Eric says.

"Thanks! I haven't done that in forever. It's kind of nice to know I still can." I look at Clay again. His expression has changed from awestruck to something bordering on mischievous.

"What?" I ask.

"I know what we're doing next year."

My brows draw together. "What are you talking about?"

"My summer project. We're doing a gymnastics camp." He bobs his head like he's picturing everything in his mind, and knowing him, he probably already has it half planned out.

I step toward him and wrap my arms around his sides. "Guess this means I have to stick around, huh?"

"Oh, you're sticking," he says, his voice low as he brings his lips to mine.

"Aaand I'm going back to painting," Kiki announces with a laugh.

The guys shout, "Same!" and sprint back to their places on the wall.

"Aww, come on, have some respect!" Paige calls after them. "This is a real-life romance book right here!" When it's clear her words are having no effect on the Rhoads men, she turns back to Clay and me and holds up a finger. "Just know I'm calling dibs on a front-row seat to y'all's HEA."

Clay squints at her. "HEA?"

"Happily ever after." She bounces once on her toes and pads back to her section. A quiet "hmm" is Clay's only response, but that doesn't bother me.

Not with the way he tightens his grip on my shoulders.

Mom's face pops up on my screen, her eyes instantly assessing me. "You're not sleeping well," she declares after several seconds.

I sigh. There's no use denying it or coming up with a bullshit excuse that she'll see through before the words even leave my mouth. "Things are a little stressful at Battles right now, that's all."

"Are they overworking you? I think you should take some time off and come home to rest."

"I'm working my normal hours, Mom. We're just busy with getting everything ready for the grand opening."

She pauses, scanning my face again. "Not buying it. The last time I talked to you, you said everything was on track for the opening."

Dammit. I did say that. Other than a couple of hiccups, our plans are progressing as scheduled. The flooring was installed yesterday, the equipment will be delivered next week, and we'll do a soft opening the week after that.

"Why don't I call you this evening and we can finish our chat then?" I suggest.

Mom's voice shoots up an octave. "What are you not telling me? Are you feeling sick again? Did you find a lump somewhere?"

"No! Jesus, calm down. I'm just having a personality conflict with one of the guys at work."

"What does 'personality conflict' mean?"

"Stupid stuff. He's been pulling seventh-grade pranks for a month now. It almost feels like he's trying to get me to quit."

Mom laughs. "Well that's dumb. Hasn't he figured out that no one can make you do anything you don't want to do?" Her comment makes me smile. Growing up, she'd tease me about changing my middle name to Stubborn. "Why does he want you to quit, anyway?"

I'd rather not get into the specifics, so I choose my words carefully. "I don't think he likes having a woman taking over his position and doing it better than he did. I've found so many things that he's messed up. It was little stuff at first, but the more I look, the more shit I'm finding." I release a long breath, thinking about the bank statement that came in two days ago. "I think I have to tell Clay."

Mom nods. "That's why you're not sleeping well."

"Mm hmm." I've been in some tough situations in the Army, but none of them have prepared me for something like this. How am I supposed to tell my boyfriend that there's a good chance his best friend has been stealing money from Battles?

I sigh again, dreading the conversation already. "I should probably go."

"Keep your chin up, sweetie. From what you've said about Clay, he's got a good head on his shoulders."

"Thanks. Love you."

"Love you too."

I end the call and set my phone down as Marshall strolls into the office with his eyes trained on me. "Good morning."

"Hey," I squeak. *Shit*! Did he just get here? Or was he standing outside the office the whole time? I casually smile and search his face for signs of anger. He doesn't look any different than he usually does, except... "Are you wearing contacts?"

He unzips his bag and retrieves a water bottle. "Yeah. Pharmacy was out of the clear ones I normally get, so they gave me blue instead."

I'm surprised they look so real—I can't see any light-green showing through. Rebecca's blathered on more than one occasion about how beautiful Marshall's natural eye color is, but I'd cut off my left arm before admitting I agree with her.

Speaking of Rebecca, I reach around Marshall to grab a stack of freshly printed gym membership forms and deliver them to the front desk. "Oh good! These just came in and I need your help." She pulls up the proofs for the family photo shoot she had last weekend. "I'm torn between this one," she points to an image of Bristol with a red and yellow wildflower tucked behind her ear, "and this one." She scrolls to a photo of her lying on the grass with her chin propped on her hands. Both are adorable, but then again, taking a bad picture of that kid is impossible.

"The flower one," Marshall interjects, coming up behind us. He leans down to kiss Rebecca on the cheek. She smiles, and I gag.

"Yeah?" She enlarges the photo and tilts her head to the side.

"Absolutely. She's a beautiful kid as it is, but this is stunning. You should print it on one of those big canvases. I could even come over and help you hang it once you move."

She beams up at him and then remembers I'm standing here, too. "What do you think, Leilani?"

I glance at the computer screen again. As much as it pains me to say it, he's right. That picture belongs in a magazine. "The flower one."

"Thanks!"

"No prob." I turn to leave when Marshall calls my name.

"Yeah?"

"Are you feeling okay?"

What the hell kind of question is that? "I'm fine. Why?"

He shrugs. "You just look like you haven't been sleeping well. Is something wrong?"

My knees threaten to buckle and my blood turns to ice. *Fuck, fuck, fuck!* That's exactly what my mom said. He must've heard our entire conversation. I force the corners of my lips upward and meet his gaze. "Like I said, I'm fine."

"Glad to hear it." He places another kiss on Rebecca's cheek and pushes off the desk. "See you at lunch, babe."

"I've never met anyone who's as thoughtful as him," she

gushes when he turns the corner into the main gym. "Isn't he the sweetest?"

"The sweetest," I echo, my mind whirling. Now that I know he heard me on the phone, the clock is ticking.

I need to get to Clay before Marshall does.

Rather than panicking, I think about the two things I have in my favor: Marshall's morning clients and the fact that Clay's in Oklahoma City meeting with the team of counselors who will work at the new gym.

I walk as casually as possible back to the office and click through a series of sub-folders on the computer until I reach one called Interior Paint Colors that contains my evidence against Marshall.

A few minutes later, I'm at Rebecca's desk with a folder in my hand. "Clay called and asked me to bring the hiring stuff he forgot to take. I'll be back in a little bit."

I release a string of profanities when I see Clay's blue truck in the Battles parking lot.

My mission to intercept him was more like a wild goose chase. The receptionist at the office in Oklahoma City said he left ten minutes before I got there. I thought about calling him, but what the hell was I supposed to say? *Can we meet for coffee? I think your best friend is screwing you and your business over.*

Clutching my folder to my chest, I take the side entrance to the gym and fly into his office. "Thank God you're—"

The rest of my sentence fades into silence when he glances up from his desk, rage etched in sharp angles on his face. I've only seen him angry twice before—at Cattlemen's after those guys were rude to me and the night Travis showed up at my apartment. Neither of those times come close to the way he looks right now.

"What's wrong?"

"Close the door." His voice is low, icy, and the relief that flooded me moments ago vanishes. "What the fuck, Leilani?" he asks as soon as the latch clicks shut. "Did you really think you could get away with it?"

My face twists. "What are you talking about?"

"This!" He explodes out of his chair and rounds the desk, his eyes boring into me as he thrusts a handful of papers into the air. "After everything I've done for you, *this* is how you repay me? By *stealing*?"

The fuck? I stare at him, like that'll help me make sense of what he's saying. "I haven't stolen anything."

"So your signature magically showed up all by itself?"

"I didn't—" His glare cuts me off, and that's when I know.

Marshall got to Clay first.

He lets out a disgusted snort as his eyes scan the length of my body. "I can't fucking believe I fell in love with a thief," he says, his lips drawn into a snarl.

Shock over his admission and confusion about this entire conversation give way to my own dose of rage because fuck him for pulling the same bullshit he did after Travis left. I'm not going to stand here and beg him to take my side. "And I can't believe you have your head shoved so far up your ass you can't see what's right under your fucking nose," I shoot back. "You deserve everything that's coming to you. My only regret is not being here to see it."

The muscles in his jaw clench and the veins in his neck

bulge. "You have one hour to get your shit out of DH's apartment, or I'm pressing charges."

His venom-laced words hit their mark, but I refuse to let the bastard see me break. I drop my folder, lift my Battles polo over my head, and throw it at his feet. "Wouldn't want to steal company property," I spit out.

DH is at the apartment when I get there, standing guard like a sentinel to make sure I don't take anything that's not mine. Fuck him.

I yank my suitcases off the top shelf of the closet and haphazardly shove my clothes inside, saving one shirt to wear so I'm not making a nine-hour drive in my sports bra. I don't have any moving boxes, so I stuff my dry groceries and toiletries into garbage bags and add those to the back seat of my Jeep, then toss my house key at DH and hit the road.

On the way out of town, I call Dr. Anderson's office to cancel my surgery next month and send a voice-to-text to Kiki.

Something came up. I'm driving back to Colorado. I don't feel like talking, so I'm turning off my phone. I'll let you know when I get there. Love you.

Two counties over, my tears finally fall. When I came to Oklahoma, I had no boobs and no boyfriend, but I had hope.

Of all the things I lost today, that one hurts the most.

Clay

Blue Falcon

THE WORLD GOES ON. THAT'S WHAT AN OLD COUNSELOR used to tell us in group therapy. While we were holed up inside, seeking comfort at the bottom of a bottle or the tip of a needle, the world kept spinning. People kept living.

I know this is true because for the rest of the week, my clients showed up at Battles like they always did, expecting me to help them with their problems. I could've canceled their sessions or brought in one of my new hires to fill in for me, but that would've meant Leilani got the last laugh and that wasn't happening.

I didn't mind, though. Every appointment became a performance, and by the end of each day, I was too exhausted to think or feel or do anything except catch a few hours of dreamless sleep on my couch.

My mission to distract myself continued on Saturday, when I made the hour-and-a-half drive to Charon's Garden in Indiahoma. I hiked the trail three times and would have gone for a fourth if I hadn't rolled my ankle. It still hurt a little bit this morning, so I traded my rock climbing plans for an afternoon of kayaking at Lake Hefner instead.

I wanted to take Leilani there after the grand opening. They have stand-up paddle boards similar to the ones we rented in Hawaii, and I found an adaptive paddle online so she could do more than sit on the front of my board. It was going to be a thank-you present for all the extra work she did for Battles 2.

"Clay?"

My eyes focus on the head peeking around the front door. "Hey, Mom," I say with as much enthusiasm as a kid going to the dentist.

"Are you okay? I knocked twice."

"Sorry, must not have heard you." I lean back on the couch and prop my feet on the coffee table.

"Where have you been? I've hardly seen you this week."

"Just busy with work." That's not entirely untrue. Between my clients and trying to figure out where I'm at with the grand opening, I *have* been busy.

She lifts a brow as she plucks a pair of cargo shorts off the couch and sits beside me.

"What? It's not that messy." Sure, there's a stack of empty Boston cream pudding cups on the table beside my feet and a few days' worth of clothes on the arm of the sofa, but isn't a guy entitled to a break every now and then?

"I dropped off the baby quilt I made for DH and Paige."

If this were any other week, I'd actually give a shit. Right now, all I can muster is a half-assed, "That's nice."

"He mentioned there was an incident with Leilani but didn't give me any details. What happened?"

Hearing her name is the equivalent of stubbing my toe—it hurts, and it pisses me off. "There's nothing to talk about. She screwed up. I fired her. End of story."

Mom's jaw falls slack. "You fired her for making a mistake? That seems a little… harsh."

"Nineteen mistakes," I clarify, picturing the stack of papers Marshall found in the filing cabinet. "She sold nineteen six-month memberships to Battles."

"Why is that a problem?"

"I don't offer six-month memberships."

She pauses to digest the information. "Well, what did she say about it?"

"Jesus Christ, Mom!" My hand flies into the air and lands with a thud on the cushion. "There was no point in asking her! Every page had her signature on it. She deliberately and repeatedly stole money from me. From my business. Nothing she could have said would have made that okay. Can we stop talking about this now?"

Mom's lips press into a thin line, which I learned as a kid was the sign for *not a chance*. "Leilani loves that gym as much as you do. When has she ever given you a reason to doubt that?"

Last fucking Tuesday, I think to myself, pinching the bridge of my nose. "Look, I appreciate your concern, but I literally have the proof in writing. My decision is final."

I've barely dropped my hand before Mom raises hers to deliver a stinging slap on the back of my head. "Ow!" I glower at her and massage the point of impact. "What the hell was that for?"

"You might be a grown man, but I'm still your mother. I have no problem smacking some sense into you when you're acting like an idiot."

"Hold on. You're siding with a thief, and *I'm* the idiot?"

She tips her head toward the ceiling and mutters, "Lord, forgive him for his stupidity," then pushes herself off the couch. "Ten years ago, your father and I could have taken one look at you lying in a pile of vomit on our bathroom floor and decided you weren't worth the effort. We could have judged you on the evidence we saw in that one moment and walked away. If we had, I doubt you'd be alive right now. You'd do good to remember that."

I pull into the Battles parking lot just after midnight. Insomnia isn't my favorite way to start out the week, but at least I can catch up on the grand opening stuff without any distractions. Jesse's supposed to send the photos from our shoot in a couple of days, and once I have those, I can finalize the print ads. The rest of the details are anyone's guess. Hopefully I can go through Leilani's folders on my computer and figure out what's left.

Scratch that.

I *will* figure out what's left. I opened this gym without her, and I can do it again.

I park next to Marshall's truck, which is parked next to the side entrance. The only time he doesn't text me when he's coming to the gym late is when he's pissed and wants to work out alone. My phone's been quiet all night, so I make a note to steer clear of him as I unlock the door.

Halfway to my office, I see him coming from the locker room side of the building. That's not abnormal, but the wide-eyed girl trailing two steps behind him takes me by surprise. Her hair's wet and she's wearing clothes from the donation bin that Marshall suggested we start.

"What's up?" he asks, shaking my hand and clapping me on the back.

"Couldn't sleep. Figured I'd get some shit done."

Marshall tips his head toward the girl. "This is Brandy. I told her she could shower here and then I'd take her to grab some food."

Brandy's eyes are even rounder than they were seconds ago, and she's hugging herself so tight her fingers are digging into her arms. She reminds me of the kids I met in Hawaii.

Hungry.

Tired.

Terrified.

Like them, she looks like she's seen too much in her short life. I fucking hate that.

"I'm glad to have you here," I say, offering up a warm smile. "You're in good hands with Marshall, but if you need anything from me, just let me know."

She nods slightly but doesn't say anything.

"Well, we'll let you get to it." Marshall glances at Brandy and tips his head toward the door.

They make it a few steps past me when I stop him. "Do you remember what you did with the folder Leilani threw on the floor before she left?"

He turns back to me with his brows scrunched. "I probably tossed it. Why?"

"I just wondered if it was stuff for Battles 2. That's what I came here to work on."

"Sorry, bro. If you want, I can help you when I'm done with my clients tomorrow."

"Sounds good. Hey… uh… thanks for all your help with that shit last week. I'm glad you had my back."

He wipes a fake tear and sniffs. "I love it when you're sentimental."

"Fuck you," I mutter, lifting my middle finger for emphasis.

That makes him laugh, but his smile fades when he looks over his shoulder. "Where's Brandy?"

I shrug. "She walked outside a few seconds ago."

"Shit. I'll see you later." He jogs the short distance to the door, and then he's gone.

His reaction catches me off guard. I know he's been helping homeless people out all summer, but this is the first time I've actually *seen* him give a shit. The Marshall I met two years ago never would have chased after a homeless girl just to make sure she had a hot meal.

I feel like a proud father.

When I get to my office, I power on the computer and grab a sheet of paper to make a list of everything I need to do. As expected, it's lengthy. I guess that's what I get for letting Leilani take over everything, including my office.

Everywhere I look, I see signs of her. The Battles ball cap she stole from me that's sitting on top of the filing cabinet. The hoodie on the coat rack she used to wear religiously. Her stash of candy in the top drawer, right behind the tray of pens. Those are bad enough, but the photo on the corner of my desk is the worst.

We're standing with the kids from Helping Hawaii on the last day of camp. While most of us are looking at the camera,

Leilani's grinning at the kid standing on her right. Her whole face is lit up, and even now it's hard not to smile when I look at the picture.

Resting my elbows on my desk, I press the heels of my hands to my eyes like that will somehow erase the last three months. I wish I had a switch to turn off this part of my brain.

Instead, I shelve the ache in my chest and focus on crossing items off my list.

Upcoming equipment deliveries.

Schedule of interviews and ads.

Spreadsheet of new employees.

Hiring packets—dammit.

I glare at the blinking light on the printer. I've learned I can count on three things in life: death, taxes, and the fact that this piece of shit will jam every fucking time I add new paper. Whoever coined the phrase *sure-feed printing system* can choke on a dick.

"All right, you smug bastard, let's do this." I take a deep breath so it won't sense my anger and grab a small stack of paper from the cabinet. "Rainbows and puppies. Rainbows and puppies." I continue my chant while easing the tray open, refilling the paper, and nudging it closed with the finesse of a Tai Chi master.

The machine whirs to life. I find myself monitoring its noises the same way I did my dial-up internet connection when I was in middle school—crossing my fingers and praying.

It hums. It spins. It grabs the paper. Good. Yes. GODFUCKINGDAMMIT!

The printer switches to a series of clicks and then stops, and I fill the silence with a string of curse words that would make my drill sergeants proud. I should take a sledgehammer to this fucking thing. Who needs tractor tires when you've got shitty office equipment?

I flip the plastic door open and peer into the bowels of the printer. Sure enough, there's a sliver of white mocking me from the back. Five minutes, one papercut, and a scrape across my knuckle later, it's out and I'm back to making death threats to an inanimate object if it pulls this shit again.

I double-check the paper tray and push the "okay" button. It starts up again, and this time it spits out papers like it's supposed to. "That's what I thought," I mutter.

Now maybe I can get some damn sleep.

Rebecca hits the red button on her cell and peers up at me through watery eyes. "I think something bad happened."

I want to tell her she's overreacting—that there's a logical explanation for Marshall not showing up for work yesterday or today—but I can't. His phone has gone straight to voicemail every time we've called, and he's not returning emails. Yesterday afternoon, Rebecca pulled his emergency contact info and tried reaching his parents in Seattle. She got as far as the tri-tone beep and a message saying the number wasn't in service.

At first, I thought he overslept. If he took Brandy to get some food Sunday night, he probably didn't get home until after 1 a.m. Then I wondered if he got in an accident. Now I don't know what to think. Do I file a missing person report? Or did one of my best friends just ghost me?

The front desk phone rings and Rebecca all but pounces on it. "Battles, how may I help you?" Her hopeful expression fades instantly. "Hi, Mrs. Donahue. Yes, I'd be happy to renew your membership."

I motion toward my office, letting her know where I'll be until my ten o'clock shows up. Between my regular Monday clients and three of Marshall's who didn't mind training with me instead, I didn't have a chance to assemble everything I printed Sunday night.

I grab the stack off the tray and plop down in my chair. The first document must have been something Leilani printed because it's not part of my hiring packets. "Of course, you're the reason I ran out of fucking paper," I mumble. I start to set it aside when the words at the top catch my attention.

Marshall got a new watch. Acted funny when he saw me looking at it.

Six missing receipts.

Two purchase orders that I can't reconcile.

Overheard him bragging to Rebecca about paying for his truck in cash.

Each entry has a date beside it. The rest of the page is blank except for the number 2 at the bottom. I flip through the pile for the first page, but all I see is the stuff I printed.

Is this what she was holding in her hand when I fired her? I glance at the carpet in front of my desk and play back that moment in my mind. A bunch of papers fell on the floor, but I never saw them because Marshall came in my office to see what happened and helped me clean up.

Fuck me. He was the one who found the fake gym memberships, too.

Dread swirls in my gut as I spin my chair around and yank open the bottom drawer of the filing cabinet. It's the same form Rebecca uses at the front desk, but Leilani's signature is at the bottom of the page instead. I've watched her sign credit card slips, so I knew the first time I saw these forms that the loopy Ls and slightly angled letters were legit.

Except...

I compare the first sheet with the second, and then the third. When I layer one on top of the other and hold them up to the light, my stomach sinks and my heart and lungs start a race that leaves me with my head between my knees and one hand on the trash can.

They're all the same.

The *exact* fucking same, right down to the gap in the signature line like someone cut out Leilani's signature, taped it on a membership application, and ran copies of it.

"I can't believe you have your head shoved so far up your ass you can't see what's right under your fucking nose. You deserve everything that's coming to you. My only regret is not being here to see it."

Marshall was trying to get rid of her. He knew she had something on him and he wanted her gone, and now *he's* gone, and I have no idea what the hell is happening.

Well, aside from the part where I fired-slash-dumped my girlfriend for no fucking reason. That part is perfectly, painfully clear. I also know it's a good goddamn thing that asswipe skipped town before I found out what he did.

My office phone rings, reminding me I'm still at work and my personal problems will have to take a backseat to everyone else's for the next eight hours. "This is Cl—"

"The police are here," Rebecca whispers.

I pop my head up. "What do you mean?"

"Two cop cars just pulled in the parking lot. Wait. Make that three." Her voice is caught somewhere between fear and panic.

"You think they're here to tell us Marshall's dead?"

It takes a conscious effort not to reply with *I fucking hope so.* "I'll be there in a sec." I debate whether to take the stack of papers with me but ultimately decide to wait to file a report. I want to go back through my computer to find anything else Leilani dug up, and I should probably call DH to nail down an alibi in case Marshall is stupid enough to show his face again.

When I make it to the front desk, the only thing I see is Rebecca staring through the glass door while her leg taps out a Morse code message on the carpet. Sure enough, three cars are parked outside, so it surprises us when the door swings open and Stephen, my ten o'clock, walks in. I force my rage aside because none of this is his fault. "What's up, old man?"

"Old man?" He leans toward me with a lowered voice. "That's not what my girlfriend said last night." My jaw drops and Stephen laughs, adding, "I hope you're ready for some burpees."

I groan. Burpees rank right above a root canal, but I'll gladly do them because him reaching this milestone is huge. Last summer, he told me he'd never be able to get past the loss of his wife and be able to start a relationship with someone else. I empathized with him then—anyone would've—but after losing Leilani, I can sympathize with him too.

Of course, he didn't singlehandedly destroy the best thing that ever happened to him the way I did. I don't deserve sympathy from anyone.

"You okay?" Stephen's bushy brows draw together.

I nod, pushing all thoughts of my failed love life out of my mind.

"Good, because I'm getting this on video." He holds his phone in the air and grins, already enjoying the torture he's about to put me through.

We head toward the main gym when the front door opens again. This time, a police officer barrels inside, shouting words like "search warrant" and "arrest." It takes a few seconds and more shouting to realize he's directing them at me.

Me.

My jaw drops for the second time in as many minutes while he spins me around, cuffs my wrists, and informs me of my right to remain silent. Instinct has me jerking away, but a twist to my right arm reminds me I'm not in charge of anything right now.

"What the fuck is this?" It's hard to hear the officer's response over Rebecca's shrieks and the echo of pounding boots as more uniforms flood the lobby, but I catch a few key phrases like *jail, child sex trafficking*, and *sick bastard*. Someone shoves me forward, and then I'm stumbling down the hall amid a swarm of Kevlar vests and curious stares while my entire world crumbles around me.

I wait for my parents doing the same thing I did last night in my cell and this morning during my arraignment—thinking of Leilani. How right she was, how wrong I was, and how I'd give anything to delete the last nine days.

I've been up since yesterday. Even if it was possible to find a comfortable position on a jail bed, my mind wouldn't let me sleep. I saw her every time I closed my eyes. The images varied, but they always came back to one: Her standing in front of the painted wings in Hawaii.

She was the angel who wanted to save me, and I'm the

asshole who pushed her away.

The only good thing is knowing my parents are on their way with their bank account intact. My only stipulation when they came down to the station to post my bail was that they didn't pay for it. I've already caused enough problems for the people who love me. I'm not dragging anyone else down in this mess.

A guard retrieves me when they arrive. Mom did her best to put on a brave act when I called them this morning, but the dark shadows under her eyes tell me otherwise. Dad doesn't look much better.

"I guess this means you got the money?" I ask.

Dad nods and then I nod because there's not much to say about where it came from. Selling my Chevelle to Kurt stung like a sonofabitch. So did hearing the charges against me this morning. I've spent the last ten years building a business and a reputation based on helping people, and it only took three words to destroy it all.

Child sex trafficking.

The worst fucking part is not knowing the full story. I know Marshall's involved—that much was obvious before they started questioning me—and with the nature of the charges and how young Brandy looked, I'd bet money she's one of his victims.

But that's all I have.

I want to shout to the world that I'm innocent, but how fucking cliché is that?

Dad nudges my arm. "Ready?" I nod again, and after some paperwork that further documents the level of hell my life has become, we leave.

Hypertrophy, atrophy, and muscle memory. In terms of physical training, they're all related. We gain muscle when we start going to the gym, and we can lose it during an extended period of detraining. But thanks to the myonuclei that produce muscle protein, our body doesn't forget all the work we did. That means when we start going to the gym again, our muscles remember what we did the first time and it's easier to get back in shape.

Then there's the type of muscle memory that deals with how the brain processes tasks and repetition. Practice makes perfect, so to speak. It's the reason we can ride a bike without falling even if it's been years since we last rode.

With sleep eluding me yet again, I'm counting on both tonight.

Going to Battles to work off my anger is out of the question, so the counselor in me moved to the next item on my list of possible solutions—if I couldn't exhaust myself into slumber, I'd numb myself there instead.

I mean, what else did I have to lose?

Not a goddamn thing.

So muscle memory took me from my couch to my truck to a store I haven't been inside since Michael Phelps stole the Beijing Olympics. I used to take pride in my sobriety. I wore that shit like a badge of fucking honor. Now it's time to see if I can remember how to forget.

Muscle memory brings the vodka to my lips without spilling a drop, and the slow burn down my throat reminds my body of its old routine. Every pull from the bottle takes me one step closer to not giving a damn about Leilani or Marshall or lawyers or anything.

They say it's called "falling off the wagon," but make no mistake, I'm not falling. I'm jumping.

Freely.
Willingly.
I don't care where I land.
It doesn't matter if I can pick myself back up.
Who knows?
Maybe this time I won't.

Leilani

Face Your Battles

DAD SHUFFLES INTO THE KITCHEN JUST AFTER SUNRISE with his thin blue robe sashed around his waist. "Thought I heard you in here. When did you get up?"

"Around five, I think." I don't mention that I didn't fall asleep until two-thirty. Although Mom's the one who's obsessed with my health, Dad's still prone to asking questions if he sees probable cause.

He walks past a spread of chocolate chip cookies, brownies, and homemade Almond Joy bars on the way to the coffee pot. "Whatcha making now?"

"Nutter Butters. Kiki should be here in a couple of hours and I wanted to have something fresh for her."

Dad hums his approval. He's a sucker for anything peanut

butter. He slathers it on waffles and pancakes, and routinely cooks with it too. Yesterday he used it to make a stir fry sauce that put the restaurant stuff to shame. In his eyes, the only thing better than peanut butter itself is adding chocolate to it. On my second night home, we made knock-off Reese's cups and half the batch fell victim to his obsession.

I expect the same for my Nutter Butters, which is why I doubled the recipe.

With his coffee sweetened to his liking, Dad joins me at the counter. He doesn't say anything. I hope that means it's too early for deep father-daughter conversations, but it seems he just needed some caffeine first.

"When are you going to tell us what happened?"

"I already did. We broke up."

"That's not—"

I flip the mixer to medium-high and point to my ear, mouthing, *I'm sorry, what*?

He hides his smile behind his mug, knowing I can't cream the butter and sugar forever. Still, I wait a full thirty seconds longer than necessary before turning it off to add the eggs, vanilla, and peanut butter.

"Out with it. You've been home for more than a week and we've let you wallow long enough."

"Wallow's a little harsh, don't you think? That implies lying in bed all day watching re-runs of *Chopped* while avoiding personal hygiene habits. I've showered almost every day since I've been back, and I even *shaved* yesterday." I lift a brow and turn the mixer on again.

"Fine," he says above the whir of the motor. "You've been *stewing* long enough."

If stewing means focusing on the ninety-nine percent of

you that wants to stab someone in order to block out the other one percent that wants to buy stock in ice cream and chocolate syrup to numb the sadness, then yeah, I'm a damn pot of beef bourguignon.

"Dad, I told you, we broke up. It's no big deal. It happens to hundreds of thousands of people every day." I bring the mixer to a stop again, this time adding the dry ingredients to form the dough.

"If it's no big deal, why do you look so upset?"

"Maybe because he's an asshole and fired me when I was only trying to help him. Or because I thought for once, things would go right for me. But nooo." I fling the flour in the bowl, sending a cloud of white dust into the air. "Apparently, the universe gets off on giving me the cosmic middle finger when I least expect it." So much for avoiding deep conversations.

"The universe doesn't have any fingers, Limp."

I huff out a laugh. Hearing my childhood nickname in this context is oddly fitting. The heart is a muscle too, and damn if mine isn't bruised right now. "I assure you she does, but it's probably like those death horses in *Harry Potter*. You can't see them unless she's shoving them in your face." I plunk the half-mixed dough on the counter and use my indignation as fuel while I incorporate the last of the dry ingredients.

"Are you more upset about being fired or the breakup?"

"Both. He was supposed to trust me, not just as his girl-friend but as an employee."

Dad supplies an understanding nod. "And instead, he pushed you away when you were trying to help."

"Exactly!" My one-handled rolling pin makes a hearty thud into the dough. Kiki got it for me last Christmas after I joked that I was going to use a paint roller covered in plastic wrap to

207

make snowman sugar cookies. "It's ironic—he's the one who always said asking for help wasn't a sign of weakness. He should know that accepting it isn't either."

"In his defense, accepting help is much harder than asking for it."

My jaw falls to the floor. "Excuse me? In his defense?"

Dad ignores my murderous stare. "I seem to know someone else who was hell-bent on doing things on her own when other people wanted to help her." With that, he downs the last of his coffee.

Oh. Hell. No.

"So this is my punishment for not wanting Mom up my ass after I got cancer? Because there's a huge difference between me being capable of taking care of myself and Clay being oblivious to what was going on in his gym."

Dad holds up a hand. "I'm not saying there isn't."

"So what *are* you saying?" I trade my rolling pin for a knife to slice the dough into small squares.

"That it's hard to see the people we love struggle, and it's even harder when they push you away." He rises and deposits his mug in the sink.

"That's it? That's all you've got? I thought you were going to have some wise words about how all men are assholes or advice on how I can get out of this damn rut that I've been in all year."

He studies me as I roll a piece of dough against the counter, flatten it, and pinch the center to make a peanut shape. "Did you feel like you were living in a rut two weeks ago?"

Let's see... two weeks ago, I had a job I loved, a hot boss, and a decent fucking future. Right now, all I have is a burning desire to eat my weight in junk food.

"I'll take that as a no," Dad continues, giving me a pointed

SAVED

look. "You of all people understand that life isn't fair or easy, but did you ever consider that you're right where you're supposed to be?"

"Coming back to my parents' house with my tail tucked? Hot damn, it looks like I'm the poster child for adult success. Maybe I should head to the animal shelter this afternoon to get a head start on a cat collection."

That makes Dad laugh, which pisses me off even more. "Keep it up, and I'll hide the Nutter Butters," I mumble.

"Relax, Limp." He steps beside me, gently nudging my shoulder, and grabs a piece of dough. "You want sage wisdom and advice? Yes, men are assholes. We do stupid things for no reason. It's a genetic thing. Some of us are just better at suppressing it than others. But I don't believe for one second that your life was spared twice for nothing. And just like with gymnastics, you have to figure out what's worth digging in and fighting for and what you should let go."

"It's not like I can do physical therapy to fix everything that happened last week."

"No, but there's this awesome thing called a telephone that lets you talk to people who live in different states. I think part of what you're feeling right now is a lack of closure. Remember that while there's nothing wrong with coming home and turning your phone off, you can't hide forever. The sooner you face everything, the sooner you'll feel better."

"Face your battles," I whisper to myself. Clay's voice instantly pops into my head. *We can't always choose our battles. Sometimes life chooses them for us. All we can do is turn and face them head-on.*

I don't know whether to laugh or cry with my next breath. Since I was little, Dad's always had an ability to help me sort

209

through my problems—it didn't matter if it was about boys, school, gymnastics, or the Army. And rather than tell me what to do, he'd help me get all the puzzle pieces on the table so I could fit them together myself. "*We all see the same thing differently,*" he'd say. "*As long as you're happy with your solution, that's all that matters.*"

As much as I hate to admit it, he's right.

Still, the thought of talking to Clay sends my stomach into a flurry of nervous cartwheels. I don't know if he'll answer the phone or what he'll say if he does.

"Fine," I huff, "you win. I'll call him."

A satisfied smile spreads across Dad's face. "That's my girl."

"But not before Kiki gets here. I'm going to need moral support and Nutter Butters to get through this."

"You're stalling."

"No, I'm checking my email. That's called being productive."

"Whatever makes you feel better," Kiki says, crossing her feet on the coffee table.

I purposely chose radio silence when I got back to my parents' house—no cell phone, email, or social media. It may have been a cop out, but I couldn't handle the thought of anyone from Oklahoma contacting me. Well, anyone other than Kiki, and I had the house phone for that.

The downside is the hundred-plus emails waiting in my inbox. Seeing unread messages makes me twitch, so I have no choice but to go through one by one to get rid of that little red alert.

Halfway through my backlog, I come to a message from Jesse Pritchett Photography. "Hell no."

"What?" Kiki leans over to look at my screen.

"The pictures for the Battles advertising campaign. Jesse said he'd email them to me when he was done with the proofs." I click on the trash can icon and continue plowing through the list.

"You can't delete it before you even look at them!"

"I can, and I did."

"Aren't you at least a tiny bit curious about how they turned out?"

Yes, I admit to myself. "Nope."

"Liar." Kiki yanks the computer off my lap and retrieves the message from my trash folder. Part of me hopes Clay looks like a troll because my heart can't cope with seeing his gorgeous face and rock-hard body before I call him. In fact...

I step over Kiki's legs and head to the kitchen. "I'm getting some water. Let me know when you're done."

Several seconds later, she breaks her silence with a gasp. "I know him."

"Duh." God bless her, she must be delirious after her nine-hour drive.

"No, not Clay. The other guy." She pops off the couch and crosses the living room, laptop in hand, and turns the screen toward me.

"That's Marshall." Jesse's photography skills are even better than I realized. He managed to make him look like a friendly trainer instead of a slimy shit biscuit.

A line forms between Kiki's brows as she studies the picture. "The name doesn't sound familiar, but his face..."

My skin prickles. "I said the same thing when I started

working at Battles—that I recognized him but couldn't figure out how I knew him. I chalked it up to chemo brain."

"Hang on." She sets the laptop on the kitchen counter and opens a new browser window, then types *Nathan Powell stolen valor* in the search bar. She switches to the image results and sure enough, a photo on the second row looks exactly like a blond-haired, blue-eyed Marshall.

"No fucking way," I whisper. Kiki's first big news story after she was assigned to Fort Bragg was on a guy who was arrested for impersonating a soldier. She said it was the first time in her career she felt like a true journalist. That's where I remember seeing his face. "Oh my God, his contacts. It makes sense now."

"Contacts?"

I pull Jesse's email up again and point to Marshall's eyes. "They're green. A couple of weeks ago, he showed up at work with blue eyes. He said it was because of some pharmacy mix up with his contacts. I bet these ones are fake."

"Along with the black hair."

Neither of us says anything for several moments as we process this development. I told her about Marshall embezzling money, but this? It's a whole new level of fucked up. "You think Clay knows?" she asks.

"I'm not sure." Now I'm even more nervous. I can't *not* tell him about Marshall's real identity, but after the way he treated me in his office I have no idea whether he'll hear me out or call me a liar all over again. I sigh and sink onto the bar stool.

"Where's your cell?"

"On my night stand."

She disappears and returns with my phone. The screen is already lit up, showing me I have thirty-seven missed texts and half as many missed calls.

"I feel like I'm going to hurl."

"That would be a waste of Nutter Butters. You can do this."

My stomach twists into knots as I navigate to my favorites list and press Clay's name. His number goes straight to voicemail. I hang up before the beep because I have no idea how to tell him any of this, let alone say it in a recorded message.

"What about calling Rebecca?"

I shake my head. "She's dating Marshall. I doubt she'd believe me after everything he's probably told her about me in the past week."

While I figure out what to do next, I switch over to check my voicemail. The first four are from Rebecca.

Kiki gives me a reassuring pat on the shoulder. "Don't freak yet. Maybe she's reaching out to see how you're doing."

"Maybe," I mutter, playing the most recent one on speakerphone.

"Leilani, it's me again. Please call me as soon as you can."

I skip the next two and tap on her first voicemail.

"Hey Leilani, it's Rebecca. I…" She pauses and clears her throat. *"Clay was arrested for child sex trafficking today and Marshall hasn't been to work in two days and no one can get ahold of him and Battles is closed while they investigate Clay, and I have no idea what's happening except that everything's gone to shit and I really hope you call me back."*

Kiki's wide eyes mimic mine as we absorb Rebecca's frantic run-on sentence. How the hell did we just go from Marshall embezzling money and pretending to be in the military to *this*?

"Call her back. I'll pack your bag." Before I can argue, she's gone.

Kiki pulls into Clay's driveway just before midnight. Our nine-hour road trip turned into twelve, thanks to construction and an accident in New Mexico. "You sure you don't want me to stay?"

"No, I'll be fine." The lights aren't on, but his truck is parked on the side of the house and I can see the glow of the TV through the blinds.

Rebecca didn't have much information when I called her except that according to DH, Clay has been lying low at home since he got out of jail. Regardless of what happens between us, I know I can crash here for the night. I'll figure out tomorrow when it comes.

"Okay. I'm grabbing a hotel, but I'll call you in the morning."

I wait until her headlights disappear before knocking on the door. He doesn't answer, so I knock harder.

Still nothing. Just as I lift to pound on the door for a third time, it opens. His hand fumbles along the wall, and when it connects with the switch to the porch light, I gasp. To say he looks like shit would be an understatement. The man I left a week and a half ago has been replaced by a haggard substitute in baggy sweatpants.

"I'm dead, aren't I? But wait." Clay scrunches his face like he's working something out in his brain. "Hell's not s'pposed to have angels. Oh fuck, are you dead too?" He drops his hand on top of my head and lifts my right brow so he can peer into my eye.

I smack his arm away before he gouges me. "I'm not dead,

but…" I lean forward and sniff. "Oh my God, you're drunk."

"I'm numb," he corrects. "Numb. That rhymes with thumb." He wiggles his thumb in front of my face. "How come we don't say the 'b'?" He pronounces the word again, this time adding the silent letter. "Well that sounds dumb. Ha! Dum-b." He laughs at his joke and makes a sweeping motion toward the living room.

I follow his lead and close the door behind me. The first time I came here, I was impressed by the cleanliness and order. Right now, it looks like nine bachelors have taken up residence.

"You shouldn't be here. Good girls like you don't need to be around convicts like me." He reaches for a bottle of vodka on the coffee table.

Clay has never showed any signs of violence, even when we argued, so I pray he's not a mean drunk. "Why don't we sit down and watch—" For the first time, I notice what's on TV. "Sesame Street? You're watching Sesame Street?"

He starts in on a slurred rendition of the theme song and plops onto the couch. If this were any other scenario, I'd be laughing and recording him for future blackmail.

There's nothing funny about rock bottom, though.

Clay

The Fifth Smile

ALCOHOLICS DRINK FOR A NUMBER OF REASONS. LAST night, mine was because I didn't want to feel anything. That's funny considering I feel everything right now...

The elephant stampede in my head.

The fire under my eyelids courtesy of the sunlight pouring through the blinds.

The stabbing sensation in my back. I fish my hand between the cushions below me and pull out my remote control. Look at me solving problems like a boss.

Stifling a groan, I push myself to a sitting position and scrub a hand over my face. It takes a few seconds for my vision to focus enough to see the glass of water and four ibuprofen on the coffee table. In the Army, an eight hundred milligram Motrin is called Ranger candy. These days, anything less than that doesn't work. If I wasn't so stiff, I'd pat myself on the back for planning ahead.

On the way back from the bathroom, I realize my living room and kitchen are spotless. Everything Mom silently judged me for has been wiped up, put away, or thrown away. It wasn't her though—she and Dad stayed in Dallas last night to watch Hamilton for their anniversary. He scored tickets months ago, and I refused to let them miss out on it because of me.

I guess that means I got drunk and cleaned my house before I passed out. Damn, that's a whole new level of pathetic.

My stomach still isn't ready for food, so I opt for more hydration and grab a Gatorade from the fridge. That's when I see her, frozen in the hallway with my laundry basket propped on her left hip. Her expression is impossible to read, but I know mine isn't.

I have an arrest record. I'm hungover. I'm a failure. Let's add a heaping dose of shame to the list of shit I'm feeling this morning, shall we?

I want to tell her how fucking sorry I am. That she was right about everything, and that I'll spend the rest of my life regretting the moment I let Marshall's lies cloud my judgment, but I wait because Leilani deserves to speak first.

She slowly rests the basket on the counter and slides her hand over her yoga pants. I love those pants. "Hi. How do you feel?"

"Hungover." I use my drink to wash the gravel from my voice. Was she here all night? Is she staying today? Why did she clean my house?

And most importantly, *how much does she hate me?*

"I got in the car yesterday as soon as I heard what happened."

217

Her gaze bounces from the basket to the floor to the dining room window before returning to me. Whether it's because she's nervous or because she can't stand the sight of me is anyone's guess. "I thought maybe you could use another person in your corner."

Okay. That's good. I can work with that. "I don't deserve it, but thanks." Her mouth forms a flat smile, and then she's looking at other things in the kitchen that aren't me.

I never knew it was possible to be jealous of a toaster.

"Uh, I'm going to rinse off before I drown myself in coffee."

The moment she tucks her bottom lip between her teeth and glances at my bedroom door, I know what she's thinking about. I was perfectly happy with sex in the dark because my biggest concern was making sure she felt comfortable. But the night she walked into my shower and wrapped her arms around me? I nearly blew my load when I saw her. Nothing could have prepared me for how fucking beautiful she was.

Ever the opportunist, my dick uses the memory to make it clear that he doesn't have a hangover and is more than happy to rise and shine. I can't say I blame him—the morning scenery is incredible—but the goal is to get Leilani to stay, not run for the hills. I casually lower my Gatorade bottle to my crotch and flee the kitchen.

To my surprise, she's on the couch when I come out of my room. More specifically, she's the only thing on the couch.

"They're in the washing machine," she says, answering my unspoken question on the whereabouts of the pillows and blanket I slept with last night. I didn't even know you could wash throw pillows. Based on the before and after in my living room, I wonder if I have any laundry soap left.

I sit on the opposite end of the sofa. The middle cushion is only a couple of square feet, but it might as well be a mile wide with a neon sign that says *Friend Zone*. Christ, this is excruciating.

"Thanks for cleaning. You didn't have to do that."

"It gave me something to do. I was too worried about you to sleep."

My jaw falls slack. "You've been up all night?"

"Most of it. I dozed on the chair sometime around four." She lifts a mug off the table and brings it to her lips.

"Joining the dark side?" I ask, extending a tiny olive branch. Leilani only drinks coffee when she's desperate.

"Hot chocolate. You still had some pods in the basket."

This time her smile is real. Small, but real. The vice around my heart relaxes slightly knowing she's using the stuff I bought for the mornings she was here.

"Yours is high-octane though." She tips her chin toward a mug on my side of the table. I guess I was too distracted by the fact that she was still here to notice it.

I grab the handle and make a show of peering into the black liquid. "Any poison I should worry about?"

Her subsequent laugh, albeit soft, is the most beautiful sound I've ever heard. "I thought about it, but you're too heavy. I wouldn't be able to properly dispose of your body."

Now it's my turn to laugh. "It should bother me that you put that much thought into it, but it doesn't."

"No?"

I shake my head. "You have a great sense of humor. It's one

of the things I like most about you." I take a swig of coffee while giving myself a round of fist-bumps for not slipping up and saying "*love*." I've been awake for a whopping thirty minutes without scaring her off and I'd like to keep it that way.

We sit in mostly-comfortable silence for a few minutes before she speaks again.

"Why'd you drink last night?"

Ah, yes. The golden question. I could fill the rest of the day with answers, but it all boils down to the same thing. "Because I had no reason not to. I lost everything. Even if my attorney is able to clear my name, the damage is already done. The idea of having to completely start over in my mid-thirties is…" I take another sip of my dark roast in hopes it'll kick my brain into gear. "It's a pain in the ass is what it is."

"What makes you think the damage is done?"

"Come on, Lei. People don't recover from sex charges involving children. In the real world, you're guilty until proven innocent, and even if the charges *are* dropped, the rumors will always be there. My entire business is based on trust. I'll never get that back."

"I wouldn't be too sure about that."

"Thanks for your vote of confidence, but I've already accepted it."

She tips her head, studying me. "We're going to play a little role-reversal game." She stands up, sets her cup on the coffee table, and motions for me to do the same. "Lie down."

Despite my misgivings, I comply while she angles the chair toward the couch and takes a seat. I keep my eyes trained on the ceiling above me because looking at her while I'm horizontal won't go well for me. Not when she's close enough to touch.

"Is there anyone you feel you've hurt in the past two weeks?"

My parents. My staff. My clients. "Yeah."

"Who do you feel you've hurt the most?"

I release a long breath. "You really want me to answer that?"

"Mm hmm."

"Um. My girlfriend. Ex-girlfriend, I mean." *Fuck, this is awkward.* "I trusted the wrong person and believed stuff about her that wasn't true. I never even gave her a chance to defend herself."

Her soft sigh is the only indicator that I've stuck a nerve. "And did you have any contact with this woman after she left?"

I move my head back and forth.

"So despite hurting her and having no contact with her, she came back on her own."

"It appears that way."

"Why do you think that is?"

I blow out a breath. "I have no fucking idea."

"Maybe it's because she doesn't need an investigation to know you aren't guilty of the charges against you, and I'd be willing to bet she's not the only one."

God bless her, her heart's in the right place, even if she is living in La La Land. "I appreciate what you're trying to do, but it's going to take more than a few loyal friends to save Battles."

"I disagree. You built that gym when no one believed you could, and look what it turned into."

"I didn't do it by myself. I had help."

"You still do. Only this time, you're not starting from scratch." She shifts, leaning forward several inches. "The members of that gym trust you with their lives, Clay. Literally, for some of them. Give them a chance to support you the way you've supported them."

The student has become the master. A slow smile spreads

across my face. "If you're ever looking for a career change, you should consider being a life coach."

She smirks. "Well I *am* unemployed."

And there it is.

Regret settles around us like a wet blanket. She meant it as a joke, but it doesn't stop the sting of our reality. The one I created. How is it that she's here after everything I put her through? That has to mean there's hope for us, right? I turn my head to the side and peer up at her. "Why don't you hate me?"

"I did for about five days. I hated you like it was a full-time job and I was the star employee."

That's not surprising. Leilani has always been a fierce competitor, no matter if she's going up against an opponent or simply trying to outdo herself. "What made you change your mind?"

This time she meets my eyes. "I figure you're hating yourself enough for everyone."

She's got that part right. The consequences of my relationship with alcohol mean I'm no stranger to self-loathing, but this is a whole new level of disgust. Everything that's happened in the past two weeks is my fault.

"I'm still mad at you though, and I won't apologize for it."

"You have every right to be. *I'm* the one who needs to do the apologizing." I sit up, careful not to disturb the gap between our knees despite my intense need to touch her. "I will never be able to tell you how sorry I am. Every day, I wish I could take back the things I said to you. God, there's so much I wish I could take back." Exhaustion and shame pull my head down.

"I know you're sorry, Clay. I wouldn't still be here if you weren't."

That brings up a good point. I shift, leaning back on the couch to gauge her response. "Why *are* you still here? Not that

I want you to leave, because I don't," I quickly add. "It's just that most people wouldn't give their ex the time of day after the shit I did to you."

Her shoulders bounce once. "Anger and compassion aren't mutually exclusive."

"Um, could you elaborate? I'm still a bit hungover."

"I had a big blow-up with one of my college friends earlier this year. But when I told her I had cancer, everything from before no longer mattered as much. Yes, we were still mad at each other, but that took a backseat to what was happening and the fact that she was my friend."

"I guess that makes sense."

"And, despite what you may think, I'm not completely innocent in our breakup."

A deep line forms between my brows. "How so?"

"I didn't realize that I'd put you on a pedestal. You're so different from other men. You're not an asshole. You know how to communicate. You understand that being sensitive to someone else's needs isn't a sign of weakness. Somewhere along the way, you became the perfect boyfriend. The perfect boss. It was so easy to overlook your flaws because there aren't many of them.

"But some of your worst qualities are borne from the best parts of you. You're incredibly loyal. When you let someone in, it's like having your own personal cheerleading squad made up of bodyguards."

I can't help but laugh. "That's quite the visual."

"It's true! You protect those closest to you, and encourage them to overcome their obstacles. Except, sometimes you're loyal to a fault. Earlier, you said you never gave me a chance to defend myself. You were right, but I never forced you to listen, either.

"I could have stood on your desk until you at least looked at the papers I was holding. Then, maybe you would've had a lightbulb moment and realized you'd been loyal to the wrong person all along. We were both to blame for me going home. Of course, it's like ninety percent you, ten percent me…"

A smile finishes her sentence. It's the fourth one I've seen this morning. "One thing I've learned is that when you care about someone, you keep pushing. You don't let them shut you out no matter how hard they try. I didn't do that, and I'm sorry."

This is the weirdest post-breakup visit ever. I expected tears and shouting, maybe some name-calling for good measure. But cleaning my house and making a list of my good qualities? It's like an episode of *Jerry Springer* in reverse.

"Thank you for coming down here and making sure I was okay. For a second, I thought I was hallucinating when I saw you in the hallway."

"Last night you said I was an angel and asked if I was dead."

"Oh God," I groan, covering my eyes with my hand. "I'm sorry you had to see me like that."

"What do you tell your clients when they hit rock bottom?"

"It varies, depending on what brought them there in the first place, but one common theme is reminding them they don't have to repeat the same mistakes they made yesterday. That every day they choose to abstain from their addiction is a win."

"Okay, then. Are you going to be a winner today?"

The corners of my mouth curve up. "You should *really* consider being a life coach."

"Right now, I'd consider a nap."

For the first time, the logistics of her visit cross my mind.

"How'd you get here, anyway?"

"Kiki drove. She stayed at a hotel last night and headed back to Fort Sill this morning."

"Have you talked to Rebecca?"

She nods. "That's who told me you were arrested."

"Did she say anything about staying with her parents?"

"She briefly mentioned moving into her new house at the end of the month. With both of us out of the apartment, DH can bring in two new people, which makes sense." Leilani walks her mug into the kitchen, then makes a detour down the hallway. I guess that means our role-reversal game is over.

Panic has me racing around the couch, much to the dismay of my lingering headache, to meet her in the laundry room. "Where are you staying tonight?"

"I haven't gotten that far yet." She closes the dryer and spins the knob to start it. "The only thing I was concerned with yesterday was getting down here."

Coffee swishes in my stomach when I ask her the next question. "Are you planning to go back home?"

She rubs her palm on her thigh as if the answer is hidden under a layer of Lycra. "I haven't figured that out either."

Thank Christ. Relief washes over me, but I keep a neutral expression. "Stay here and sleep for a while. It'll be easier to decide what to do once you've gotten some rest."

"Uh..."

I hold my palms up. "You can stay in the spare bedroom at my parents' house or crash here on the couch. I promise I won't bother you."

Her bottom lip disappears between her teeth while she considers my offer and finally says, "The couch is fine."

Hell motherfucking yes! My brain knows this doesn't mean

anything—we still have a bunch of shit to talk about, and there's a huge chance we won't get back together—but my heart feels like Rocky Balboa when he reached the top of the steps at the Philadelphia Museum of Art.

I make a beeline for my room to get a pillow and blanket off the bed I haven't slept on since Leilani went back to Colorado. I tried, but there were too many memories tied up in those sheets.

After closing the blinds, I grab the remote and turn the TV on. A cartoon tiger in a red jacket appears on the screen, singing about friendship. Jesus, how drunk was I last night? On the plus side, I remembered to stay away from the news. That was one of my attorney's three rules, along with "Don't turn on your phone" and "Lay low."

I quickly change the channel, not bothering to ask Leilani what she wants to watch. As long as it's one of those shows on house hunting, fixing up, or flipping, she's happy. "I'll just be in my room," I say, keeping my promise not to bother her. "Let me know if you need anything."

"Uh, you can watch too, if you want." She gives me my fifth smile of the morning. By far, it's my favorite because there's a hint of hope in the corners of her lips. Even though HGTV has never been my thing, my ass is on the other end of couch before she changes her mind.

Today's show follows newlyweds as they turn a run-down house into their dream home. How they have a sixty thousand-dollar renovation budget on his salary as a dental tech is beyond me. There's no place for logic in television, though.

They've just finished the demolition when I feel it—her feet on the side of my leg.

When I sat down, she had her knees angled enough that

they didn't leave the middle cushion. Does she know she's touching me, or did she stretch out in her sleep?

Please be awake. Please be awake.

I risk a peek in her direction and suppress a grin.

Her eyes are open.

Leilani

A New Lease

"THAT SONOFABITCH."

I don't think I've ever seen Clay's nostrils this big before.

"I can't believe I never caught on. Do you know he used to tell me I was too trusting?" He downs the rest of the water in his bottle and crushes the plastic with his fist, muttering, "fucking irony" on the way to the trash can.

"You're not the first person he conned and at the rate he's going, you probably won't be the last." Mrs. Prescott's words do little to improve Clay's mood.

His parents got back shortly after I woke up from my nap. She said how great it was to see me again, gave me a bear hug, and insisted that Clay and I join them at their house for dinner.

I'm not one to pass up a roast, so here we are.

After he was arrested, Clay finally fessed up to his parents as to why he fired me. To my surprise, being around them for more than a few minutes wasn't as awkward as I feared it would be. All Mrs. P said when we walked into the kitchen was, "Do you mind grabbing the rolls out of the oven?"

I waited until after dessert was over to bring up Marshall's previous stolen valor charges. Given that I fell asleep after this morning's heart-to-heart, I still hadn't had a chance to tell Clay about it. At that point, it made sense to wait until his parents were there, too. He and I still need to talk about his drinking and his assurance that it was a one-time mistake, but we can only have so many heavy conversations in one day.

"I'm sorry to have killed the mood tonight," I say to the room, though my eyes are on Clay.

Mr. P's response is immediate. "Don't be. The more information we have on this bastard, the better."

"He's right, this is actually great news. Our hands are tied right now because our lawyer is still waiting on the search warrant report. This gives us more ammo to show that Marshall... Nathan... whatever his name is," Mrs. P waves her hand, "is the one behind all of this."

Clay only grunts. I hate that there's nothing I can do to fix this.

"Oh, I forgot to tell you—I've decided to demo the back bathroom. Your mother's been wanting some fancy tile in there for years and I'm not getting any younger. Feel like coming over tomorrow and helping your old man?"

"You think giving me a sledgehammer is a wise move?"

The elder Prescott grins. "Might do you some good, and it'd save me money on labor."

I'd bet anything that Mr. P had no intentions of remodeling the bathroom, especially not tomorrow, which makes his gesture even sweeter.

Clay silently considers his offer before pushing off from the kitchen counter and collecting the dessert plates. "You hear that, Mom? Child labor. I thought you said that would end when I turned eighteen." His sarcastic smirk is a welcome sight, and the rest of us breathe a sigh of relief.

"I said eight-*y*," she clarifies, a grin crossing her face.

"Eh, it looks like you've got forty-six years'-worth of muscles in there. You shouldn't have any problems." My neck and face flush as soon as the words leave my mouth. What the hell am I doing talking about his muscles in front of his parents?

Floor, swallow me whole please.

Clay, thank God, never misses a beat. "I told you guys she was good with numbers."

They smile as I make my escape, tucking the bowl of walnuts in my arm and grabbing the chocolate syrup on a desperate dash to the kitchen.

Mrs. P follows, either oblivious to my state of mortification or thoroughly enjoying it and ready for more. "Are you staying at the cottage again?"

I stand there, mouth agape, not knowing how to answer. Clay and I haven't discussed that yet, though his body language today has been a clear indicator of what he wants.

"Mom!" he coughs, shooting her a warning look.

"What?" She points to the brownies. "I was going to send the rest back with you. I just didn't know whether to put them in one container or two."

"Mm hmm." The look on Clay's face says he's not buying it.

My phone rings from inside my purse, signaling my reprieve.

I excuse myself and make a beeline to Mrs. P's sewing room—the same one I was in when she fixed my breast form earlier this summer. My, how things come full-circle.

"Hey, I'm glad you called." I texted Kiki a few times today, but we haven't been able to talk. When her editor found out she came home early from her weekend pass, he stuck her on an assignment at the artillery range.

"How's it going?"

"Good."

She pauses. "What aren't you telling me?"

We purposely avoided conversations about Clay and Marshall during our road trip yesterday. Instead, we played ostrich by discussing Kiki's next duty station options, singing along with the radio, and sleeping—me, not her. This is the first time I've told anyone what's on my mind as far as Clay goes. "I want to give him another chance."

"You sound like that's a problem."

I plop down on a chair in the corner of the room. "I feel like I'm not supposed to want to."

"Why?"

"Because of the Travis thing and him firing me. That's two major strikes. What happens when the next one comes?"

"He earned his first strike fair and square, but the second one wasn't entirely his fault."

My forehead furrows. I didn't tell her about me taking part of the blame for that one. She was already out covering her story when that happened. "What do you mean?"

"He ended things under false pretenses. None of that would have happened if that dickwad wasn't in the picture."

Huh. "I guess you're right."

"No guessing. I'm older and wiser, remember?"

I can hear the smile in her voice, which eases some of my anxiety. Kiki may not be in a relationship of her own right now, but she's always been a damn good source of advice. "So I'm not crazy for still having feelings for him?"

"No! Stop worrying about what other people think. And as far as counting strikes goes, you can't keep tally like that. It's not fair to either of you, because you'd just spend your whole relationship waiting to scratch another mark on your scorecard. Besides, what does Dad always say about fear?"

"It makes a terrible compass."

"Exactly." She starts her car and the phone switches over to Bluetooth. Knowing she called me before she even got the air conditioning going makes me love her even more. "If you're too stubborn to listen to your heart or your gut, then listen to me: Give him another chance. No one is perfect—"

"—except Nick Bateman," we finish in unison, laughing. Kiki used to tell me that before every gymnastics meet during my senior year of college to help with my pre-match nerves.

"Seriously, Lei. You deserve happiness. I, on the other hand, deserve a shower. I'll call you tomorrow, okay?"

"Thanks, Kiki."

Three pairs of eyes hone in on me when I return to the kitchen, but in typical fashion, Clay rescues me. "We should probably head out before it gets too dark…"

There's still plenty of light out, but his dad takes the hint and walks us to the back door. "I want to get started on that demo early tomorrow. Say, six thirty?"

"I'm sleeping in until at least eight. Don't you show up here one minute before then." Mrs. P points a finger and shoots Clay her best stern look, which isn't stern at all, then turns to me.

"It was wonderful to see you again. Don't be a stranger,

okay?" She leans in for a hug and then passes the brownies to me.

In one container.

"See you kids tomorrow!" With a glint in her eyes, she pulls the door closed, leaving us on the deck overlooking their property.

"Please don't pay attention to her," Clay begs, taking the dish from me. "This doesn't mean—"

He glances down and watches me reclaim the brownies. "One bowl is fine."

"It is?"

I nod.

"And by that you mean…" He controls the arch of his brows, a sign that he's trying not to get his hopes up for the literal or metaphorical meanings behind my comment.

"It means I was wondering how you felt about trying this—us—again."

"Really?" Control be damned, his brows meet his hairline and his jaw hits the ground, making me laugh.

"I know, it's not something I thought I'd say a few days ago, either."

We step off the deck and amble down the walkway to his place. The flowers lining either side of the cobblestone are in full bloom, adding a lingering sweetness to the warm evening air. I should ask Mrs. P what they are.

"You sure about this?"

I cast a glance at him, appreciating the way the setting sun illuminates him from behind. He looks angelic. That is, if angels had scruffy jaws, big muscles, and wore fitted black t-shirts. "I would have loved it if my feelings for you disappeared when I went back to Colorado, but they didn't. And, at the risk of going out on a limb, I'd say neither did yours."

"I failed miserably at getting you out of my head. The more I tried, the worse it got. It's fitting, considering how stubborn you are."

"Ha, ha." I playfully roll my eyes while he enjoys a smile at my expense.

"What made you change your mind?"

"Several reasons. One, we were both victims of Marshall and it's not fair that the bad guy wins. I don't want him taking any more from us than he already has."

"Cock-sucking bastard." He kicks a piece of loose cobblestone into the grass.

"Moving along," I continue, "I slept today. *Really* slept. That hasn't happened much lately. And when I woke up and saw you crashed out on the other end of the couch, it just felt… I don't know. Normal and right and like how it's supposed to be."

Clay nods. "I was afraid I'd fall asleep and wake up to an empty house."

"That sort of ties in with my last reason. I've never seen anyone as remorseful as you. Hell, I think your clothes are even sorry for what happened."

"My clothes? You should see my dishes. Those poor guys will never forgive themselves."

My head flies back as laughter bursts from my chest. God, I've missed this—our easy banter and his ability to inject some levity at the perfect moment.

When we reach the front door, he stops and faces me. "So, I guess this means you're staying in Oklahoma?"

"Yep."

He returns my smile, but he's a bit slower on the delivery of his next question. "Do you, uh, need help finding an apartment?"

"Nah. I saw this cute cottage when I drove in, and I was thinking of asking the landlord if he has room for me."

Clay's entire body inflates. "He does. He has all the rooms. Ones with beds and couches and showers, and even one with a washing machine. Oh, and he has a pool." He opens the door and pulls me inside.

I set the brownies on the small entry table to our right and tap my chin, enjoying the hell out of our little game. "Hmm. Does he offer a long-term lease?"

"He prefers it."

One step closes the distance between us, and then his hands are on my hips. Damn, that feels nice. "But what if I need more space one day? A few extra bedrooms and maybe a yard?"

"The lease is transferrable to another property."

Clay's palms take a journey up my arms and come to a rest on either side of my neck. From this angle, it's impossible not to fall victim to the pools of hazel staring back at me.

"I really like this landlord."

"That's good," he murmurs, lowering his lips to mine, "because he really likes you."

Following the "come inside, we're out back" instructions taped to their front door, Clay and I let ourselves into Paige and DH's house, stow a fruit and veggie tray in their fridge, and join them outside.

"Hey!" DH pops up from his lounge chair and rounds the pool to greet us. "I hear congratulations are in order."

"What?!" Paige shrieks, dropping her half-inflated raft.

He laughs at her sudden interest in our conversation. "Relax, babe. Not those kinds of congratulations."

Unconvinced, Paige follows DH's path and lifts my hand, then Clay's, before turning back to her husband. "Andrew Lucas Rhoads, if you're lying about this, I'll murder you in your sleep tonight."

So that's his real name? Huh.

"No, you won't."

She props a fist on her hip and arches a brow. "What makes you so sure of yourself?"

"Because who else would take the four a.m. feedings?"

Her face screws into a scowl, but she can't hold on to her narrowed gaze for more than a few seconds before she admits defeat. "Dammit, you're right. Way to steal my ammunition, kid." She throws a wry smile over her shoulder at Poppy, who's hanging out in one of those travel cribs by the patio table. "What's all the fuss for, then?"

DH tips his head toward Clay. "He survived the first meeting of the parents."

"Ahh." Paige nods.

"Hey, at least he didn't meet my mom during one of the most embarrassing wardrobe malfunctions of his life."

"At least your first conversation with my mom wasn't, 'Hi, it's nice to meet you. Do you have any questions about my arrest record?' And let's not forget the reason you went home in the first place. I half expected your dad to shake my hand with a baseball bat."

"Don't let him fool you," I tell Paige and DH. "My parents loved him. Hell, when they pulled up, Mom couldn't get out of the car fast enough to hug him. Of course, that probably has something to do with being drawn to people in crisis, but still…"

I only brought my toothbrush and a couple of days' worth of clothes when I came back to Oklahoma last weekend. The night I decided to stay, I called my parents to give them the news and figure out the logistics of getting my Jeep and the rest of my stuff back here.

Dad said he was one step ahead of me. He'd already swapped the adaptive cup on my gear shift with a regular knob and loaded the backseat with everything I'd brought to their house. They got here Wednesday evening and, thanks to the Prescotts' hospitality, stayed in their guest bedroom.

Mrs. P cooked half of a Thanksgiving dinner that night and the conversation flowed easily with the men trading Army stories while Mom told Mrs. P about growing up in Hawaii.

As far as Mom's obsession with my diet went, she didn't say anything about my Fruity Pebbles or junk food shelf when I caught her sneaking a peek in Clay's pantry. Maybe it's because she knows someone else has picked up her "look after Leilani" baton.

Still, I wasn't sure she was going to leave without a fight. Dad said he was one step ahead on that, too. They never got to see the Southwest during his military service, so he rented a car Friday morning and told her they were going to the Grand Canyon before heading home.

"Austin, wait a—!"

"CANNONBALL!"

A boy wearing blue and green swim trunks sprints out of the house and dives into the pool, splashing everything in a six-foot radius—including us.

A woman wearing a resigned smile joins us seconds later.

"Sorry, y'all! He's been looking forward to this all week. I could hardly get him to keep his seatbelt on when we pulled into the neighborhood."

DH doesn't hear her apology because he's too busy scooping Austin into his arms after he climbs out of the pool.

"You dare splash me? You're going down, little man!"

"Uncle D, no!" Austin punctuates his plea with squeals of delight as DH leaps in the air for a two-in-one cannonball, showering us for a second time.

"They can't even wait ten seconds, can they?" The woman shakes her head in amusement and turns to me, extending her hand. "You must be Leilani. I'm Eric's wife, Maggie, and the youngest child in the pool is my son, Austin."

Her playful jab at DH makes me laugh. It's hard to reconcile the stories he's shared at Battles about his PTSD with the guy dunking his nephew in the deep end. Knowing Clay played a large role in that makes me even more proud of him.

"Where's Eric?" Clay asks, draping an arm over my shoulder.

"Right here," he replies, joining us on the deck. "Had to get this one suited up. Jordan, can you say hi to Clay and Leilani?"

Eric's daughter extends her chubby toddler fingers and waves, then points at the pool. "Yummy?"

"We have to find your floatie."

"Yummy!"

Paige holds her arms out to Jordan. "Come here, sweetheart. I know where it is."

"Yummy!"

Clay and I exchange confused looks. "She wants to eat the pool?" I ask.

Maggie shakes her head. "Anything she likes is yummy. Food. Animals. Swimming. Even Austin, sometimes."

"Oh my gosh, that's adorable! And also brilliant. She's a girl after my own heart."

"It's not so great when we have to figure out which yummy she's talking about." Eric adds. "It's turned into a running joke in the house: Show me the yummy!" He says it in the voice of Rod Tidwell from *Jerry Maguire*, which makes it even more hilarious.

A short time later, Paige's parents and little brother arrive with Rebecca, Bristol, and Blake in tow. Although we've spoken on the phone several times, it's the first I've seen her since I went back to Colorado.

I can't imagine what's been going through her head in the last two weeks. Marshall may have gotten me fired and attempted to destroy Clay's business, but neither of us are dealing with the level of shame Rebecca feels for being in a relationship with him.

"*It wouldn't be as bad if it was just the sex*," she'd confessed the last time we talked. "*But I brought him around my children. I keep thinking about all the times he played with Bristol and the pictures he took of the kids. What if he sent those to someone?*"

Clay told her to make a list and focus on the things she could control. Instead of moving into her new place next week, she's staying at her parents' house, and she got GPS trackers for her kids that are made to look like tiny smartwatches.

DH even put her in contact with one of his friends at the Moore Police Department who volunteered to give her handgun training. When Rebecca joked about putting Marshall's face on the targets, I knew she was going to be okay.

She pulls me in for a hug, and despite already apologizing for believing the things he said about me, she does it again. "Thanks for inviting me out here. I didn't realize how much we needed a break from reality until the kids saw the pool," she says. "And speaking of, nice bathing suit." She points to the red bikini I'm wearing under my tank top.

I laugh, remembering my murderous thoughts when I opened my suitcase in Hawaii. "Yeah, I had this friend who shoved me out of my comfortable nest when I took a trip with my hot boss. Turned out she had pretty great taste."

"Any word on your surgery?"

"I called Dr. Anderson's office and they're squeezing me in next Friday for my initial consult. He can't guarantee anything, especially since he hasn't seen me yet, but based on the general timeline, I could be looking at getting my reconstruction sometime around Valentine's Day."

The arch of her brows tells me she understands the significance of the date. "That's awesome! What about you and Clay? Are you guys okay now?"

His name draws an immediate smile. I don't even care that I look like a dorky seventh grader talking about her crush. "All things considered, we're doing so, so good." Instinctively, I scan the deck for him.

He and the guys are over by the grill having a deep, meaningful conversation about—you guessed it—cars. He hated giving up his Chevelle to cover his bail and legal fees, but earlier I overheard Eric and DH say they'd help him look for a new project. I get the feeling that being elbow-deep in engines and grease with friends is exactly the kind of therapy he needs right now, so I don't mind.

I'm just about to suggest some pool time before we eat when my phone buzzes in my back pocket. "Oh shit," I mutter, glancing at the screen.

"What happened?" Worry washes over Rebecca's face.

"It's Clay's attorney."

"Why does he have your number?"

"Clay's had his phone off since his arrest. He was using his mom's phone to contact his attorney, but now that I'm back, Mrs. P gave him my number."

"Well, what did he say?"

"He wants Clay to go to his office on Monday at three." That's two days away, which is more like seven years when you're in the crosshairs of the court system.

"What for?"

"I'm not sure. Clay said he already told the attorney everything he knows, so this has to be something about the charges against him."

I keep watching the screen, but nothing else comes. I don't know the etiquette about conversing with attorneys. Am I allowed to respond with follow-up questions?

The guys laugh about something, making the knots in my gut twist tighter. "What do I do, Bec? This is the first time I've seen him relax all week. I don't want to take that away from him."

As if he can feel me looking his way, he turns and smiles, and that's all I need to make my decision. Right now, what he doesn't know won't hurt him.

I tuck my phone in my pocket and turn back to Rebecca. "This conversation never happened, okay?"

Clay

Feel the Burn

ELEVEN HOURS.

That's how long I have to wait to find out if this nightmare is over.

Like the thunder outside, the sharp cracks of anger and rumbles of dread storming through my mind show no signs of letting up. I keep replaying the last two years in my mind. All the warning signs and red flags were there. How could I have been so goddamn stupid?

He never liked talking about his family or where he grew up. He only volunteered stories about his "service" when other people asked him, and even then, it wasn't much.

The secretive phone calls and plans he'd cancel at the last minute. His sudden interest in helping the "homeless"... I'd save the court system the trouble and kill him myself if I could.

"Hey." Leilani runs her hand over my brow and down the side of my face. "How long have you been awake?"

"A few hours." I shift, pulling my arm from beneath her, and sit up. "Go back to sleep, I'll take the couch."

"Nope."

"It's okay, babe. There's no sense in both of us being up."

To her credit, Leilani tried to spare me the worry. She managed to keep the meeting with my attorney a secret until last night when I mentioned going on a hike this afternoon. She kept saying we should stay in town and suggested we go for a walk around Lake Hefner instead.

I almost agreed until I realized she was chewing the inside of her lip and made her tell me what was going on.

She lightly smacks my side. "When are you going to realize I won't let you go through this alone?"

"Stubborn, stubborn," I tease. The truth is, I do feel better having someone to talk to right now. If that's what being pussy-whipped means…well, beat me with a bag of bearded clams.

"What are you most worried about?"

That's like sorting through a bucket of torment and choosing the worst one. It's impossible, because by default, knowing about something takes some of the fear away.

"That's the thing—I don't know. Literally. What if he's out there pinning more shit on me? What if the stuff we *do* know about him is just the tip of the iceberg? I'm so fucking afraid I'm going to walk into my attorney's office and hear a whole new list of charges. Can they even do that there? Or would I be arrested all over again?" I blow out a frustrated breath hoping like hell this won't be my last night lying next to Leilani.

"Okay, first of all…" She sits up and straddles me. "Stop

going down the rabbit hole of what ifs. The police will find him eventually. Second, I find it hard to believe your lawyer would ambush you like that. He's on your side, remember?"

She waits until I nod to continue.

"And third, remember the advice you give your clients. Focus on what you can control." Leaning over, she turns on the lamp and pulls a pen and small notebook from my nightstand drawer.

Our nightstand drawer. In *our* room. Next to *our* bed. That thought cuts through a layer of my anxiety, making it a little easier to breathe.

Once she settles beside me, Leilani flips the notebook open. "This guy I know told me that by helping others, I help myself."

"He sounds like a really smart man."

The corner of her mouth lifts as she pops a shoulder. "Eh, he's okay, but more importantly, he's right." She taps the pen against the paper for emphasis. "We're going to make a list of three things you can do today to help someone else."

"We are, huh?"

"Mm hmm."

Watching her write *one*, *two*, and *three* along the margin makes me think of our conversation in Hawaii about her being a numbers person and me being a people person. I had no idea she'd be able to perform both roles so flawlessly, at least where I'm concerned.

For someone who's spent his career helping to slay other peoples' dragons, it's really fucking nice to have a partner who's willing to pick up a sword for me.

On that thought, a flash of light illuminates the corners of the room, drawing my attention to the one thing Leilani hasn't been able to do in years.

But maybe I can help her.

I grab the pen and jot "take Mom's old vanity to the Habitat ReStore" as the first item on the list. I needed to do that anyway now that Dad and I have installed the new one. While I have donations on the brain, I write "pass out more toiletry bags" for number two. As sad as it is, I know I'll see a couple of homeless people on the drive back from Oklahoma City.

With the first two items done, I stare at the blank space beside number three. Leilani's right about helping myself while I help others, because this is something I want as much for me as I want for her.

"Help me sing?" Her eyes dart from the notepad to my face.

"You told me how much you used to love playing acoustic covers when it rained. It'd be a shame to miss out on a chance just because of one pesky missing limb."

Her mouth is still agape when I return to the bed with her guitar in my hand. "What are you doing?"

"Between the two of us, we have everything you need. I don't know why I didn't think of this before." I slide behind her and bring the guitar around, setting it on her lap. She's small enough that my arm easily reaches the strings, so I give it a test strum. The resulting cacophony makes us both laugh—and cringe.

"Yeah, it's been a while." With expert fingers and a trained ear, she alternates between twisting the pegs and plucking the strings. "Try it now."

I run my thumb from top to bottom. "Sounds like we have a winner."

"What do you want me to sing?"

"Normally, I'd say anything, but it has to be a song I know, or I won't be able to help you play."

"Well, you're old, so let's do something from the nineties."

"Old?" I challenge, dipping my lips to her neck. "I thought we already established that I'm just coming into my prime."

"Fine," she giggles. "How about 'seasoned?'"

"I'm going to pretend I didn't hear that."

She leans her head back against me. "Oh, come on, you know you love me." Her entire body goes rigid as her Freudian slip claims the remaining laughter in her voice. "Um, I didn't mean that the way it came out. I was just—"

"I do." It's an easy response, and one I don't mind sharing. "I love the shit out of you. Have for a while now. I just feel bad because technically, the first time you heard me say it was when I was firing you." The memory makes me cringe. "It definitely wasn't one of my finer moments."

"I already told you that you're forgiven. Besides…" Leilani twists so she can see my face. "I happen to love the shit out of you, too, Clay Prescott."

"Yeah?"

She nods, matching my grin inch for inch. Our relationship is so different from most of the couples I know, but it works for us.

She tips her chin up for a kiss, then faces front again and slides her fingers down the neck of her guitar. "How about some Tupac?"

Steam swirls out of the secretary's mug in lazy spirals. "How can she drink coffee right now?" I whisper. "This place is hotter than Kuwait in August wearing full body armor."

Leilani smooths her hand over my back. "It's not *that* bad."

"Fine, Baghdad in April in full body armor."

"What about Hawaii in July in a red bikini?" She smiles at me with a look that belies the wicked thoughts she's putting in my head.

The mental image that follows diverts some of my body heat to my dick, which doesn't give a shit about the temperature of my attorney's office or my current state of legal limbo.

I cast a quick glance over my shoulder to make sure the secretary isn't eavesdropping. "I appreciate the distraction, but if you keep it up, I'm going to have an embarrassing situation in my shorts *and* a public indecency charge."

"Fair enough. How about some food porn instead?"

"Food porn? That's a thing?"

She nods and casts a purposeful glance at my lap. "A very big thing."

My quiet groan makes her laugh because she's evil like that, but she follows through on her suggestion. By the time the secretary calls my name, I've learned how to make eight different cookies using one box of cake mix.

Nerves carry me across the waiting room and into Dan's office. Mom's the one who recommended him. Apparently, he's the grandson of one of the ladies in her quilting group. That doesn't hold any weight for me, but his track record in the courtroom does.

Leilani sits in the chair next to mine and rests her hand on my knee. It's only then I notice how badly it's bouncing.

"I'm sure you're anxious for an update, so I'll get right to it."

I grip the arm of my chair and hold my breath, reminding myself that bad news today doesn't mean anything. I have appeals. I can hire more lawyers. Of course, I'd probably have to sell all of my other possessions...

"The DA's office is dropping the charges against you."

It takes a few seconds for my brain to catch up to my ears. To be safe, I glance at Leilani to make sure she heard the same thing. Her eyes and mouth are just as wide as mine. "They are?"

He nods and leans back in his chair. "The victim's original statement and several emails you exchanged with Marshall about showering at your gym made it seem like you were complicit in the trafficking ring. However, upon further review of your statement and a lack of any other evidence linking you to this crime, they agreed to drop the charges."

It's my turn to fall back in my seat. In the past, acute relief has looked like combat boots on American soil after a deployment or a suicidal client who decided to give life another chance. Today, it takes the shape of a house and a future I desperately want to have with Leilani but was too afraid to hope for, given the circumstances.

"What happens next?"

"You'll have another court date in about two weeks to finalize everything. I'll give you the details once I have them."

"What about Marshall?" Leilani asks.

"You'll have to ask the investigators about that. Anything they're able to tell you is more information than I have."

Right now, I don't even care about Marshall. Like Leilani said earlier today—the police will catch up to him eventually. I refuse to let that bastard occupy any more of my time or thoughts.

I rise and extend my hand. "Thanks, Dan. I appreciate your help."

"Glad it all worked out. I'll be in touch."

We turn to leave when Leilani spins back around. "What

about Battles? When can Clay get his keys back and open the gym?"

Oh yeah. I guess I should figure that out. So far, I've been able to keep everyone on my payroll like normal, but that won't last forever.

"Let me make a call to the DA's office. I'll text you as soon as I hear something."

Leilani's phone pings twenty minutes later with a message saying I'll have my keys back no later than my court date. That's fine by me. God knows we can use a couple weeks of lazy, stress-free mornings.

When we get back to the house, I grab my phone and turn it on for the first time since my arrest. As expected, the number of missed calls, texts, and voicemails is in the double digits. I ignore them for now and tap out a message to DH letting him know the latest while Leilani does the same for her parents, Kiki, and Rebecca.

"I'm going to run up to Mom and Dad's to tell them in person. Will you be okay here for a little while?"

"Yep. I'm going to change clothes and start on one of those cake mix cookie recipes for dessert tonight." She flashes a wicked smile and disappears into our bedroom.

Just before I walk out the door, I spot her phone on the counter.

Perfect.

I tap on her contacts and take a picture of Kiki's number, but wait until I'm about fifty feet away from my house before I dial it.

"Hello?"

"Hey, it's Clay. Can you do me a favor?"

"Sure, what's up?"

"I need to know Leilani's ring size."

DH snaps to attention in front of Paige. "Permission to install the tiki torches, Drill Sergeant."

"Permission granted. And stop calling me that!" She swats his arm and goes back to arranging the silk flowers and tropical leaves for the centerpiece on the patio table. Just as he pokes the first torch in the grass, Paige stops him. "That one's supposed to go right there." She points to a spot two feet over.

"Isn't this close enough?"

"Almost only counts in horseshoes and hand grenades. We need *perfection* for tomorrow night." DH grumbles but obeys, knowing he won't win this argument.

Kiki was more than helpful with ring information when I called her last week. I told her about my plan to propose at sunset the following Saturday, and she offered to invite Leilani to her place on Friday night so I could get everything set up while she was out of the house.

The first thing Mom said about the proposal was, "When are you going to give me grandbabies?" which was oddly similar to Mrs. Moretti's "I can't wait to be a grandma!" when I FaceTimed them to get their blessing.

Apparently, Hawaii wasn't the only thing our moms had talked about.

Ring shopping was a breeze thanks to a store in Honolulu. I explained the significance of the ring I was looking for and the woman immediately said she had two pieces in mind. One video chat later, I was the proud owner of Leilani's engagement ring, a small wedding band that nestles next to it, and a titanium and koa wood band for me. Cart before the horse, yes, but I'm not worried about Leilani's answer when I'm down on one knee.

As far as the actual proposal, I'd planned on hanging some garden lights and putting floating candles in the pool. When Paige heard the news, she joined forces with my mom and threw my plan out the window.

"*Trust us*," they'd said. Famous last words from women who get high off happily ever afters.

Armed with forty-percent-off coupons, they stormed two craft stores, invading aisles and decimating clearance bins while somehow managing to keep the total price under fifty bucks at each store. Now, they're transforming my deck into a miniature Hawaiian paradise at eight o'clock at night because Paige was too excited to wait until tomorrow morning to set up.

"Clay, honey. I think you have a message." Mom blindly feels for my phone under a stack of unassembled paper lanterns that will hang from a pergola DH and Kurt are building tomorrow morning.

I don't recognize the number, but I know the name.

Hey. It's Stephen. Something happened tonight and I need someone to talk to.

While logic says to call him, instinct says to keep using the method of communication he established so he doesn't shut down on me.

Me: Ok. Where are you?

Stephen: Battles.

Dammit. I don't want to encourage him to drive anywhere else because he could be under the influence of something.

Me: It's not open yet, but I'll meet you there. Give me

fifteen minutes.

Stephen: Ok.

I stow the phone in my back pocket. "I have to go up to Battles. One of my clients is there and he's had suicidal thoughts in the past. Why don't you guys pack up? We can start again tomorrow morning."

"Is that safe? It's getting dark." I stifle a smile and give Mom a reassuring hug. Sometimes I wonder if she knows I'm thirty-four.

"It's fine, Mom. There's a diner just down the road. I'll take him there for some coffee and if it looks like he needs more help than I can give, I'll call in reinforcements."

She holds my gaze for several seconds before relenting. "Okay. It's getting to be my bedtime anyway. Drive me up to the house?"

Paige promises she and DH will leave as soon as she finishes the centerpiece. At the rate she's going, they'll both still be here when I get back, but I keep that comment to myself.

I reach the gym sooner than expected thanks to the light traffic. I don't see Stephen in the parking lot or on the bench outside the main door. Which is shattered.

Fuck.

My compassion for whatever situation he's in has just vanished. I haven't even gotten my goddamn keys back from the DA and I already have another mess to clean up. Careful to avoid the shards of glass, I step through the broken frame and follow the sounds of destruction coming from the main gym.

The smell hits me first.

Then, something hard.

A fist maybe?

Whatever it is hurts like a motherfucker and sends me

stumbling to the floor with a metallic taste in my mouth and a deafening roar in my ear. I clutch the left side of my face and fight to gain my bearings again.

The fumes are stronger.

I can't see out of one eye.

Move.

Take cover.

My attempt to stand is cut short by a five-pound weight plate flying toward me like a frisbee. It demolishes the mirror behind me, embedding tiny razors into my clothes and skin. Instinctively, I cover my face because I can't afford to lose vision in the other eye.

What is that fucking smell?

"That's it, cower like the little bitch you are."

Not. Stephen.

"You are so fucking predictable. One cry for help and you'll come running."

Rage pushes me to my feet. Ignoring the piercing pain in my head, I spit the blood out of my mouth and come face-to-face with the devil. "Better than you can say for yourself. You come running and they cry for help."

"You don't know the first fucking thing about help! I *was* helping them. They *needed* us."

I still can't hear for shit in my left ear, but Marshall doesn't sound like he's high on anything. That's good. Then again, that means everything he's doing is straight from his cold, dead heart. I take several steps forward, erasing the advantage he had by ambushing me. "Right. They needed you so much they ran away the first chance they got."

The acrid stench in the air burns my nose. I know that smell. I just can't think of what it is right now.

"How's that little cunt of yours, by the way?" The light reflects off something sharp in Marshall's hand. "All this is her fault. If she would have kept her fucking nose out of my business, none of this would've happened."

My jaw clenches. I know he's trying to bait me. Still, it takes every ounce of self-control not to let loose on him. When he shifts to the left, I counter his movement. It works to my benefit anyway. Just another few feet and I can grab the empty weight bar off the squat rack.

He takes another step, but this time an evil grin spreads across his face. "This is going to be so much fun."

A flash of orange catches my eye half a second before he attacks. The distraction lands me on my back with a gash down my forearm and two hands vice-gripping my neck. That's when I see the flames consuming everything in the lobby.

Oh shit.

The smell.

"You motherfucker," I choke out. I lock on to his left side and thrust outward, reversing our positions to put me on top. My fists move of their own accord. Cheek. Nose. Jaw. Repeat.

Fire spills into the main gym and follows the trail of paint thinner snaking through it. The heat and smoke flip a switch in my brain, replacing the need for safety with the need to destroy the devil beneath me.

"Is the savior gonna take a life with his bare hands?" It's the last thing he says before I tighten my grip around his neck.

"Yes." It's the last thing I say before the room explodes.

EPILOGUE

Leilani

Three Days Later

EIGHTY MILES SEPARATE LAWTON AND MOORE. KIKI made it back in an hour.

It was the second time in two weeks that she'd taken me to see Clay. Both of us white-knuckled it the whole way—me gripping her hand, and her gripping the steering wheel—while I replayed Mrs. P's voicemail in my head.

"Hi, it's Beth Prescott. I'm so sorry to leave a message like this, but there was an accident at Battles while Clay was there meeting a client. The only thing we know is that he's alive and in surgery at Barton Memorial. Please call me back as soon as you get this."

It'd taken me three tries to get my trembling hand to tap the right buttons.

When Kiki and I got to the hospital and saw DH and Paige flanking the Prescotts, I had an instant understanding of what my mom and dad went through. No parent should ever have to sit in a sterile room waiting to hear their child's prognosis, no matter if he's four or thirty-four.

But in typical Clay fashion, it'd been impossible to deny the small miracles that happened in the midst of all the bad.

The fire was the leading story on News 9's nighttime broadcast. Seeing the silhouette of Clay's little blue truck against the roaring flames made bile slosh in my stomach. Though the volume was muted, the closed captioning told us firefighters had pulled two bodies from inside and both were rushed to Barton Memorial in critical condition.

Ten minutes later, the sliding glass doors opened. It was Jonathan, the man Clay saved on the bridge earlier this summer. He'd seen the news and got to the hospital as quickly as he could. Over the next couple of hours, a steady stream of clients, employees, and friends had joined our vigil. I'd willed Clay to pull through, if only to see his community—the one he feared had abandoned him—was rallying around him instead.

The second miracle had come in the form of a doctor pushing through a set of swinging doors marked "Hospital Personnel Only." The six of us—me, Kiki, Mr. and Mrs. P, DH, and Paige—met him in the hallway, unable to wait one more second for an update.

He'd said things like burns, skin grafts, and smoke inhalation that made our eyes and mouths go wide until Paige turned to us with a translation.

"He's going to make it. He'll be fine." She'd barely gotten the words out before I'd crushed her in a hug, sobbing with relief into her shoulder. Mr. and Mrs. P were sharing their own tearful embrace, so DH and Kiki walked back into the waiting room to give everyone else the news.

The doctors had moved Clay to the intensive care unit, which came with a set of strict visiting rules—one immediate family member at a time and no more than fifteen minutes per person. I'd resigned myself to knowing I'd have to wait several days before I could see him when the third miracle happened.

Paige extracted herself from my clutches and approached the surgeon for a brief discussion, then turned back to me with a big, fat, watery-eyed grin on her face and said I could go to his room immediately.

I'd lost it all over again.

Somehow I'd managed to choke out, "You guys should go first," to his parents, but Mrs. P politely shushed me.

"We already decided this before you got here," she'd said, rubbing my back while Mr. P nodded. "You're going to be the first person he asks about, so it only makes sense."

I spent my allotted time with my hand on his chest and my lips pressed to the patch of skin just above his left elbow while he slept. When I visited the next morning, he was awake, and for the next two days, I heard bits and pieces about what happened the night of the fire.

Well, what he remembered anyway.

When his doctors moved him to a regular room today, we got an extra treat—seeing an officer camped outside Marshall's intensive care room. DH checked with his buddies at the police department and found out they had enough evidence to arrest Marshall for the fire, thanks in part to Clay's statement and the security cameras outside the building. I know we'll hear more about it in the coming weeks, but for now they're holding up their promise to give Clay some peace and quiet while he recovers.

Paige did some digging today, too. Nurses can't share personal information with another member of the hospital who isn't involved in their care, so she was mindful of her phrasing. It turns out that if someone hypothetically spilled a flammable liquid on his pants while dousing a building, that person could be burned severely over a large portion of his body.

The firefighters said they found Clay about ten feet away from Marshall. The explosion was in the opposite corner of the gym, making it too far away to have directly affected them, so all we can guess is that Clay tried to crawl to safety.

None of that is important, though. If my Humvee accident taught me anything, it's not to drive myself crazy trying to reconstruct the details. The only thing that truly matters is that Clay survived. He'll have some scarring from the third-degree burns on his forearms and legs, but that's nothing considering how much worse it could have been.

"If I didn't know better, I'd say someone had a hot date tonight." Jennifer, our favorite nurse, drops Clay's chart into the rack outside his room and waggles her eyebrows at me. I'm not *that* dressed up—just some jeans, a cute floral top, and some flats—but I suppose that's a far cry from the yoga pants and t-shirts I've been wearing.

"I do. I even brought dessert." I lift my bag of Boston cream pudding cups as proof.

"I just checked Mr. Clay's vitals, so y'all should have a couple hours to yourself." She shoots a mischievous grin at me and heads back to the nurses station.

I push his door open and start to move the curtain aside when I notice the lighting is different. "Are those..." I open the curtain the rest of the way and gasp. Clay's room has been transformed into some sort of tropical paradise, complete with garden lights, paper lanterns, and flowers on his bedside table.

If that wasn't enough, he's wearing a Hawaiian shirt over his bandages and sitting in a chair for the first time since he's been in the hospital.

"What is all this?" I set my bag on his bed and scan the room again, still unable to make sense of what I'm seeing.

"This is plan B." His lips curve upward as he gestures for me to come closer. "I was supposed to do this Saturday night. Instead, DH and Paige hid the evidence for me and brought it here when you went home to shower this afternoon."

He lifts his hand, revealing a little black box. It's still closed, but it doesn't take a genius to know what's inside.

Oh. My. God.

"At the risk of being cliché and corny, you really are the most incredible woman I've ever met. I used to be afraid that settling down would mean I'd have to give up my business because I'd never find someone who loved Battles as much as I did. Then you came along and proved how wrong I was. I could sit here all night listing the things I love about you, but in the interest of visiting hours, I'll just say you're one hundred percent perfect for me."

Tears spill over my cheeks when I laugh. "There's only ninety-seven percent of me left." I hold up my stump and gesture to my chest, making Clay chuckle.

"Then you're ninety-seven percent perfect." He pauses before he opens the black velvet box. "It's oddly fitting that we're doing this here because it represents one of the reasons why I chose this ring."

He lifts the lid, revealing a pearl that's nestled within a halo of little white diamonds. It's hard to say which is more breathtaking—the ring itself or the significance behind it. "Making something good out of the bad," I say when the lump in my throat eases.

Being on the receiving end of a smile as big as Clay's is like winning the lottery. "Exactly. And without further ado…" He sets a folded towel on the floor and carefully drops onto his good knee, burns and bandages be damned. "Will you do me the honor of being my wife?"

I nod vigorously until I can get my brain to cooperate with my mouth. As soon as he slides the ring on my finger, he tips his head toward the door and shouts, "She said yes!"

A chorus of muted cheers erupts in the hallway, and then the nurses are back with a bottle of sparkling white grape juice and plastic champagne flutes. As they take turns toasting us, I think back to the reason I ended up in Oklahoma in the first place.

It's crazy what a little dose of perspective can do.

After the nurses leave, I sit on the arm of Clay's chair and lift my glass for a toast of our own. "I never thought I'd say this, but here's to cancer, for giving me far more than it ever took."

Clay

Ten Years Later

Leilani's hair whips around her face as we cruise down Kamehameha Highway in our rental Jeep. You'll never hear her complain, though. In her words, tangles are a privilege.

"Eyes on the road, mister."

"What? I'm just checking out the view."

"The ocean's out *your* window," she teases, flashing a bright smile.

We started dating the last time we were in Hawaii, but neither of us had any idea what the rest of that year would hold. That's probably a good thing—telling a brand-new couple that they'd deal with embezzlement, arson, and attempted murder before Halloween would've been catastrophic at best.

I spent months in therapy after the fire at Battles.

I'd wanted to kill Marshall that night. I might've been successful if not for that explosion. I'd even thought about shuffling down to his hospital room while no one was looking and disconnecting whatever tubes were keeping him alive. My only consolation at that point was knowing he'd be brought to justice.

Except, that never happened.

Three days after I was released, Marshall died from an infection.

An infection.

Fitting, yes, since that basically described him as human being, but not at all what any of us wanted.

Anger became my constant companion because Marshall was dead, but not by my hands. Then shame would take over because what kind of counselor wants to hurt someone? To *kill* them?

It was springtime before my therapist got me to understand that everything I was feeling—even the fucked-up stuff—was part of the grieving process. I'd lost an employee and someone I thought was one of my best friends. I'd lost seventy-five percent of the building my business called home. I'd almost lost the woman of my dreams.

Any one of those things would've been difficult for a person to handle. All of them at once was a recipe for disaster.

But Leilani was there every single day, loving me, supporting me, and calling me out on my shit. It was like being married to my drill sergeant. She even issued me a ninety-day random acts of kindness challenge, and the ornerier I got, the harder she'd made it. During one of my rougher weeks, my words were "paisley," "vitamin," and "eyebrow."

She'd also been right about not having to rebuild Battles by myself, though we had no idea the word "rebuild" would take on the literal definition. The new gym opened the summer after the fire, but Battles 2 kept us plenty busy in the meantime.

Kiki keeps pushing us to open a third location in Norman where she and Alex live. Once they got serious, she traded her Army boots for civilian life and took over the website and marketing for Battles. Her efforts even landed Alex and me on the cover of *Men's Health* magazine's "Fitness in Your Forties" issue two years ago, but I think that was just as much for her and Leilani's enjoyment as it was for the business.

"Oh my God!" Leilani's shriek startles me back to the present.

"What happened?"

She holds her phone out toward me while she happy dances in her seat.

I laugh. "Babe, I'm supposed to be watching the road, remember?"

"It's a girl! She's eight pounds, three ounces, and has a head full of hair. They haven't decided on a name yet, but Rebecca and the baby are doing well!"

That was a romance no one saw coming. Jesse and Rebecca have known each other for ten years, but something clicked for them the last time he was at Battles taking headshots of the staff, and that was that. Leilani was ecstatic when she found out. I think Paige's obsession with happily ever afters has rubbed off on her.

And speaking of, I pull into the parking lot at Sunset Beach. I shoot a quick text to DH letting him know we're here, then take Leilani's hand and make the short walk to where our families are waiting.

Courthouse weddings are common among service members because anything can change at a moment's notice and the government doesn't give a rat's ass about fiancées.

The fire at Battles and my subsequent visits to the doctor fell into a similar category, so Leilani and I got married at the courthouse two weeks after I was released from the hospital. Her parents came down and her dad still gave her away, but legalities and efficiency were the most important parts of that day.

We'd planned to have an actual ceremony once Battles 1 was up and running, but by that point, we figured we were just as married as everyone else. Instead, we set our sights on a vow renewal in Hawaii for our tenth anniversary. It ended up turning into an extended family vacation with both sets of parents, Alex and Kiki, along with DH, Paige, Poppy, and Matt, their seven-year-old son.

Naturally, Paige called dibs on the decorations. We made her swear on a stack of her favorite books that she wouldn't go crazy because... well... it's Paige. But to our pleasant surprise, she listened.

A path of tiki torches guides us past two rows of white chairs up to a simple wooden altar draped with flowy white fabric and accents of tropical flowers in the corners. Leilani drops my hand long enough to wave at our son, Simon, earning us a gap-tooth grin from the boy who stole our hearts five years ago.

"Dearly beloved," DH jokes from his position under the altar. "Nah, just kidding. This evening, we're celebrating the love between Clay and Leilani as they renew the vows they took ten years ago.

"Anyone can get married, but to be able to stand here today and willingly choose each other again is a testament to the strength they share as a couple and the commitment they made to loving one another in good times and bad. But before we get to the vows, Clay has something for Leilani."

She turns toward me, her lips parted in surprise, then whispers, "What are you doing?"

I glance at Simon and bob my head once. He pops out of his chair with a gift bag in his hand and rushes to the altar, shouting, "I did it! I kept the big secret! Do I still get ice cream when we're done?"

Everyone laughs, and I give him a high five. "You got it, buddy." He stands beside me, just like we practiced, and removes the tissue paper so I can retrieve Leilani's present.

She draws in a quick breath and covers her mouth when she sees the frame with three starfish representing our family.

Mine features a handful of coffee beans that I painted white and strategically glued to make biceps and a six pack. I even added a stack of metal washers to look like weights. Simon turned his into an astronaut, complete with a plastic bubble helmet and a tiny rocket made out of a sharpened pencil stub.

And of course, Leilani's is the same one I gave her on our last trip to Sunset Beach, with a small addition—long strands of brown yarn for her hair.

Tears roll down her cheeks as her eyes move between me

and Simon. "I don't know what to say. It's perfect. Thank you both so much."

She bends down to give our son a hug while I return the frame to the bag. Once he's settled in his seat, I take her hand in mine and brush my thumb over the tattoo on the inside of her wrist.

"Lei, the first time we were in Hawaii, I told you the story about the boy who saved the starfish. Up until that summer, I was that boy. But then I met you, and that story took on a whole new meaning. I became the starfish, and for the past ten years, every time life has spit me out on the beach, you've thrown me back." Not caring that I'm kissing her before I'm supposed to, I pull her close and lower my lips to hers. "Thank you for always being there to save me."

AUTHOR'S NOTE

Many of the characters in my book are named after fallen service members. Some I chose from a list, and some my husband served with. This is my very small way of honoring their service.

Corporal Jeremy D. Allbaugh, July 5, 2007,
Operation Iraqi Freedom

Specialist Eric Burri, June 7, 2005,
Operation Iraqi Freedom

Specialist Clay P. Farr, Feb. 26, 2006,
Operation Iraqi Freedom

Sergeant Trista L. Moretti, June 25, 2007,
Operation Iraqi Freedom

Specialist Brandon J. Prescott, May 4, 2013,
Operation Enduring Freedom

Private First Class Willington Rhoads, July 16, 2008,
Operation Enduring Freedom

ACKNOWLEDGEMENTS

To my readers, without you, I'd just be a lady who talks to the imaginary voices in her head. Thank you for your support, especially considering how long it's been since I last released a book. I wish I could squeeze each of you.

Bloggers, your time is so valuable, and I appreciate the hours you spent with my characters. Thank you, thank you, *thank you*.

Wellbutrin, you're the real MVP.

My NUTS! Y'all. What an emotional/incredible/amazing/exhausting year it's been! Thank you for giving me a place to come for encouragement, support, and laughs. Writing a book takes a village, and that includes each of you.

To my husband, it's been a hell of a year, but we made it. Here's to new adventures as civilians and being able to say I still really like you.

Mandy Grifka and Samantha George, I'll never be able to adequately express my gratitude for your friendship. It's always sad to see one of our book babies come to an end, but equally exciting to start a new project. I literally couldn't do this without you!

The Bourne Bitches: Brenna Rattai, Candy Fontz, Desiree Iniguez, Jonelle Espinoza, Lindsay Rodner, and Sarah Wilson, y'all are six of the best therapists out there. I'm looking forward to the day we're all in the same room at the same time!

Brenna Rattai, thanks for all the music!

Alyson Santos, I'm so blessed to call you a friend. Thank you for your notes on Saved and ensuring my jeans don't make my ass look bad. I'm eternally grateful to the universe for allowing us to cross paths. I can't wait to see Imagine Dragons with you!

Jennifer Mock, you are nothing short of incredible. Thank you for filling my life with music and love.

Dawn Chiletz and Misty Marcum, thanks for always putting a smile on my face. One of these days, we're all going to be at the same signing and I can't freakin wait!!

Stacy Kestwick and RC Boldt, let's do face masks again SOOOOOON!

Jennifer Van Wyk (that's wick, not wyke! lol) with JaVa Editing, I appreciate you more than you know. Thank you for your edits and awesome suggestions. #assholeforever

To the gals of DND and FTN, I'm beyond blessed to be surrounded by amazing women. Thank you for the advice, support, and friendship.

Cassie Roop with Pink Ink Designs, thank you for designing another beautiful cover. I bow down to your skills!

Stacey Blake with Champagne Book Design, I love knowing my baby is in such great hands. Thank you for adding the perfect finishing touches.

Ryn Hughes, Kristine Barakat, and Renee Kubisch, thank you for making one of my dreams come true this year! And to the rest of the SAE 2018 attendees, massive high fives for being part of the magic pill I needed to get back to writing. Reese's peanut butter cups and Butterfingers for everyone!

Christine Maree, Jared and I are looking forward to our next adventure with you! I'm so grateful for your hospitality and friendship.

Give Me Books, thanks for handling all the details and helping to spread the word about Saved!

Depression Self-Assessment

I'm not a doctor, and this chart is not meant to treat, advise, or diagnose any medical condition. My hope is that it can help start a conversation with yourself or someone you know who might be suffering from depression. There is no shame in making an appointment with a medical professional.

Over the last two weeks, how often have you been bothered by any of the following problems?	Not at all	Several days	More than half the days	Nearly every day
1. Little interest or pleasure in doing things				
2. Feeling down, depressed, or hopeless				
3. Trouble falling or staying asleep, or sleeping too much				
4. Feeling tired or having little energy				
5. Poor appetite or overeating				
6. Feeling bad about yourself—or that you are a failure or have let yourself or your family down				
7. Trouble concentrating on things such as reading the newspaper or watching television				

8. Moving or speaking so slowly that other people could have noticed? Or the opposite—being so fidgety or restless that you have been moving around a lot more than usual		
9. Thoughts that you would be better off dead or of hurting yourself in some way		

If you selected any problems above, how difficult have they made it for you to do your work, take care of things at home, or get along with other people?

Not difficult at all
Somewhat difficult
Very difficult
Extremely difficult

Reference

Based on *Patient Health Questionnaire-9 (PHQ-9)* Developed by Drs. Robert L. Spitzer, Janet B.W. Williams, Kurt Kroenke, and colleagues, with an educational grant from Pfizer Inc.

No permission required to reproduce, translate, display, or distribute.

PLAYLIST

Dylan Scott "My Girl"

Ed Sheeran "How Would You Feel (Paean)"

Jason Mraz "I Won't Give Up"

Jaymes Young "Moondust"

Ron Pope "A Drop in the Ocean"

Kodaline "All I Want"

Tiger Lou "Like You Said"

Andrew Belle "Pieces"

Billie Eilish "Ocean Eyes"

Seafret "Wildfire"

Seafret "Oceans"

Erick Baker "Comfort You"

Kenny Chesney "You Save Me"

Imagine Dragons "Believer"

ABOUT THE AUTHOR

Hazel James is an Army veteran, and her greatest loves include her family, lip gloss, Diet Coke, and the beach. You can find her at:

www.instagram.com/realhazeljames

www.facebook.com/realhazeljames

www.facebook.com/groups/hazelsnuts

For a complete list of other works, visit www.authorhazeljames.com.

Made in the USA
Columbia, SC
09 June 2019